WAITING
Queen FOR MY

A DARK MAFIA ROMANCE

NEW YORK TIMES BEST-SELLING AUTHOR
GEORGIA CATES

Imprint: Georgia Cates Books, LLC

ISBN: 978-1-948113-21-2

Editing services provided by Lisa Aurello

Formatting by Jeff Senter of Indie Formatting Services

Cover design by Georgia Cates

ABOUT WAITING FOR MY QUEEN

THE HERO AKA THE ANTIHERO

Luca Rossini is very hatable, but I ask you to give him time before you decide that he's unredeemable. He just might surprise you.

1

EMILIA BELLINI

"*Some…one… has a birthday next week.*" Nic says the words as though this year's birthday is a happy occasion and something to be celebrated.

It isn't. Not by a long shot.

"God, Nic. Why'd you have to bring that up and right now of all times?"

His kisses against my neck, his warm breath skimming my skin, his hands gripping my waist. I was enjoying all of it, and now he's completely killed the mood.

I push at his shoulders, but the big oaf doesn't budge. Pulling me closer, he presses his mouth to my ear and whispers, "Twenty-one, Em. It's an important birthday."

I may be turning twenty-one, but that milestone means nothing for me. I still won't be allowed to make my own choices or decisions. I'll transition from being told what to do by my father to being told what to do by my husband. Literally. I'll be trading one cage for another. My wings will remain forever clipped.

"What's wrong?"

I don't want to talk about this now. "Nothing."

"You know you can't do that with me." Nic places his finger beneath my chin and lifts, forcing me to look up at him. "Tell me what's going on."

I don't want to tell him about the conversation between my parents I overheard last night. But I know in my heart that he deserves to know the truth. Nic and I don't keep secrets from each other. We never have.

"It's not good news."

"Judging by the expression on your face, I wasn't expecting it to be good."

Despite pretending that it would never come, the day has arrived. "The Rossinis are coming to see Papà next week. I overheard him and Mamma talking about it."

Nic inhales deeply and slowly releases the breath, his cheeks puffing out. "Wow. I thought you were going to tell me that you didn't get the lead in the new production."

"I'd give up the lead a million times over if it meant avoiding—" I can't even finish the sentence. Saying the words makes it all too real.

Nic pulls me against his chest, squeezes hard, and kisses the top of my head. "I won't let him have you."

Him.

Luca Rossini. Regal. Mafia. Bastard.

My betrothed.

"Unfortunately, you don't get a say about it." And neither do I.

Nic was born into this life but at a very different level than me. He understands how things work. He's known his entire life that I was promised to another man. We both knew, but it didn't keep us from falling in love.

"This isn't the way I wanted to have this conversation," he says.

"What conversation?"

Nic loosens his embrace and cradles my face with his hands. "I have loved you for as long as I can remember. In fact, I can't remember ever *not* loving you. Even when we were twelve and you kicked me in the nuts for kissing you."

In spite of the pain and fear I feel in the moment, I giggle under my breath as I recall the incident.

"It may not have felt like it at the time, but I loved you then too."

"There's never been a time when you weren't by my side. I don't want to know what it feels like to not have you there anymore."

"I don't want to know what it feels like either." But I'm going to know. And I'm going to know very soon.

"You're *my* Em, not *his*."

"I will always be *your* Em. There's nothing he or anyone else can do to take that away from us."

"I'm not a Rossini. I don't have an empire, and I never will. I can't give you the lifestyle that he can. But I'm the one who loves you with all of his heart."

Our fathers are best friends, and we've been raised together since birth. I, a Mafia princess. He, the son of a soldier in my Italian family's organized-crime outfit—Cosa Nostra. And now he's on the inevitable path to becoming a soldier for my father.

I've never cared that he was at the bottom of our strict hierarchical structure. He's always just been *my* Nic, the beautiful boy I love.

"You know empires mean nothing to me."

With his hands still cradling my face, his thumbs stroke my cheeks. "I want you to marry me. Not him."

My head spins with elation. My gut flutters with joy.

And my heart breaks.

"Nic—"

"I know what you're thinking: it isn't possible. But I

want to try. We have to try... that is, if you'll have me as your husband."

I've dreamed so many times of a moment like this one —being with a man who wanted me for *me*. Emilia Bellini, the woman, not the Mafia princess.

"This is a very dangerous conversation to be having."

"I don't care. I will not be intimidated by the Rossinis."

Maybe not, but he should be. They're a very powerful family. I don't want to think about what would happen to Nic if the wrong person overheard him saying such a thing.

Reaching up, I place my fingertips over his lips. "Shh... don't say those words so loudly. You never know who's listening."

He kisses the tips of my fingers and takes them away from his lips. "I have to say it because it's how I feel. I can't hold it in any longer, Em. I want you to be mine. *My* wife."

I look into Nic's beautiful deep-brown eyes, and I only see one thing: my soul mate. "I would be the luckiest woman in the world to have you as my husband, but it isn't possible. I belong to Luca Rossini. It might as well be written in stone."

Stone and blood.

"Help me chisel away those stupid words. Say yes, and together we'll write our own fate."

All I've ever wanted was to marry for love. But girls like me don't have that luxury. We are used as pawns in a game we can't control.

But it's 1978. We live in a modern world, completely different from that of my parents and grandparents. And I want to try and change the rules.

"Let's do it."

Grasping the sides of my face, Nic presses a soft kiss

against my mouth. "Did you really just say yes to being my wife?"

"I did, but you have to ask for a meeting with Papà. Soon. Before he meets with Marco and Luca Rossini next week."

Could this really work? Is it possible that my father would give me to Nic instead of Luca Rossini?

He loves Nic's father like a brother, so maybe.

Hopefully.

I wrap my arms around Nic and jump, circling my legs around his waist. "I love you. God, I love you."

"I love you too."

Nic's mouth devours mine, and my back thuds against the house when he pushes me against the exterior wall. "Shit… sorry… did I hurt you?"

"I'm fine."

"I would hate myself if I ever hurt you."

"You would never hurt me." I dig my heels into his flanks, coaxing him onward like a jockey on horseback. "Just shut up and kiss me."

And kiss me he does, like never before.

Light-headed, I break our kiss and gasp for air. "If we don't stop, we're going to need to go to confession and visit Father Michael."

"I want to do a lot of things with you that'll require a confession with Father Michael."

My laughter sounds like a squawking bird. "Nicolò Moretti! You… you are so—"

"I'm so what?"

"Naughty." And beautiful and lovable and perfect.

"Naughty doesn't begin to cover what's on my mind. You'd blush if you could read my thoughts right now."

"I bet they're the exact same thoughts going through my head."

Releasing the hold of my legs around Nic's waist, I slide down his body, deliberately dragging my crotch over the bulge of his jeans. The contact only lasts a second, but it's enough to elicit a deep, throaty groan from him.

"I don't have to read your mind. I can read your body just fine."

He tightens his grip and squeezes me against him. "You can feel that, huh?"

Is he kidding me? "Of course, I can feel that."

"You cause this to happen to me more often than you know."

"You're confused if you believe that I don't know when it happens."

Turning my hand over, I flatten my palm against the zipper of his jeans and slowly move it up and down the bulge.

"Damn, Em —"

"Does that feel good?"

"Yes," he croaks out, and the break in his voice reminds me of a boy going through puberty. But Nic is well beyond puberty. He is a man. And I am a woman who doesn't want to stop touching him. Consequences be damned.

Nic murmurs a profanity under his breath when I tug open the button on his jeans.

"Do you want me to stop?"

"No." He shakes his head. "Keep going."

Gripping the tab of his zipper between my thumb and index finger, I pull downward, slowly separating the brass teeth holding his pants together. His breath becomes a warm pant against my ear, and the anticipation of touching him makes my hands tremble.

This is wrong in the eyes of God. I know that, but I don't want to stop.

Flashes of light. Once. Twice. Three times.

Not lightning in the sky above. Not a flickering bulb on the porch.

Jolting, I yank my hand away from Nic's fly when I register that headlights are approaching the house. "Someone's coming."

Would the Rossinis show up early and unannounced at this time of night on a Thursday? I don't know anything about them, so I have no idea what they're capable of.

"You need to go before someone sees us."

Nic steps away from me and goes to work refastening his jeans while muttering profanities beneath his breath.

Smoldering one minute.

Snuffed out the next.

"I love you."

I want to kiss him before he goes, but I don't dare risk it.

"I love you too, but you need to get out of here before something really bad happens."

Relieved when Nic makes his escape without incident, I enter my dark house and tiptoe across the floor. My heart leaps into my throat when I hear my father say my name.

Oh shit. Was he at the window watching? Listening?

"Yes, Papà?"

"Come into the living room please."

I navigate through the dark by holding out my hands. A quick double-click later, the lamp in the corner suddenly illuminates the room, and I see my father sitting in his favorite chair.

I'm afraid to ask, but I force out the words. "What are you doing?"

"I sometimes sit alone in the dark when I have a lot on my mind. It helps to quiet the chaos in my head."

"Is everything all right?"

Papà points to the sofa next to him. "Come join me. Let's talk."

My father's face is typically devoid of emotion, giving nothing away. He's the most stoic man in the world when it comes to dealing with his men, but with me he's different. I can always read the turmoil brewing beneath his surface.

"Something's wrong."

"With your twenty-first birthday around the corner, the time is here. The Rossinis have called, and they're coming to see me next week. They're going to insist on a wedding."

"I know." And it's so unfair.

"Your grandfather and I made a promise to the Rossinis twenty years ago, and it's time to deliver on it. You understand that, don't you?"

I actually don't understand why anyone would think it was a good idea to decide that a one-year-old and five-year-old should marry when they grow up. It's ridiculous.

"I don't want to marry him." I look down at my hands on my lap, the same hands that just unzipped Nic's pants and almost touched him for the first time. "I'm in love with someone, Papà."

"Love doesn't matter, Emilia. You're promised to Luca Rossini. You've known this your entire life."

"I didn't set out to fall in love. It just happened."

"Who is it?"

"Nic."

"Nicolò?"

I nod. "He wants to marry me. And I want to marry him. We're in love."

Lines form over my father's face, and he shakes his head. "I'm sorry, but that's not possible."

"Nic is strong and intelligent and loyal, more loyal to you than Luca Rossini will ever be. He's already like a son to you. Wouldn't you want him to be your son-in-law?"

"You know how much I love Nicolò. I would like nothing more than to formally make him part of this family, but it can't happen. Too many things have been set into motion with the Rossinis. Those things can't be stopped. It's too late."

"Nic is coming to see you. He's going to ask permission to marry me."

"My agreement with the Rossinis goes back two decades. They've delivered on their part of our agreement over the years, and now it's our turn to reciprocate. We can't back out."

"There are plenty of other girls out there. Prettier girls. Smarter girls. He's a Rossini. He can have whomever he wants."

"But he wants you."

I'm the eldest Bellini granddaughter, and Luca is the eldest Rossini grandson. Of the five Italian crime families in New York, our marriage will join the two most powerful. The power is what they're after.

"So you'd condemn me to a loveless marriage and make me the glue joining our two families for the purpose of becoming more powerful?"

"It's a matter of honor. I can't go back on my word."

"They want me because they're greedy people. Offer them something of value in exchange for my hand."

"It doesn't work like that and you know it."

"Try for me and Nic? Please Papà."

"They'll never agree to anything less than a marriage."

"I've never asked you for anything in my life, but I'm begging you for this favor."

He's bending. I sense it. Now isn't the time to let up. "Do this for your *passerotta*, and I'll never ask you for another thing as long as I live."

Passerotta. Papà's special pet name for me, meaning little sparrow. Yes, it may be a dirty trick to use that endearment to persuade him, but I'm desperate.

"I can't marry Luca." I won't.

My father sighs. "All right. I will make Marco an offer, *passerotta*."

Relief pulsates through my body with each beat of my heart. "Thank you, Papà. I will never forget this."

This is going to work. I have a very good feeling about it. Because love has a beautiful way of making you believe that everything is going to be okay.

And if it doesn't work, Nic and I can run away and elope. Marco and Luca Rossini won't be able to do a damn thing about that.

No one can.

2

LUCA ROSSINI

"THIS HAS BEEN A LONG TIME COMING. TWO DECADES IN the making. I'm only sorry that our fathers aren't here to see the fruit of the partnership we forged all those years ago." My father holds up his whiskey glass. "To the marriage of my son Luca and your daughter Emilia."

Turning up my glass, I gulp the warm amber liquid. It's high quality, and I'm guessing that Alessandro probably opened his finest bottle. As he should. This is an occasion to be celebrated.

The burn of the whiskey on the way down isn't sufficient to keep me from noticing what's happening over the rim of my glass.

Alessandro Bellini isn't toasting with us. And that is concerning.

"Things have changed since we last spoke about the betrothal between Luca and Emilia."

Things have changed. I don't care for statements like that. I like plans to go as intended because change causes chaos. Chaos results in panic. And panic leads to shit going sideways.

"When you say *things have changed*, I hope you mean that Emilia is now eager to take her place as my wife."

"I'm afraid not." Alessandro Bellini's eyes leave mine and focus on my father's. "I'd like to discuss other options. Offer an alternative plan."

"Don't disrespect me by looking at my father. Look into the eyes of the man with whom you're dealing."

Bellini continues looking at my father. "The agreement was between our fathers, which has passed to us, but I'll negotiate with Luca if that's your wish."

I'm twenty-five fucking years old. I'm not a child.

"My son is a man, and Emilia is to be his wife. You should speak with him concerning his marriage to your daughter."

My fist clenches so tightly that the tips of my finger-nails dig into the fleshy area of my palm. "There will be no negotiation. I want my bride, and I intend on having her this time."

She should have been mine three years ago, but I granted Alessandro's request to let her stay with her family a little longer. I wanted to please my father-in-law-to-be. And Emilia.

"Hear me out, Luca. I believe you'll find my offer to be more appealing than having Emilia as your wife."

I doubt it, but I'll hear him out. "I'm listening."

Bellini pleads his case, and his offer is generous. He wants to gift me three separate properties, each turning a million-dollar profit a year, as a trade for dissolving my betrothal to his daughter. The topping on the bountiful proposal is that I'll have the right to marry a woman of *my* choice.

But holdings aren't the only thing I'm after. Bellini should know that.

"Why is Emilia opposed to marrying me?"

"She's in love with someone else."

My father's grunt is laced with laughter. "She's a silly girl who fancies herself in love. She probably falls in love with someone different every week. It's what girls do, Alessandro. You know this."

"Emilia isn't a typical silly girl. Her thought process is very methodical. She's serious about her love for Nicolò, as is he about his love for her."

"Nicolò Moretti? Paolo Moretti's boy?"

"Yes."

"She means to marry the son of a soldier over the son of a boss who will inherit a powerful empire?" My father chuckles. "She isn't a methodical thinker. Your girl is a little fool."

A little fool who, I'm certain, has tainted herself by whoring around with a man who will never be more than a soldier. A nobody.

"My daughter is not a fool, but if that's the impression you have of her, then I would expect you to be more than happy to dissolve the betrothal."

"She was promised to me. To dissolve our betrothal so easily would send the wrong kind of message to our adversaries. We would appear weak. But also, I'm not one for giving up what belongs to me. Even if she is a whore."

Bellini's eyes widen. "You dare to call my daughter a whore? Insult her in my own home?" He turns and looks at my father. "This is the way you've taught your son to deal with the head of another family?"

My father narrows his eyes at me.

"My son chose his words foolishly. He lashed out because he's angry, Alessandro. Surely you can see why."

"I understand your disappointment, but my offer is generous. More than generous and we both know it."

"I would never argue that three million a year isn't generous, but holdings won't give me sons."

"Another woman can give you children."

Another woman can't give me sons who are half Bellini.

If Emilia had upheld her part of the deal and married me when she was supposed to the first time, we would already have a child by now. Maybe even a second one.

Alessandro believes he can withdraw his agreement and substitute it with a few holdings and the promise of another woman? Emilia Bellini believes she can turn her back on our marriage? Both are wrong, but I choose to let them find that out the hard way.

"I accept your offer."

I'm not sure who looks more surprised, Alessandro or my father.

"Luca? What are you doing?" my father says.

"Emilia and Nicolò are in love. They want to be together and they should be. Who am I to stand in the way of true love?"

"Luca. You'll be relinquishing your Bellini bride. Half of your children's inheritance. I think you should step away and think about the repercussions before you make a rash decision."

"There's nothing to think about. My decision is made."

We stand and Alessandro offers his hand. "I'm truly sorry this didn't work out. I thank you for your compromise, and your kind gesture won't soon be forgotten."

To compromise is to show weakness. I haven't compromised. I've reevaluated and decided upon a plan that better suits me and my ambitions.

"One day when you have a daughter of your own, you'll understand why I had to do this for Emilia."

My children won't whine and convince me to bend to

their wills. They will know who rules our home, and they will marry who I say they marry.

My father's voice is low when we leave the Bellini mansion. "Do you have any idea what you've just done. What you've just lost?"

"I have a plan. I'll explain everything after we're in the car."

"You have no idea what the fuck you've just done," he says.

My father is a wise man, but he has tunnel vision. Everything he does must be done according to "the old ways." He fails to see opportunities when they are right in front of his face.

"I've lost nothing and gained everything."

"No. You just walked away from multimillions and settled for a measly three per year."

Does he really believe that I'd leave a fortune like the Bellini family's on the table and walk away?

"The three holdings Alessandro offered to gift me are nothing compared to what I have in mind."

"That show you just put on was part of a bigger plan?"

"Not just a bigger plan. It's the master of all plans."

I'm going to be king of everything.

Including Emilia Bellini.

3

EMILIA BELLINI

AUNT CONNIE FINISHES CURLING MY HAIR AND PRESSES THE comb of my veil against the back of my head. "Here?"

"Higher I think."

She adjusts the placement and assesses me in the mirror. "Closer to the crown of your head like this?"

"Yes, I think so. What do you think, Mamma?"

My mother stands behind us and studies the positioning of my veil. "I think it's perfect."

My cousin Mara holds out a glass of bubbly for me. "Here. This'll help calm your nerves."

I take the offered glass and tilt my head back, sipping carefully so I won't mess up my lipstick.

"I'm not nervous."

Why should I be? I'm marrying my best friend today and with my family's blessing. Hands down, this is the happiest day of my life. And there are going to be so many more happy days to come with Nic.

Anniversaries. Babies. Lots of babies.

And our escape.

Nicolò Moretti. My best friend. My lover. My husband.

My future children's father. My hero. The man who is going to take me far, far away from here and this Mafia life.

"Come on, Em. Every bride is nervous on her wedding day," my cousin Natala says.

"Not me." I expected to be, but it's the opposite. I'm very much at ease about marrying Nic today. Because it feels right. Because it *is* right. We're perfect together. Of that, I have no doubt.

A wicked grin spreads across the face of my youngest sister, Isabella, and she giggles, sounding like the twelve-year-old child that she is. "What about later? Are you nervous about your wedding night?"

My sister Micaela snorts. "Good Lord, Isabella. Don't be so naïve."

"I'm not naïve. I happen to know that the first time hurts," she says, grinning and looking so proud of herself for having that kind of knowledge.

"You can be such a child sometimes." Micaela rolls her eyes. "Em isn't nervous about tonight because it won't be their first time."

"Micaela," my mother warns.

"Come on, Mamma. We all know that Em has kept Father Michael's confessional booth hot since she and Nicolò got engaged."

Micaela isn't wrong. I've had to visit Father Michael on a routine basis since Nic asked me to marry him.

"Tell us, Em. How long have you and Nic been doing it?" Micaela asks.

I'm not discussing something so personal in front of an audience, and especially not in front of my grandmother. "Can we please change the subject?"

Isabella giggles and adds, "I bet Father Michael knows."

I love my three sisters, but I'd like to strangle the two youngest ones right now.

"Girls, not another word about this nonsense. This is your sister's special day."

Today is a special day indeed. But in some distant part of my mind, I'm ready to have this day over and done. I'm eager to breathe easy tonight because everything went well.

With hair and makeup complete, my sister Gemma plucks my dress from where it hangs. "Time for the most important part."

Yes, the dress is important, and I love the one I chose. But for me, Nic is the most important part of today. That's something my sister doesn't understand yet because she's never been in love. It's still all about the wedding in her mind. But she'll understand one day. Hopefully. I pray that my sisters will have the same good fortune as me: to marry for love.

A tulle, lace, and pearl veil flowing from the crown of my head.

Seven pounds of lace and satin swathing my body.

Three-inch pumps on my feet.

Mamma stands behind me, and together we look at my image in the mirror. "You are a beautiful bride, Emilia."

"Thank you, Mamma."

My grandmother, Caterina, who's been silent until now, gets up and comes to me. Opening a pink velvet box containing a strand of pearls, she says, "Your great-grandmother wore these when she married Salvatore. I wore them when I married Franco. Your mother wore them when she married Alessandro. And you'll wear them when you marry Nicolò."

"These are beautiful, Nonna, and I'm honored to wear them."

Bending at my knees, I lower myself so my petite

grandmother who barely stands five feet in heels can fasten the strand around my neck.

"*Bellissima*."

"Thank you, Nonna."

Bang.

POW. POW. POW.

The nine of us drop to the floor with hands covering our heads, just as we've been taught. Every shred of excitement I felt today is now gone, morphed into sheer terror.

No. This can't be happening. Not today.

Luca Rossini and his men coming here to kidnap me on my wedding day—that's the nightmare I've been having every night since my betrothal to him was broken. And it always begins the same in my dreams: shots downstairs while we're upstairs getting ready for the wedding.

"They've come for me, Mamma. The Rossinis. They're here."

"Don't be afraid. Your father left plenty of men here to protect us. We're safe."

We wait silently, listening for more shots. None come.

"What do you think could be happening down there?" Isabella asks.

"I don't know."

Micaela lifts her face from the floor. "Do you think it's safe to get up?"

Mamma sits up a moment and listens. "I think the situation must have been defused since there have been no more shots."

Isabella bolts to her feet. "Let me help you up, Nonna."

Gemma and Micaela see me floundering on the floor in my wedding dress and grab me beneath my arms, helping me stand.

One creak. Two. A third and then a fourth.

Isabella's eyes widen. "Someone's coming up the stairs," she whispers.

My heart pounds so hard that I'm certain it will crack the bones containing it. Because we're trapped. We have nowhere to run.

Correction. *I'm* trapped. *I* have nowhere to run.

My mother's name follows a few taps on the door, and my body relaxes when I recognize the voice.

"Bono?"

"Yes, ma'am."

"What in the world has hap—" Mamma swings open the door but stops midsentence and gasps.

I take a single step to the right so I can see Bono, and I too gasp when I see his blood-soaked shirt.

"Are you shot?"

"No, ma'am."

"Obviously someone was. Who's injured?"

Bono stares at my mother for a moment. "I don't know how to tell you this."

Nonna goes to the door. "Just say it, boy. You know that's how it's done."

He shakes his head. "They're all dead."

"Who's dead?"

Bono stares at my mother for at least three heartbeats. "I'm so sorry, Mrs. Bellini."

"Tell me now, Bono. Who's dead?"

"All of the men except the ones who were here with you."

"Names. I need names," my mother screeches.

"Alessandro and Giovanni."

A sharp inhale of air catches in my mother's throat, and her knees fail, forcing Bono to catch her limp body as she goes down. "No. Not Alessandro! Not my sweet boy, Giovanni!"

Bono searches the room and makes eye contact with Nonna. "Ricci, Emeril, the boys."

"My sons and grandsons are dead?" Nonna asks.

"All of them."

I wait for it, knowing that Bono is going to look for me in the room next. And then our eyes meet. "Nicolò and Paolo."

Despite blinking rapidly, all I see is darkness. The wails I hear from the women surrounding me confirm that I haven't completely blacked out. At least not yet.

I'm hot. So damn hot. But my face feels ice cold. As does my heart.

One of my sisters, I'm not sure which one, catches my arm and cushions my fall as I collapse to the floor.

My father.

My little brother.

My beloved Nic.

Nic's father, Paolo.

My uncles.

My cousins.

My father's most loyal men.

DEAD.

All dead.

"Dammmn them. Damn every last one of them to hell," Mamma wails.

Them. The Rossinis. They did this. They did this because of me.

The Bellini and Moretti men are dead because of me.

4

LUCA ROSSINI

Sofia Bellini is sitting on her living room sofa. Her face is stoic, her back stiff as a board as we approach. Although customary, she doesn't make a move to stand and receive us into her home.

It's been a month since the wedding day massacre, and she's still dressed in black from head to toe. A little dramatic. And pathetic.

She lifts her black veil, and I'm pleasantly surprised when I see her face. She's still a lovely woman at her age, hopefully a predictor of how her daughter will be lucky in her looks now and years down the road. I don't want an ugly wife. But this isn't about good looks. Taking possession of the Bellini assets trumps Emilia Bellini's outward appearance.

Sofia Bellini holds out her hand, and my father kisses the ring on her finger, the ring worn by her husband while he was the reigning Mafia king. The ring that would have passed to their son Giovanni had he lived to adulthood.

"Thank you for having us in your home," my father says.

Her face is expressionless because she is a woman who has learned to disguise her fear and anger and pain. She looks calm on the exterior, but I'm certain that inside her mind, she has killed us at least twenty different ways since we walked into this room, none of them mercifully.

I kiss the ring on Sofia's finger. A formality. A formality that ends today.

"It is a pleasure to meet you, Mrs. Bellini."

Sofia pulls her hand away and places it on her lap, saying nothing. I recognize the catty act for what it is— respectfully disrespecting me.

Looking up, I watch a woman, probably in her sixties, enter the room. Her chin is high and the grace in her stride would rival that of any queen. If she's whom I believe she is, then this woman should walk with the grace of a queen. Because she once was a queen.

"Caterina," my father says.

Caterina Bellini, widow of the brilliant Franco Bellini, a mid-century legend among the New York Mafia five families. He was a pioneer in criminal organization. People are still trying to mimic what he had the foresight to create decades ago.

"Marco," she counters.

"I hope you're well."

"As well as I can be considering that the entire Franco Bellini male line has been wiped out."

"I'm sorry. I know that it must have been difficult for you to lose all of your sons and grandsons."

"Difficult?" she mutters. A few heartbeats pass and she continues, "Until you've experienced a loss like ours, you can't imagine the *difficulty*."

Sofia toys with the ring on her finger, spinning it round and round. "You haven't come to deliver condolences, so let's get on with why you're here, shall we?"

Direct. I like it, so I'll be direct in return. "I've come for my betrothed."

Sofia's head tilts and her lower jaw tenses. "I'm afraid your trip has been a wasted one, young man. There is no bride here for you."

"Emilia was promised to me twenty years ago. An agreement was made between the elders. She was to be mine when she turned eighteen, but we graciously gave her three extra years at home to prepare for her role as my wife. I'm done waiting."

"It is well known that Alessandro compensated you greatly for dissolving the betrothal. He was more than generous."

"Oh, I think I understand what this is about. This greedy little bastard doesn't intend on settling for a few assets when Emilia stands to inherit the largest portion of the Bellini empire. Am I right?" Caterina Bellini says.

Sofia looks at her mother-in-law and then back at me. "I thought you murdered my family because you felt slighted and insulted over the broken betrothal, but that's not it at all. You want Emilia's inheritance."

"Of course, I want it."

"You're crazy if you think I'm going to give you my daughter after you murdered my husband and son."

"I wiped out the male half of your family within a matter of minutes. Do you really think I'd *ask* you for anything?"

Sofia looks at me, saying nothing.

"I'm taking Emilia, and you're going to sign over all of the Bellini assets. Immediately."

"You're out of your mind if you think I'd ever do that."

"You will do it. Because if you don't, the Bellini women will meet the same fate as the Bellini men."

"How will we live if you take everything from us?" Sofia says.

"You will be my wife's family. I will provide for you financially, and of course, all of you will come under my protection."

Caterina laughs. "You'll use our family's money to provide for us. How very generous of you."

I resist the urge to tell her that I could take everything and leave her family to fend for themselves.

"I want to see my bride. Call her to come down and meet me."

"Emilia isn't here."

Of course, Sofia is going to say that. "Don't lie to me."

"I'm not lying. She isn't here."

"Where is she?"

"The cemetery. She sits by Nicolò's grave every day. She'll be gone for hours."

Nicolò Moretti. I despise his name upon my ears. But I take solace in knowing that in the end, I won and he lost.

I hope that Nicolò is enjoying the view from his dirt room. And if by chance he's watching over his beloved Emilia, I'm going to give him a real show when I fuck her until she screams and begs for the mercy and forgiveness that she doesn't deserve.

"Deliver Emilia to my father's house on Friday night."

"For an initial meeting?"

Sofia already knows the answer to that question; otherwise, she wouldn't be asking.

"No. You'll be leaving her with me permanently."

"But you aren't married. It wouldn't be suitable to leave her with you."

"Bring her to me. Because if I have to return for her, you won't enjoy the way things go."

5

EMILIA BELLINI

THEY SAY TIME HEALS ALL WOUNDS, BUT WHOMEVER CAME up with that couldn't be more wrong. I'm wounded to my core by the damage done to my heart. It's shattered and will never heal. Nothing will ever erase these scars on my soul.

I am so broken that I have become unbreakable.

"Emilia," my mother calls out when I enter the house.

"Yes, Mamma?"

"Come into the living room please."

My family, or at least what's left of it, is gathered there. And I instantly get the feeling that Mamma, Nonna, and my sisters aren't together in one room because they want to socialize. They've assembled for a reason.

"Did someone call a family meeting?"

Nonna pats the sofa next to her. "Come and sit. We have much to discuss."

Everything about my grandmother's words, tone, and expression is troublesome.

"What has happened?"

"We had a visit from Marco and Luca Rossini today."

The thought of those snakes being inside our home makes me cringe.

"Did they come alone?"

"Yes."

No soldiers? They must think we're really weak.

"Did they take responsibility for the massacre?"

"Yes."

We already knew the Rossinis were responsible for it, but hearing the affirmation is a fresh tear in the wound of my heart. It confirms what I feared most—that all of this is my fault. The Rossinis butchered innocent people because of me. None of this would have happened if I hadn't tried to change the rules of the game.

"Did they come to gloat?"

My mother sighs. "Gloating would have been preferable to the reason those bastards came."

That doesn't sound good. "Well, go on. Let's hear it."

My grandmother nods. "Tell her."

My mother isn't one for beating around the bush, so I'm baffled by how long it's taking her to say the words.

"Luca still considers you his betrothed."

What?

How?

"Papà ended my betrothal to Luca when he transferred sole ownership of the three assets to the Rossinis. Everyone in the five families knows that. *Everyone*."

"He has never stopped thinking of you as his betrothed."

What is he? Stupid?

"My God! I was going to marry another man. What part of that doesn't scream broken betrothal?"

"He's ordering us to hand you over to him."

Ordering? Who the hell is he to order anything where I'm concerned?

"We can't give Emilia to those terrible people," Gemma says.

"He's insane if he thinks I'd ever marry him after he killed my family and the man I love." It's ridiculous to think I'd even consider it.

"He isn't proposing marriage, Emilia. He's demanding it, and he's quite serious about it."

Quite serious means he made threats.

"What happens if you don't hand me over? If I don't marry him?"

Mamma looks at each of us, ending with me. "He says the Bellini women will meet the same fate as the Bellini men."

He's threatening to kill us.

How is this possible? We were the most powerful family out of the five, and now we've been reduced to doing as the Rossinis bid?

"Marriage isn't his only demand. He wants all Bellini holdings transferred over to them immediately."

"That's insane."

"Nonna and I made phone calls today pleading for aid. The other families want to help us, but no one is willing to go head-to-head with the Rossinis after the massacre."

Because they're cowards. All of them.

"I didn't think I'd ever live to see the day that the Bellinis were at anyone's mercy, but that is what we have come to." Nonna sounds so defeated. I've never known her to act this way. She's usually such a fighter.

My mother won't give in to the Rossinis so easily. She's far too crafty to not have a strategy for managing this problem. "What is the plan?"

"We have no choice but to meet their demands."

That's not the tactic I was expecting to hear. "I'm to be a sacrificial lamb?"

"Not a sacrificial lamb. Our secret weapon."

Yes, I grew up a Bellini, but I'm unschooled when it comes to the affairs of this lifestyle. I'm a girl. Papà didn't discuss Mafia things with me.

"How in the world can I be used as a weapon?"

"Luca Rossini is greedy but also highly intelligent, a dangerous combination. He's very good at making moves that will ensure that he gets what he wants. This is only the beginning for him. He's well on his way to being very wealthy and powerful. The bastard is the new and upcoming king of everything in New York. Your father's replacement."

Does she hate him or admire him? I can't tell the difference.

"And you'll be his queen," Nonna adds. "What's a queen without a king? More powerful."

I'm failing to hear the part about how I'm to be a weapon.

"The empire will pass to his oldest son when he dies. *Your* son. It will be our opportunity to take back what is ours plus everything belonging to them."

"Luca Rossini is young. Unless he has some kind of terminal illness that I'm unaware of, he's going to live for a long time."

"Without intervention, probably so."

Intervention? "You're talking about killing him? *Me* killing him?"

"That's exactly what I'm talking about. But not before you give him a son."

This is nonsense. I'm not an assassin. "How do you propose I kill him without ending up dead myself?"

"I haven't thought that far ahead, but we have at least a year to come up with a foolproof plan."

"I don't like this at all. Isn't there another way?" Gemma says.

"I don't want to give my daughter to these monsters, but without allies willing to fight for us, we're out of choices. We are the only people who can help us now, and we must be calculating. Hit them in a way they won't see coming."

Half of my family has been murdered. I can't allow the other half to meet the same fate when I have the ability to prevent it. "When am I to be delivered to them?"

"Friday night."

Luca Rossini isn't wasting any time. "That soon, huh?"

My mother comes to me and grips my upper arms. Looking into my eyes, she says, "Marry him and you can fight him and his family from within their circle. You can avenge the wrong done against our family while you're right beneath their noses, and they'll never even know it."

Becoming his wife means that I'll be going to war. And my marriage will be the battlefield.

"The sooner you give him a son, the sooner we can get you out."

"Marco Rossini isn't going to let me walk away with his grandson."

"He will if he's dead."

"So now we're talking about killing two people?"

"Well, yes… plus Luca's three younger brothers."

"*Five* people?"

"And anyone else who gets in the way."

Five dead Rossini men. That number is still smaller than the Bellini death toll.

This won't be easy, but I owe this to my family. I owe this to everyone who lost their lives on my wedding day.

"A queen will always turn her pain into strength and strength into power. Walk through your despair, Emilia.

When you reach the end of your path, you'll be where you want to be. You'll have more money and power than you can dream of, and the Bellinis will reign once again."

I've never wanted money or power. Love and happiness have been my only true desires in life. But now? Now is a different story. I feel like something is waking up inside of me.

Something dark and sinister.

A powerful thirst for revenge.

I will pretend to his face that I am the weak woman he believes me to be. But behind his back, I will be sharpening my hidden dagger. Patiently, I'll wait for the perfect time to strike against him and his family.

Go ahead, Luca Rossini. Underestimate me. That'll be fun.

6
_____

LUCA ROSSINI

MY FATHER'S CONSIGLIERE, ARRIGO, ALSO KNOWN AS HIS right-hand man, comes into our conference room where we're sitting around the table. He's one of the few people without the last name Rossini who are allowed into this room.

"The Bellini women have arrived. They're waiting for you in the living room."

My father goes to the wet bar and chuckles as he pours six glasses of whiskey. "They came. You know what this means, don't you?"

"It means they have no allies willing to go to battle for them. They're out of options," my brother Stephan says.

"Exactly. And that means we've won the war. The Bellini assets are ours."

And Emilia Bellini is finally mine.

Everyone takes a glass of whiskey, even my youngest brother Enzo who is only sixteen.

"You should be the one to lead us in this toast, Luca. This is your victory."

I didn't do this alone. It began with my grandfather's

foresight so many years ago. "From long ago until now, here's to all of the decisions that led us to this place."

"But mostly *your* clever decisions, son. Your bravery," my father says.

We click our glasses together and toss back the whiskey. Enzo coughs and sputters much like I did the first time I had a shot of whiskey.

"Such a mamma's boy." Dante loves ragging on Enzo.

I place my hand on top of my baby brother's head and muss up his hair. "What's the matter? Can't handle your liquor?"

"I can handle it. It just went down the wrong way."

"Sure, it did, little bro."

I was younger than Enzo when I had my first shot of whiskey. I still remember the way it burned on the way down. I also remember pretending that I could handle it although I wasn't certain that someone hadn't swapped the liquor out with lighter fluid.

My father slams his glass on the table. "Come on, boys. Time to collect our spoils of war."

This moment has been a long time coming. As I walk to where the women are waiting, it suddenly doesn't feel real to me. I'm so accustomed to delays that I find myself wondering what the next one will be. But I remind myself that we're in charge now, and there'll be no more excuses. Emilia is going home with me tonight.

The six Bellini women are seated when we enter the living room, and my eyes bounce back and forth between the daughters seated on each side of their mother. Both are beauties and very similar, but one is much lovelier than the other. I can't decide which one is Emilia because it's been too many years since I've seen her.

"Welcome to our home," my mother says as she comes into the room.

Sofia smiles, but the hostility in her expression isn't disguised. I don't fault her for that, though. We've earned her hatred a hundred times over.

"Your home is as lovely as I remember it." Her tone is ice cold.

"How long has it been since you were last here?"

"Many, many years."

"That's a shame. Looking back on it now, you and I should have spent more time together and raised the children to know each other. Perhaps things would have gone differently if we had."

"Perhaps."

I focus my attention on the girl sitting to Sofia's left. The more beautiful one. The older-looking one. The more frightened-looking one with tears pooling in her lower lids.

Dark brown hair cascading over her shoulders and down her arms, the ends nuzzling against her bare skin like a frightened child clinging to its mother. Almond-shaped deep-caramel eyes surrounded by lush dark lashes. A few scattered freckles across the bridge of her perfectly shaped nose. Plump, glossy coral lips.

In my wildest dreams, my betrothed didn't grow up to be this beautiful. And it annoys the hell out of me because I don't want to be attracted to her.

I want to make her suffer.

Sofia Bellini grips the hand of the girl in question. "Please, Marco. Swear to me on your honor that my daughter will be safe with you."

My father chuckles. "Emilia is going to give us babies, heirs to the Rossini empire. There is no safer place for her than with our family. You know that."

Sofia and the girl beside her, my Emilia, embrace one another and sob. Her grandmother and sisters cluster around her, doing the same. It's pathetic. I would have expected less of a display from Bellinis. Certainly not this spectacle.

My betrothed has weaknesses. Those will need to be eliminated before she influences our sons with that nonsense.

"That's more than enough of that," I tell them.

She lifts her chin, and her eyes meet mine for the first time. Inside those deep-caramel orbs, I see something I like very much: rage. There during one heartbeat and gone the next, it was only a fleeting flash. But I saw it, and I don't mistake it for what it is.

This girl is going to be so much fun to break.

"Come, Emilia. I'm ready to take you home."

"She won't be living here?" the grandmother asks.

"I have my own home. She'll live there with me."

"You didn't mention anything about her living outside of the Rossini compound."

"I don't think we're obligated to tell you anything more than we wish to tell you, Sofia. In case you've forgotten, we have full control," my father says.

Soft murmurs pass back and forth between Emilia and her mother, and I'm unable to decipher what they're saying. And it pisses me off.

Reaching for her upper arm, I tug. "That'll be all of that."

When she's on her feet, I realize just how small she is. A dainty little princess to break. That'll be fun.

"Where's your suitcase?"

"The foyer."

"We'll pick it up on the way out."

There's an overlapping of goodbyes and I-love-yous as Emilia and I leave, but her mother's voice bleeds through the noise. "When will I see her again?"

It's never been my intention to keep Emilia from her

family. I see no value in separating them, but that's something I'll keep to myself for now.

Continuing to walk forward, I don't look back. "You'll see her when I decide I want you to see her."

I'm pleased when I manage to get her into the back seat of my car without a bunch of carrying on.

"Where to?" Sal asks.

"Home."

"Yes, sir."

During the drive to my house, I don't say a word to Emilia. I want her fear to escalate to the highest level possible. And I believe I'm successful as I listen to the sound of her rapid, unsteady breath filtering through the silence.

She takes a final deep breath and blows it out slowly through pursed lips when Sal parks the car inside the garage. I'd love to know what's going through that mind of hers right now.

"Welcome home, Emilia."

No response from her.

No surprise from me.

I fetch her suitcase from the trunk, and she follows me through the house as I lead her upstairs to the bedroom. *Our* bedroom. "You'll get the full tour tomorrow. Right now, you and I have some loose ends to tie up."

"What kind of loose ends?"

"You'll see."

I place her suitcase on the bench at the foot of the bed and point at the door to our left. "That's the bathroom. There's a pregnancy test waiting for you on the vanity. When you've finished, show me the results."

"I don't know how to take a pregnancy test."

"You can read, can't you?"

"Of course, I can."

"Follow the directions on the box."

"Why are you making me do this?"

"I have to be certain that you aren't pregnant with Moretti's bastard."

"I'm not pregnant."

"Then take the test and prove it."

"Fine."

There it is again. That flash of anger in her eyes.

That's it. Come out, angry princess. I want to play with you.

She marches into the bathroom and shuts the door with a firm thud. A brave little princess she is to do that under my roof.

Several minutes tick by, and she emerges from the bathroom. "The directions say it takes two hours for the results to appear."

"I'm aware."

Two hours. What shall we do while we wait?

She crosses her arms, looking around my bedroom. Avoiding my eyes.

"Come and sit next to me. I won't bite… unless you're into that kind of thing."

"I'm fine where I am."

"I'm not asking." I pat the bed. "Sit beside me."

She does as I tell her, but the scowl on her face lets me know that she isn't pleased about it. "*Happy?*"

"No."

"You've gotten everything you wanted. What do you have to be unhappy about?"

"Our union should have been a joyous occasion. A beautiful wedding where our friends and families came together to celebrate our marriage."

"A marriage between us was never going to be a joyous occasion."

"It could have been, but you chose to make things difficult and unpleasant. That means I was forced to do things I would have preferred to avoid."

"I know the specifics of how you murdered Nic. You took pleasure in what you did to him."

"Yes. I rather enjoyed it."

"Only someone evil could admit that."

I expected her to bring up Moretti sooner or later, but hearing his name on her lips pisses me off more than I anticipated.

"Would you like to know what his last words were?"

She looks at me a moment before answering. "No."

"You really don't want to know what your beloved boy said to me while he was lying there in a pool of his own blood dying?"

"I doubt anything you tell me would be the truth. And I know what Nic's last words to me were. Those are the ones that I'll always hold dear inside my heart."

There's my confirmation. Marrying Moretti wasn't about *not* marrying me. She truly loved him.

"Suit yourself. If you can live without knowing what he said about you, then I can live without telling you."

"I can live with it. The question is how do you live with yourself after brutally taking the life of an innocent man?"

"Moretti wasn't innocent. He tried to take what belonged to me."

"Contrary to what you may believe, I have never belonged to you."

"We were promised to each other by our grandfathers. Betrothed. I was told my entire life that you were to be my wife."

"It's 1978. A betrothal between us when we were children should never have happened."

"But it did happen. And you will always belong to me whether you like it or not."

One of her brows lifts. "Unless that pregnancy test proves that I'm carrying Nic's baby? You won't have me then, will you?"

I had hoped that Emilia's Catholic faith, or maybe Nicolò's fear of Alessandro, had persuaded them to not have sex. I see now that any hope I had was in vain.

The thought of Moretti putting his filthy, inferior hands on my betrothed enrages me. But what's even worse is that she let him. She wanted him to touch her and he did. Now, she could be pregnant.

I can't handle it.

I'm so pissed off that I don't trust myself to be in the same room with her right now.

I get up with the intentions of leaving, but I stop when I hear Emilia's low chuckle. Moving to stand in front of her, I lean down until we're so close that I have to blink a few times to focus on her eyes.

She doesn't blink.

She doesn't cower.

She stares right back at me.

"I'm going to do you a kindness, which is very out of character for me, and I'm going to leave this room. While I'm gone, I'd suggest that you get on those little Catholic knees of yours and pray very hard that the pregnancy test you just took is negative. Or we're going to have a huge problem on our hands."

7

EMILIA BELLINI

Unless that pregnancy test proves that I'm carrying Nic's baby? You won't have me then, will you?

The expression on Luca Rossini's face when I said those words was priceless. I laughed out loud, not to myself as I should have, but I couldn't help it. It was the first time that I'd had the upper hand with the bastard, and I enjoyed it. But I see now that toying with him for my own pleasure isn't the safest thing for me to do.

The look I saw in his eyes was murderous. He looked as though he was thinking about putting his bare hands around my neck and squeezing the life right out of my body. It's a look and a warning that I won't soon forget.

I'm unable to resist lying on the bed after the restless night I had. I close my eyes with the intention of only resting for a little while, but Luca is standing over me when I open my eyes again.

"Wake up, princess. Time to read the verdict that will dictate what I do next with you."

"It's been two hours?"

"It has indeed."

I sit up and hang my legs off the side, taking a moment to finger comb my hair.

"Stalling?"

"No. I'm ready."

He walks ahead of me and stands aside at the door. "You spent the last two hours sleeping instead of on your knees praying. That isn't the action of an unmarried woman who is worried about being pregnant."

"Because I'm not worried. I'd love nothing more than to be pregnant with Nic's baby."

That's not a lie. For one, it would put an end to this nonexistent betrothal that Luca believes still exists between us. And two, I'd give anything to have that special piece of Nic growing inside me.

I flick my hand in the direction of the test. "The absence of a brown ring in the mirror is a negative result. Go on and look."

"You don't want to have a look for yourself?"

"I don't need to. I already know the result."

He steps forward and looks down. "Negative." A slight grin tugs at the corners of his mouth. "I'm relieved I'll never have to question the paternity of my son."

"What son?"

"The one we're going to conceive before I marry you."

"Why would you think we're going to do that?"

"I need to know you're fertile before we marry."

"No. That's not the way."

"I can't divorce you if you're unable to give me heirs, which means I'd have to kill you. Can you not see that I'm doing you a favor by giving you the opportunity to prove your ability to bear children before we're married?"

This is what he considers a favor?

"If you do this and I don't conceive, my fault or not,

everyone will know. I'll be unfit for marriage after you've had me."

"That ship sailed a while ago. You're lucky I'm still willing to have you after you've given yourself to Moretti."

Is he kidding me? "I'm *lucky*?"

"Many women would be happy with being my betrothed."

Then they can marry the bastard because I sure as hell don't want him.

"You're Catholic? Devout from what I hear. Am I safe in assuming that you aren't on birth control?"

"I'm not."

"Which is it? You're not Catholic, or you're not on birth control?"

"Yes, I'm Catholic. No, I'm not on birth control."

"Good."

He goes to the nightstand, taking out a mirror and small bag of white powder. "Just so you know, I'm not at all happy about getting Moretti's sloppy seconds."

"That's a disgusting thing to say."

"Not half as disgusting as you spreading your legs for Moretti while you were promised to me. Didn't you know that you were supposed to remain pure for me, not whore yourself out to a soldier's son?"

"I didn't whore myself, and Nic was far more than a soldier's son."

He pours white powder on the mirror and taps a razor through the substance.

"Is that cocaine?"

"Yeah." He stops and looks up at me. "You've never seen coke? Never tried it?"

"No." Because I'm not a moron.

He returns to breaking it up with the razor. At least that's what I think he's doing. "Good. Keep it that way."

"Why would you care if I tried it?"

"Pregnant women shouldn't do drugs."

"We've established that I'm not pregnant."

"No, but you're going to be very soon."

He leans down and uses a rolled bill to suck a white line up his nose. "Ah, that is some good fucking stuff."

"You're an addict?"

"A user. Not an addict. I do a line when I feel like it. I can take it or leave it."

This has denial written all over it.

"Why are you doing it now?"

"To celebrate."

"Celebrate what?"

With his coat and tie already shed, he reaches for the top button of his shirt and unfastens it before moving on to the next button. "Finally having you beneath me after waiting so long."

"You snorted cocaine so your conscience wouldn't get in the way while you rape me."

He stops unbuttoning his shirt. "Whoa, princess. Before we go any further, let's get some fucking things straight. First of all, I don't have a conscience. I do very bad things, and I do them very well, so I'm perfectly comfortable with what's about to happen here. Secondly, nothing about this is rape."

"You may not be holding me down and forcing me, but my choice has been taken away."

"You have a choice. You can say no to all of this and walk out of my house right now if you'd like. I'm not holding you hostage."

"You're giving me the choice to leave and be killed or stay and be tortured?"

He chuckles. "Hey, I didn't say they were *great* choices."

I can't kill this man if I'm dead. "I don't choose to die."

"Not eager to join Moretti?"

"You're a horrible human being."

"Are you giving this horrible human being consent to have sex with you?"

Am I?

"Yes." I've never hated that word more than in this moment.

"Say it."

Now he's just rubbing salt into my wound. "You have my consent."

He returns to unbuttoning his shirt. "Say all of it together."

"You have my consent to have sex with me."

He grins. "That was a lot easier than expected."

Peeling away his shirt, he tosses it across the foot of the bed and stands with his hands on his hips. It's impossible to not notice how chiseled his chest and arms and abdomen are.

He wants me to notice. That much is clear.

"I've heard that cocaine gives you limp dick." I haven't actually heard that. I just want to take a jab at his manhood. Attacking his ego is the only way I'm able to hurt him right now.

A deep chuckle rumbles from his chest. "You've been badly misinformed."

He grins and then goes to the stereo, turning on the radio. "(Don't Fear) the Reaper" by Blue Öyster Cult is playing. God, I hate that song. Despise it. My sister and I argue about it all the time. She says it's a love song because it's a story about a love affair that transcends death. To me, there's nothing romantic about a song with reaper in the title.

Luca increases the volume until it sounds like Blue Öyster Cult is performing a concert in the bedroom.

"Do you have to play that so loudly?"

He smiles and some—probably most—women would find him extremely handsome. I might think so as well if I could see him as anything other than the monster he is.

"The music is to drown out any sounds coming from this room. I won't have everyone in the house hearing what transpires between us."

What's he afraid of? I'll scream? I'll reject him?

I know I shouldn't push this dangerous man, but for some reason I can't resist the urge. "I'm not going to scream if that's what you're afraid of. After being with Nic, I assure you that you don't have the capability of making me do that."

His chest roars with laughter. "Challenge accepted."

Challenging him is only going to make this harder on me. So why do I keep doing it?

He removes the throw pillows from the bed and tosses back the bedding. "Are you going to take off your clothes, or do you need me to do that for you?"

I can't bear the thought of him undressing me. "I'm fully capable, thank you."

The bastard has all of the control, but we are equals in one aspect. For entirely different reasons, we both need a son. What he doesn't realize is in giving me one, he advances himself one step closer to death. Thinking of that end result will get me through this ordeal.

I should be praying for strength and mercy and fertility as I slowly undress, but I can't bring myself to do so. My faith is withering. It has been since my wedding day. I've never felt farther from God than I do in this moment. And never more alone. I have no one.

I want to ask Nic to forgive me for what I'm about to

do, but I can't bring myself to say or even think the words. This is so much more than having sex with the man who killed him. I'm going to try to conceive a child with his murderer. It's the ultimate betrayal, and I'm not worthy of Nic's forgiveness.

Luca watches me remove my blouse and then my jeans. I recognize his intent stare for what it is: another intimidation tactic. And it's working.

I unfasten my bra and allow the straps to fall from my shoulders. I grip it as though it's my lifesaver, and I'll drown without it.

I have to do this.

I have to let him do this to me.

This is for my family.

He's standing by the bed, naked, and still watching me. My eyes betray me by glancing at his erection.

Oh God. It's big. This is going to hurt.

"Stop acting as though you've never done this before."

Maybe I'm acting as though I've never done this before because this is my first time.

I want to scream those words at him, but I refuse to give him the satisfaction of knowing that he will be the first man to have me.

He'll figure it out soon enough.

I should have slept with Nic. At least then my first time would have been special. It would have been with the man I love.

Why did I ask Nic to wait until we were married? Such a stupid idea.

I drop my bra and Luca's eyes move to my breasts. "Well, those are disappointing."

Reaching up, I cover myself. I have small breasts. I know I do, and I don't need him to humiliate me by pointing out that fact.

Again, I know I shouldn't, but I retaliate the only way I can. "Nic loved them. He couldn't keep his hands or mouth off of them." Looking at his erection, I laugh. "If anything is disappointing, it's that. Your dick is tiny compared to Nic's."

I don't know how Luca gets to me so quickly. It's as though I blink and he materializes in front of me. Scowling.

With his hand around the back of my neck, he yanks my face to his in one smooth motion. His eyes, shades of green and gold that I've never seen on another human being, are glaring at me. They're both beautiful and haunting.

"Not another word about the things you've done with Moretti. In fact, don't say his name in my presence again. Understand?"

I nod, but I'm smiling on the inside because I've gotten under his skin. "Understood."

He dips one of his fingers inside the waistband of my panties. Pulling back the elastic, he releases it, allowing the band to pop against my skin. "Take these off."

I push my thumbs into the waistband of my panties at each hip and lower them down my thighs until they fall to my feet.

"Good girl."

Reaching around, he grasps the back of my thighs and lifts me into the air. I reach out and wrap my arms around his shoulders because it feels as though I'll tumble backward if I don't.

After he takes a few steps, we fall on the bed with him on top of me. I turn my head and close my eyes when his mouth roughly drags along the length of my neck. His facial stubble is rough against my tender skin, but I fear that it'll be nothing compared to what's to come.

"I believe you mentioned something about limp dick." He presses his erection against my inner thigh and even that hurts. I can't imagine what it's going to feel like inside of me. "Does that feel like limp dick to you?"

"I can hardly even feel it." I'm pretty sure that my trembling voice comes off as less than convincing.

"Perhaps I should make you suck my cock first." A sickening grin comes across his face. "I'll be a gentleman and hold your hair out of the way while you suck it."

The thought of being made to do that almost triggers my gag reflex.

"Do you really trust me enough to put your most precious asset in my mouth? Between my teeth?"

For emphasis, I grind my teeth together.

"Do not challenge me, princess. You will not win."

"We shall see."

"Do you think provoking me is clever?"

"I do."

"All right then. Let's see how clever you feel when I do this."

He pushes my legs apart and in one motion, painfully thrusts himself inside of me. One moment I'm still a virgin, and in the next heartbeat, my virginity is ripped to shreds.

"Ohhh!" My loud gasp fills the room, and my nails bite into his flesh when I grip his upper arms, eliciting a groan out of him.

He hurts me and I hurt him back.

Good enough for him.

"Felt that, didn't you?"

I try to fight it, but the sharp, stabbing pain between my legs brings tears to my eyes.

"Barely even a prick." My voice cracks on the last word.

"*Barely even a prick*," he parrots.

He pulls back and my relief is short-lived because he thrusts again, this time with more force. I try—God, I try—but I'm unable to contain the high-pitched shriek in my throat.

"You really shouldn't let that mouth get you into something your ass can't handle."

I dig my nails into the flesh of his back and drag them down his skin, provoking a growl out of him this time.

"Still *barely a prick*?"

He wants me to break. Stroke his ego by admitting that he is hurting me. But I can't do it. I won't let him win this round no matter how painful it is.

"You're still inside me? I thought you had pulled out."

He murmurs a string of profanities and slams into me again. And again. And again.

I close my eyes and try to imagine that it's Nic moving in and out of me instead of this monster, but it's impossible. Nic would never be so rough. He would have been caring and tender.

Luca grips my jaw in his hand and squeezes. "Look at me."

I open my eyes, and the tears collecting behind my lids spill down the sides of my face, rolling into my hair. Giving me away.

"Eyes on me, Emilia. I'm not going to let you close your eyes and see him. You don't get to choose him this time."

I somehow manage to mentally slip away from him in my mind and lose myself in the damn reaper song blaring in the room. My only thoughts are of the lyrics and deciphering what they mean. And I reach an unlikely conclusion. Gemma is right. This song does tell a story about a love affair that transcends death. Just like my love for Nic.

The song comes to an end, and so does my concentration. I'm back to reality. Back just in time for Luca's finale.

He grips the top of my head and thrusts one final time, groaning loudly against my ear when he collapses on top of me.

"That was '(Don't Fear) the Reaper' by Blue Öyster Cult, and up next is a song back in the top 40 singles at number 39 this week. 'Wonderful Tonight' by Eric Clapton," the radio DJ says.

One of my all-time favorite songs. But now I'll hate it forever because I'll never hear it again and not remember this terrible moment.

I'm not experienced when it comes to sex, but I'd say that was Luca Rossini's version of a possessive fuck, intended to teach me that I belong to him.

I'm grateful when he pulls out of me and rolls away.

"That was the most pathetic fuck I've ever had."

"Dreadful," I whisper.

"I thought that I might need to check you for a pulse at one point. Do you always lie there like a dead fish?"

"I was lying still so I wouldn't puke."

"Moretti wasn't a real man if he was satisfied with a pitiful fuck like that."

Just the mention of Nic's name reminds me of how deeply I've just betrayed the man I love.

I slide off the side of the bed and rush to the bathroom, slamming the door closed. Placing a hand towel over my face to drown out the noise, I sob violently into it.

I'm sorry, Nic. I'm so very sorry.

When I feel like I can cry no more, I splash handfuls of cold water on my face and pat it dry. I still look miserable, and no amount of water will improve that.

But Luca Rossini hasn't won. He will not defeat me.

I feel wet and sticky between my legs. That's when I see

the smeared red between my inner thighs and small trickles down my legs. I'm not surprised blood is all over me after that kind of brutality.

Luca might not have taken me so roughly if I hadn't provoked him, but I couldn't help myself. He does something to me. Something that makes me throw caution to the wind and risk the punishment for the joy of the crime.

Wrapping myself in a towel, I return to the bedroom. The music is off, and he's out of bed putting on his clothes.

"You're leaving?"

"Yeah. I won't be able to sleep for hours."

Right. I guess cocaine does that to people.

I'm glad he's leaving. But not before I take another jab at him.

"You conquered me—a woman who is less than half your size. That must make you feel like a very powerful man."

"The feeling of power has nothing to do with gaining physical control over you. It was in hearing you willingly submit to me." He looks up at me while tying his shoes. "I could have easily forced you, but that's not what I wanted."

"True submission can't be forced. It must be earned."

"It takes a strong woman to fully submit."

"And an even stronger man to deserve her submission."

He smiles, not countering back, and it feels like a small triumph.

"Am I to sleep here?"

"You're going to be my wife. This is your bedroom too now."

"I'll be your wife only if I get pregnant," I remind him.

Word travels quickly within our world. If I don't conceive, everyone will know that I'm infertile, and none of the men in any of the five families will want me as his wife. Bastards. But maybe that would be best for me. At least then I could walk away from this world, and no one would try to pull me back in.

One side of Luca's mouth tugs upward. "You'll have my son inside of you soon. I'm going to fuck you every night to ensure it."

8

LUCA ROSSINI

IT'S MORNING AND THE SHOWER IS RUNNING WHEN I COME into the bedroom. I'm surprised Emilia waited so long to bathe. I would have expected her to scrub her body head to toe the minute I left.

I consider taking off my clothes and getting in with her. The princess would certainly hate that, but her unhappiness isn't what prevents me from doing so. I'm tired. I've been out all night partying with the guys, and I'm coming down hard. I need to crash for a while, so I'll be worth a damn today. I have family business to tend to.

I pull back the covers on my side of the bed and discover a blood stain on the sheet. The exact spot where I fucked her. Where I fucked her mercilessly.

Virgin's blood?

Her gasp. Her grimace. Her tears.

She was in pain. I saw it and I reveled in it.

I made myself believe that it was because she'd never had a cock like mine before, but the truth is that she'd never had a cock at all. I couldn't piece that together last night because I was high on coke.

She isn't the whore I believed her to be. She didn't give herself to Moretti. He didn't take her virginity. I did. Her innocence belongs to me. And that changes everything.

Owning her virginity gives me a thrill down my spine.

Fuck sleep. I need to sort this out in my head, and I can't do that here.

I pull the covers up and slip out of the bedroom without a word to Emilia. I'm probably the last person she wants to see right now anyway.

My father. That's who I need to talk to. He's the only person who may understand what I've done and why.

I grip the steering wheel tightly as bits of last night flash in my mind.

Well, those are disappointing.

Her tits aren't disappointing. They fit her small frame perfectly. I wanted to touch and taste them so badly, but I knew that doing so would have brought me no pleasure because she was so tense and uninviting.

Who am I kidding? She wasn't tense and uninviting.

She was in torment.

I've never experienced that before—fucking a woman who didn't want me.

I lied when I told her she was a pathetic lay. Being inside her was like nothing I've ever experienced before.

And I turned it into an absolute hell for her.

She was a virgin, and I fucked her like I was some kind of savage. I obliterated her innocence as though it didn't matter at all, but the truth is that it matters very much. More than she knows. It means everything to me.

I enter the Rossini compound, and my mother calls out for me to join her in the living room.

"Hey, Mom."

"I'm surprised to see you here. I thought you'd be spending the morning with your fiancée."

"I'm here because I need to talk to Dad."

"About a certain young lady?"

"Yeah. Some things happened last night, and I'm not sure how to proceed with her going forward."

"I'm guessing you argued?"

"You could say that."

"Your dad gives good advice, but I'm the one who understands the way a woman's mind works. Maybe I could be a little more helpful?"

My mom has a good point. "Things didn't go smoothly last night."

"What did you do?"

Of course, she assumes that I'm the problem. And she's right.

"We went head-to-head, and I didn't play nicely."

"Let's be honest, son. You've never played nicely."

"Well, last night I was at my worst."

"Let me guess. You're still nursing a wounded ego, and you retaliated against her for choosing Nicolò Moretti?"

Fuck, my mom knows me well. "Something like that."

"Essentially, you've given your fiancée every reason to hate you and love that Moretti boy even more."

"She can love him all she wants, but he's still dead."

"Have you ever stopped to consider why she was willing to give up everything for him? Why she loves him so much?"

"I don't care why she loves him." And I really don't want to have a conversation about why.

"Do you think she fell in love with a soldier's son because he acted like a barbarian with her? Of course not. He was gentle and tender with her."

"How do you know how he was with her?"

"I know what makes a woman fall in love with a man, and it isn't him acting like a jerk toward her."

I chuckle. "Are you saying that Dad made you fall in love with him because he was gentle and tender with you?"

"Absolutely."

"It's hard for me to imagine Dad ever being soft. He's always a rock."

"He reserves that side of himself only for me in private. No one sees it but me. And that's what you must do for Emilia, or you'll never win her heart."

"I don't think she'll ever give me her heart. She hates me."

"It'll take time, but begin by being gentle with her. Speak softly and sweetly. Bend. Wear a velvet glove over your iron fist when it comes to your queen."

"I don't know how to be gentle."

"Learn, Luca."

I killed her family and stole her innocence during one of my cocaine highs. How will she ever be able to give me her heart after doing those things?

It's hopeless. I've gone too far to ever gain her love. But I'm not a quitter. I'm going to give it my best shot.

She's given me her body. Now I want her love.

9

EMILIA BELLINI

THE SHOWER DIDN'T HELP AT ALL. I STILL FEEL LUCA Rossini all over me. Inside of me. Even the air around me.

The devil has crept in and gotten beneath my skin. The ugliest parts of him have seeped through my cracked exterior, and now his poison is in my veins. My bones. My heart. And I'll never be the same.

Hating him is my new disease.

I'll never be free of him.

Until I send him to hell where he belongs.

"Emilia!" Mamma, Nonna, and my sister simultaneously shriek my name when they see me walking into the living room. All of them leave their seats and surround me at once, giving me a group hug. It's exactly what I need in this moment, and I break into a full-on sob the second I feel their warmth around my body.

"How are you here?"

"I called for a cab, walked out the front door, got inside, and came here."

"You aren't being guarded?"

"Apparently not."

"I thought he would have eyes on you at all times."

"There are men at the house, but they watched me walk out the door. No one so much as asked where I was going or when I would be back."

"That seems odd to me," Gemma says.

"Nothing about it is odd. He's already ensured that he'll get what he wants. Emilia's leaving changes nothing because he knows that she'll return in order to protect us."

If you can feel another person's contempt like a tangible thing, I do in my mother's voice.

"What happened last night after you got to his house?" Micaela asks.

"I don't want to talk about that in front of Isabella."

"Come on, Em! I'm a woman now. I get my period and everything," she says.

"You are growing up quickly, Issy, but a conversation about last night isn't appropriate for a twelve-year-old to hear."

"Go upstairs," Mamma tells her.

"Man! I never get to hear about anything."

I watch my baby sister stomp out of the room, her arms crossed, and I envy her. I wish I was twelve again without a worry in the world about Luca Rossini.

"Was it terrible?" Gemma asks.

Saline fills my lower lids. "It was awful. I was angry and I provoked him. I know I shouldn't have, but I couldn't help myself."

Concern spreads over my mother's face. "Provoked him how?"

Tears fall, landing on the front of my blouse. "I spoke of Nic because I wanted to taunt him."

"Oh, Em. You shouldn't have done that."

"I also insulted his *manhood*, which resulted in him becoming rough with me."

My mother's eyes widen. "Rough how?"

I look down, unable to say the words because I'm so ashamed.

"He took you before marriage?"

I nod and more tears fall down my face. "Yes."

"He forced himself on her. He can't do that." The volume and pitch change of Gemma's voice demonstrates the outrage she feels.

"It wasn't like that. I gave him my consent."

"Because you had no choice." Mamma puts her arm around me and pulls me against her. "I'm so sorry that happened to you."

"Will it always hurt like that?"

"It shouldn't have been painful… unless he was unusually rough."

"I think he must have been." It seemed brutal at the time.

"Was it different from the times you were with Nic?"

"I was never with Nic. We were waiting until after marriage."

"Oh. I thought you and Nic were sexually active."

"He wanted to be, but it was important to me to be married first. And now I wish we hadn't waited."

"Oh, Emilia."

"Last night was excruciating. I need you to tell me if it's going to hurt like that and be so bloody every time he makes me do it."

"No. The worst should be over."

Well, at least there's that.

"He says he won't marry me unless I get pregnant."

"There was no mention of that when they made their demands."

"You should have heard the son of a bitch telling me how he's doing me a favor by allowing me to *prove my fertility* before marriage. He went on to say that because we can't divorce, he'd be forced to kill me if I wasn't able to give him heirs."

"Marco has taught him to have no respect for the old ways." Nonna slams her hand down on the arm of the sofa. "It's downright shameful."

Lines form over my mother's face as she scowls. "Luca has brought you into his home and given you free rein because he's that convinced that you aren't a threat to him. He's a fool who has underestimated you, and it's the greatest advantage we can have over the Rossini family."

"I'm going to enjoy watching all of them die, one by one, never realizing that they themselves are the ones who opened their doors and invited in their killer."

I've always seen Nonna as a devout Catholic I could look up to. Now she's talking about how much she's going to enjoy watching the Rossini men die.

"You're going to have to do some unpleasant things to gain Luca's trust."

I've already done unpleasant things. "How do I go about doing that?"

"You must be a dutiful fiancée until you become his dutiful wife. Follow their rules and stop provoking him. Stroke his ego and make him believe that you are enjoying the sex. Be the one who sometimes initiates. You'd be shocked by what that does to a man. But at the same time, you can't turn into a sex kitten overnight. It must be gradual, or he'll suspect that you're up to something. And most importantly, make the most out of his appetite for sex. Think of it as a means for getting the son you need so you can end the Rossinis."

"What if I don't get pregnant?"

"You will. You're a Bellini. And the Rossini heir will be *our boy*. He will never belong to them. And we will raise him to be strong and powerful and brilliant. You will be mother of the boy who will inherit everything. It's your destiny."

My destiny. It's a destiny that has cost me the people I love most. Cost me my freedom. Cost me control of my own body.

How will I be able to look at my own boy and not see him as a reminder of everything I've lost? How will I not see his father in him?

No. My true destiny was to be Nic's wife. We were supposed to leave this life far, far behind and raise our babies together in a tiny little house filled with love.

"I know this must seem like an impossible task right now, but you can do this, Emilia. You're stronger than you know."

This is my burden to bear. My punishment for trying to change the rules of the game when I didn't have the power to do so. But that won't always be the case. I'm going to move myself into a position where I do get to call the shots.

"I can do this. With his child inside of me, I will hold all the cards, and Luca Rossini will rue the day he takes me as his wife."

"That's our Bellini girl."

Killing Luca Rossini is the endgame, but it isn't enough. I want him to know complete devastation before he dies.

I'm going to make him fall in love with me. And then I'm going to cut him the deepest, most painful way I know how. Right where it hurts most. His heart.

Mafia life is like a razor's edge. It cuts and you bleed.

And I'm going to make him bleed.

I'm refreshed and energized after seeing my family. I desperately needed this visit with them after last night's agonizing defeat.

"Stay strong, daughter."

Luca one.

Emilia zero.

But that's about to change.

I leave my family's home and the cab drops me at the front door. I enter Luca's house, and the same men who watched me walk out this morning now watch me return. Again, not one says a word to me.

"Is Luca home yet?"

"No, but his mother has come to see you. She's waiting in the living room."

I lift my brows and shrug, my hands turned palm-side up. "I don't know where the living room is. I've not been given the official tour."

The man points to the left. "That way."

Viviana Rossini is standing at the window, and I take the stolen moment to study her. She's an attractive woman. Much taller than me, but that's not saying much. Her hair is dark brown, and I think with a closer look I'd find that some of the lighter strands around her face are gray. Her skin is firm and almost completely wrinkle-free. I bet she sleeps in some kind of cream every night as my mother and grandmother do.

She turns, looking at me when the floor beneath my foot creaks, and I find that her eyes are the same as Luca's. Green with gold flecks. Both beautiful and haunting.

"Hello, Emilia."

"Hello."

"It's lovely to see you again."

I flash a faux smile because I'm supposed to be gaining the trust of every Rossini, but I can't bring myself to say anything pleasant.

This is going to take work.

"Come sit with me. I'd like to talk to you."

I sit on the edge of the sofa, my hands on my lap. "I'm sorry. I would offer you tea or coffee, but I don't know where anything is."

Her brows strain. "Luca didn't show you around the house?"

"He said he would do so today, but I've not seen him since last night." And I'm not sad about that.

Her wrinkled forehead tells me that she wasn't expecting to hear that. "I saw him earlier today. I thought he would come home and make amends for last night."

Now I'm the one hearing something I didn't expect. "He told you about last night?"

"I'm sure not everything, but he did tell me that it didn't go well."

I have a feeling that he seriously downplayed the situation to his mother. "It didn't go well at all."

"Hmm. I thought Luca would have come home to talk to you. He must be more upset about last night than he let on."

That's not the impression I got from him last night. "He's upset?"

"Yes. He doesn't like the way things happened between the two of you."

Is she telling me the truth, or is this some kind of tactic to convince me to not be mad at her son?

I don't have a conscience. I'm perfectly comfortable with what's about to happen here. Those were his words.

"I wasn't under the impression that he was troubled by anything that happened."

"He's worried that he might have taken things too far with you. He fears that your relationship might never recover from it. Is that true?"

Wow. I can't believe he admitted that to his mom.

"He was terrible to me."

"Luca has Rossini blood running through his veins. Marco never allowed him to be anything other than hard as steel. He hasn't yet learned how to be tender. He'll need time to figure out how and where that fits into your relationship. I hope you'll be patient with him."

This woman is crazy if she thinks her son has the capability of showing anyone tenderness. He's a monster.

I don't understand how any of them could ever believe that Luca and I will have a normal marriage. We won't. Not after the things he's done.

Do they really believe they hold so much power that they can force compliancy upon me? Compel me to accept this fate?

They can't.

I won't forget.

I won't forgive.

I'll get even.

Viviana's pleasant expression fades. "You have my condolences about your family. I liked Alessandro very much. I'm truly sorry for your loss. I hope you believe that."

I don't know why, but I do believe her.

"Thank you."

"A tragedy very similar to yours happened to me when I was sixteen. Marco was my savior, although at the time I could only see him as the devil.

The devil. Interesting choice of words.

"How was your situation similar to mine?"

"My father was murdered by a rival, and I had no family to take care of me. Marco agreed to take me as his wife. I don't know what would have happened to me if he hadn't."

"He married you when you were only sixteen?"

"A month before my seventeenth birthday."

At sixteen, Viviana wasn't yet a woman. She was still a child. I'm twenty-one. I can't imagine what last night would have been like if I was still sixteen.

The men in this world have no cares for what they do to us.

"I'm sorry that happened to you."

"I'm not. I love Marco and I love our children. We have an incredible life. Although I didn't think that was possible on my wedding day."

"You didn't want to marry him?"

"God no. I despised him, and I hated being married off to a man so much older than I was. I fancied myself in love with a silly boy from school."

"How long did it take for you to fall in love with him?" Just out of curiosity.

"Marco was handsome. And he was *very good* in bed. He had that going for him early in our relationship."

Luca didn't inherit that talent from his father.

"It wasn't until I was pregnant with Luca that I began to look at him in a different light. I saw how deeply he wanted to protect us. And then I saw the way he looked at me after I gave him a son. It was as if I was the only woman in the world who mattered." She smiles. "And I fell in love with him."

"You're right. Our losses are similar."

But Marco didn't murder people you love. Luca did. And for that reason, I will never be able to feel anything but hatred for him.

"Your heartache is still fresh. You can't see it right now, but you'll discover that you're able to move forward and forgive things you once believed unforgivable."

Viviana is wrong. I will never forgive or forget what Luca has done to me and my family.

"When you come to know me, you'll find that I am

very loyal and when I love, it is with all of my heart," she says.

I want to despise Viviana simply for being married to Marco. I want to hate her simply for being the woman who brought Luca into this world. But I'm having a difficult time bringing myself to do so.

"You are a lovely girl. You and Luca will give me beautiful grandchildren."

This woman has no idea that I'll be killing her husband and all of her sons. I actually feel sorry for her because I know that kind of pain.

"Hopefully Luca and I will soon be blessed with a healthy son."

She places her hands palm to palm and rests them on her chin. "My first grandchild. I can't wait."

"Me either." That's not a lie. The sooner, the better.

"Things will change between you and Luca after you're pregnant. You'll come to know each other in a way you never thought possible. The perfect time for falling in love is while his child is growing inside of you. You'll see that what I'm telling you is true."

The perfect time for falling in love with Luca Rossini? Never.

The perfect time for planning his murder? Absolutely.

10

LUCA ROSSINI

I'VE SPENT THE ENTIRE DAY AWAY FROM EMILIA. THINKING. Wrapping my head around her motive for making me believe that Moretti had taken her. I can only come up with one rationale: she wanted to piss me off. And piss me off she did.

My brother Stephan punches my upper arm. "What's the matter with you tonight, Casanova?"

"Nothing's wrong with me."

He laughs. "You're a damn liar."

My other brother Dante chuckles. "He's not even married yet, and he's already having woman problems."

"I'm not having woman problems."

"What's the skinny on last night? How'd it go with Moretti's sloppy seconds?"

I reach across the table and fist Stephan's shirt, pulling him closer. "She's no one's sloppy seconds and especially not Moretti's. She was untouched until last night."

"You popped her cherry?"

Yeah, I popped her cherry. Big time.

The guys around the table howl and cheer, slapping high fives in the air. "Luca scored his first virgin."

"This is my soon-to-be wife we're talking about. Show some respect."

"I figured Moretti had already beat you there."

"I thought so, too."

Stephan lifts his arm to gain the attention of our waitress. "We need a round of shots. This deserves a toast."

"A *toast*? Hell no! I have something way better than a shot of whiskey." Vinny takes out a bag of coke and shakes it. "This is how one celebrates Luca finally conquering the untouchable Emilia Bellini."

"I really wish you wouldn't do that shit. Especially in here," Stephan says.

"No one is paying attention to us, bro."

Vinny divvies out a portion of coke on the table and breaks apart the rocks with a razor blade.

I don't usually do coke two days in a row, but I need a distraction after last night. And this morning.

I take the rolled bill from Vinny and quickly suck the coke up my nose.

"Damn, Luca. You can about snort the laminate off the table."

I wait for the high to start. And then it hits. "Fuck, that's tight."

"I know. Ken got some damn good coke this time. I hope he's able to keep buying from this new dealer."

Not a trace of white powder remains on the table after Vinny and I finish.

"I see some men who look like they're up to no good," a familiar voice says.

I turn and Angelica wraps herself around me, briefly pressing her mouth against mine before I pull away and untangle her arms from my body.

She knows I hate it when she does that shit.

"What's wrong, baby?"

"I hate when you do that, and you know it." And I also hate when she calls me baby.

"I can't help myself. I want everyone to know you're mine."

The guys burst into laughter, and Stephan says, "I don't think Angelica got the memo, Luca."

"Nope. She definitely hasn't heard the news traveling through the grapevine," Vinny adds.

"What news is that?"

Stephan grins. "Luca has a fiancée."

Angelica rolls her eyes and leans into me, looping her arm around mine. "Luca has had a fiancée since he was playing with toy soldiers."

"Yeah, but he went after her last night and brought her back to his house. They're getting married."

Angelica steps away from me. "You went after her?"

I grip her elbow and tug. "Come with me so we can talk about this."

I don't love Angelica. I never have, but I've known her our whole lives. Her father is a loyal soldier. Out of respect for both of them, I would have preferred to end our relationship in a private setting.

"No need to go anywhere. We can talk just fine right here."

"Hey, Angelica. Guess what else he did." Stephan pauses briefly. "Luca popped Emilia's cherry last night."

I point in the general direction of everyone at the table. "Not another fucking word out of any of you."

"I can't believe you." She looks at me, shaking her head. "I'm leaving."

I tighten my grip on her elbow and pull her away from

the table. "I've been betrothed to her since I was a boy. You knew that I would marry her one day."

"I thought you'd find a way to get out of it."

"Why would you presume that I'd ever do that?"

"Because I believed you loved me."

"I've never given you any reason to believe that what we had was more than sex. But it doesn't matter. I'm marrying Emilia and this is over."

She jerks her arm away and stumbles backward, looking at me for a moment before turning and pushing her way through the crowd of people in the club until she disappears.

"I think she's mad," Stephan says.

"You think?"

He shrugs. "She would have found out eventually."

"Yeah, but I could have handled it in a much better way."

"Why? Were you wanting to keep her on the side?"

Vinny cuts me off before I can reply. "You have Emilia. You don't need Angelica too, you greedy fuck."

"I don't want her."

Vinny slaps my shoulder. "Ah, hell. No one here would blame you if you did. She's a damn good lay. I probably would have tried to hold on to her as a side gig too."

"The girl knows how to suck a cock. That's for damn sure," Dante says.

It's in this moment that I realize Angelica has fucked every man around this table. I hadn't given that any thought before now.

Vinny leans close to me. "What about Emilia? Was she a good fuck?"

"What do you think, dumbass? The girl was a virgin," Stephan says.

"She's going to be my wife. I'm not discussing what we do in the bedroom with any of you fucks."

"Angelica looks good and she knows how to fuck, but that's because she's fucked half the men in New York. You have a beautiful fiancée at home who's only been taken once, and it was by you. It's like comparing cubed steak to filet mignon. So why the fuck are you here, bro?"

Vinny makes a good point. Why am I here?

"You should go home and school your girl. Show her how you like it done."

"Yeah. You're right."

Teach her. Yeah, that's exactly what I'm going to do.

THE BEDROOM IS DARK WHEN I ENTER. FROM THE doorway, I hear Emilia's deep, steady breathing. I guess I shouldn't be surprised she's already gone to bed. It is after midnight.

With only my familiarity to guide me in the dark, I go to the stereo and decrease the volume before turning on the radio, so it won't be loud like last night. I turn the dial, searching for something I think Emilia might like. I stop when I come across "Hopelessly Devoted to You" by Olivia Newton-John. Every girl I know loves that stupid song.

Emilia turns over and looks at me. "What are you doing?"

"I thought you might like a pretty song to be playing this time."

"*This time?*"

She sits up, turning on the lamp, and I see it again—that same flash of anger I caught a small glimpse of yesterday. Except this time, it's not so small.

"You left. I haven't seen you since last night when you treated me like some kind of whore, and now you show up after I've been asleep for hours and expect to do it again?"

"Yes, Emilia. I expect to do it again. We're going to do it many, many times because you're to be my wife."

"Your wife. Not your whore."

"Correct. And as my wife, it's your duty to give me a son."

"That much is true. But it is my duty to give you a *healthy* son. Not one who is impaired because he was conceived while you were high on cocaine and God only knows what else. And don't try to lie to me and say that you're not high. Even in this dim light I can see that your pupils are enormous."

Perceptive little princess.

"I didn't do that much."

"That's bullshit."

Emilia Bellini is brave for calling me out on this. And that's exactly what I need—a woman with a fucking spine. But the sharp tongue I'm not so sure about yet.

"Have you even considered what might happen if I became pregnant by you while you're high?"

No. The thought has never crossed my mind. But it has now.

I go to the bed, simultaneously kicking out of my shoes and unbuttoning my shirt.

"If you want sex tonight then you'll need to go find it somewhere else. I'm not doing it with you again while you're high. You hurt me last night. A lot. But more important than that, I won't risk conceiving a child with you while you have drugs in your system."

Peeling my shirt from my body, I toss it to the foot of the bed.

"Did you not hear a word I just said?"

"I heard every single word, and you don't have to worry. I'm not going to touch you tonight."

I take off my pants and lie down beside her, pulling up the sheet.

"I thought you couldn't sleep after you've done coke."

I drape my arm over my eyes. "I never went to bed last night. I'm tired."

She turns off the lamp, and I feel the mattress shift as she settles into a comfortable position.

Tired and wired. It's an exhausting combination. I want to sleep so badly, but my body won't allow me to. My thoughts are racing, and that means that I end up in the darkest corner of my mind, thinking of things better left alone.

"Why did you choose Moretti over me?"

One breath passes and then another.

"There was never a conscious decision to choose him over you."

"But surely you had been told your entire life that I would be your husband, just as I was told that you would one day be my wife."

"Of course, I was told, but it's impossible to feel betrothed to a name and not a person."

"It was different for me. I have memories of seeing you when we were younger. For me, you've always been mine."

"I'm sorry you felt betrayed because I wanted to marry Nic. It wasn't my intention to hurt you."

Anger. Jealousy. Betrayal. That's a short list of the emotions I've been feeling. But *hurt*? That's not one that I felt belonged on the list. Until now.

"What made you love him?"

"He was my best friend from the time we were small. He understood everything about me." She pauses a moment and snivels. "He was going to take me away from

Mafia life. We were going to run away together and live ordinary lives."

The man she loved was going to take her away from a life she despises. I'm the one who's going to drag her into its deepest depths. It's just another reason for her love for Moretti to grow while her hatred for me multiplies.

"I'm sorry I hurt you last night. I would have been gentle with you if I had known you were a virgin."

"I didn't think you realized."

"I didn't. At least not until this morning when I saw blood on the sheets. That's when I put it together. The realization messed with my head, and I left before seeing you so I could sort out my thoughts."

"I was a virgin and now I'm not. I don't know what there is to sort out about it."

"In spite of what you may believe, your virginity was very important to me. I wouldn't have treated it with such disrespect if I had been aware that it was still intact."

"Well, you did and now it's gone forever."

It's not gone forever. It belongs to me. And I cherish it.

"How did Moretti resist you?"

"Premarital sex is a mortal sin. I asked him to wait until we were married, and because he loved me, he was willing to do so."

Moretti was willing to wait, and I forced her to commit a mortal sin with me. Although unknowingly, I took her virginity.

The dude's dead and still beating me where this girl is concerned.

"I was angry when you made me believe you'd been with him. I wanted to hurt you because you were *my* betrothed. Your virginity was mine to take, and I thought he had stolen it from me. Last night would have been different if I had known the truth."

"You're wrong. My virginity was never yours to take. It was mine to give. And I would have given it to a man who chose to love me. Not one who chose to hurt me."

I'm doing a spectacular job of proving myself to be the monster she thinks I am.

Fuck.

Emilia is going to be the mother of my children. No woman will ever be more important to me than she is.

"I don't want to hurt you. I want to protect you. I want to protect our children."

"Okay. Then put your money where your mouth is. Protect the health and well-being of your child by being drug-free when we make this baby."

"I can do that. It's not a problem for me."

"To be safe, we shouldn't do it again until that toxic shit is out of your system."

"How long of a wait?"

"At least three days. Probably four to be safe. And you need to… *empty out* what's in there."

"I get it."

"And I don't think you should sleep with other women while we're doing this. You could infect me with something that might harm the baby."

"If I'm sleeping with you, then I won't have the need to sleep with other women. Anything else?"

"We must be married as soon as we know I'm pregnant. I won't have people knowing I'm pregnant outside of wedlock."

"Plan the wedding. Have everything lined up, and I'll put a ring on your finger the moment my child is in your belly."

And we'll begin the rest of our lives together.

11

EMILIA BELLINI

It's Monday morning. I made it through the weekend with Luca Rossini, my only scathe the punishment fuck on Friday night. And damn, I was sore for two days afterward.

I'm grateful he understands the logic behind abstaining until the cocaine has had time to leave his system. Or at least long enough for it to leave his *penis colada*.

Luca is standing in front of the mirror towel drying his hair when I come into the bathroom. He stops and his eyes follow my reflection in the mirror.

"You're up early."

"Not really. I'm actually running late for work."

He turns around and looks at me. "You have a job?"

"Yes, I have a job."

"What kind of job?"

"I'm a principal dancer at the NYC Ballet." I can tell by the bewilderment on his face that he doesn't know exactly what principal dancer means. "I'm lead ballerina."

I lean into the shower and turn on the water, leaving my hand in the spray while I adjust the temperature.

"No one told me. Have you danced for a long time?"

"My whole life."

"You must be good if you dance for the NYC Ballet."

"I'm not good. I'm *very* good."

There's no time for timidness. Besides, he's already seen me naked.

I'm in a hurry, so I yank my nightgown up and over my head, tossing it on the floor. Pushing my panties down my hips and legs, I quickly kick them out of the way and step into the shower.

Luca watches my every move, his eyes never leaving my body as I undress. And I hope that seeing me naked torments him.

"We have a new production opening in two months. I'll have daily rehearsals until then."

"You'll perform on a stage in front of an audience?"

"Yes. That's what a production is."

"You're a Bellini, soon to be a Rossini. You don't think it's dangerous for you to be in the spotlight?"

I can hear the disapproval in his voice. It reminds me of Papà's objection when I first took the job.

"I've always had a life outside of the Bellini world, and I'll have a life outside of the Rossini world." I'm not giving that up.

"You can't live in the spotlight after you become my wife. There are too many people out there who would hurt you simply to hurt me."

"I've worked my ass off for my position. I can't quit." I *won't* quit.

"You should enjoy your production. It'll be your last since I'm certain your dance company won't want a ballerina on stage with a growing abdomen. This problem will take care of itself soon enough."

Jackass.

"Sal will drive you there and back."

"Don't you need him?"

"I need you to be shielded and protected more than I need him to drive me. I'll find an alternative."

I can't believe Luca is giving me his car and driver. "That's very considerate."

"It's not considerate. It's necessary. And it's what a husband does for his wife to secure her safety."

"Either way, thank you."

"What kind of schedule do you have?"

"Monday through Friday, nine to five. And probably some Saturdays when we get closer to opening night."

"So it's like a real job?"

It annoys the shit out of me when people act as though dancing isn't a true profession.

"It isn't *like* a real job. It *is* a real job."

"When is opening night?"

"September 13. I can get front-row seats for you if you'd like to come."

He chuckles. "That's okay. I'll pass."

Shit. Why did I even offer? I don't want him there. "Okay."

"I'm leaving."

Good. "See ya."

Feeling cool air hitting my wet body, I look back over my shoulder and see Luca standing there, holding the shower curtain to the side.

"What are you doing?"

"Come here for a second."

I step toward him. "What is it?"

He grasps the back of my neck, pulling me in, and presses a kiss against my mouth before I'm able to protest.

"Have a good day at work, ballerina girl."

And poof, he's gone, leaving me standing in the shower, breathless and touching my fingertips to my lips.

What the hell just happened?

~

"GREAT REHEARSAL, EVERYBODY. I'LL SEE YOU ALL BACK here at nine in the morning."

Almost eight hours on my feet, many of them on my toes. It's been a tough day. I can't wait to get home and soak in the tub.

Wow. I just called Luca's house *home*. I must be really tired.

"Hey, Em," my dance partner, Peter, calls out. "Hold on a second."

"Yeah?"

"Great rehearsal today."

"I know my fouetté needs more work, but don't worry. I'll perfect it before the production."

"Your fouetté isn't why I stopped you."

"What's up?"

"Everyone wants an update on the case, but they're too afraid to ask. Have there been any new developments?"

Oh, there have been many new developments. My family's murderer has taken me from my home, forced me to move into his house, sleep in his bed, consent to sexual relations with him, and plan a wedding while we try to conceive a son.

And then there's the kiss this morning that I haven't been able to stop thinking about.

Yes, Peter. There have been many new developments.

"Unfortunately, the police have nothing new."

"I'm sorry to hear that."

"The people who killed my family will be brought to justice. I have faith in that." And I'll be the one who delivers retribution.

"I'm sure you're right. The police just need a little more time."

"Bye, Emilia," one of the other ballerinas says as she walks by.

I throw up my hand. "See you tomorrow, Kathy."

Peter walks toward the exit with me. "Do you want to share a cab?"

"Thanks for the offer, but I have a ride."

"Open invitation anytime you need one."

I don't know Peter well. We haven't worked together for very long, but I get the feeling that he's flirting with me.

"Thanks. I appreciate it."

He points to the left. "I'm going this way."

I point at the black Cadillac waiting for me at the curb. "That's my ride."

"Wowzers. Fancy."

"Not mine. It belongs to a friend."

"Is your friend driving?"

"No. That's his driver."

"Your friend has a lot of money."

"Yeah, I guess he does."

Luca has a lot of money. And he's about to have even more when the transfer paperwork for Bellini holdings is complete.

"See you tomorrow."

I've taken about a dozen steps toward the car when I'm approached by a man in a dark suit. "Emilia Bellini?"

"Who's asking?"

"Special Agent Reynolds. FBI."

I resume walking. "I have nothing to say to you."

"Just one minute of your time. That's all I'm asking for."

I look toward the car and then back at the FBI agent. "That black Cadillac is waiting for me. I'm sure you already know who employs the driver, so you know I'm not lying when I say that one minute is all I can spare."

"Luca Rossini is responsible for the Bellini and Moretti murders. But I think you already know that."

I stare blankly at the agent, neither confirming nor denying his accusation.

"You could be in grave danger."

I laugh on the inside because it's actually the Rossini men who are in danger. But no one suspects because their killer is a woman who stands barely five feet tall and weighs a hundred pounds soaking wet.

"The Rossinis are family friends who are helping me through a very difficult time."

"If they're threatening you, I can help. But I need you to help me help you."

"I'm sorry. I don't know what you mean."

"I don't have to tell you what the Rossini family is capable of. They're dangerous people."

"I know far better than you, Agent Reynolds, what the Rossini family is capable of."

"Then help me."

If I worked with the FBI, they would seize all assets, both Rossini and Bellini. That's all they're interested in. Not helping me or the other women in my family.

My child's inheritance would be seized, and everything I'm doing would be for nothing.

"I'm sorry but working together isn't an option."

"I know they murdered your family, and now they're threatening you and your surviving loved ones."

"I don't know what you're talking about."

I walk away and Sal gets out of the car, coming around to open my door. "Good evening, Miss Bellini. I trust that today's rehearsal went well?"

"It went very well, thank you."

When I arrive at Luca's house, I find him in the living room watching television. I stop in the doorway, taking advantage of the moment to study him and wonder how a creature as beautiful as he is can be so vile and cruel?

He turns, looking at me in the doorway, and smiles. "What are you doing?"

"Nothing. I just got home from work."

Home. There's that word again.

He pats the cushion on the sofa. "Come sit next to me."

I'm reminded of our first night together, but this time he's in a much better mood.

I sit beside him and kick out of my shoes, curling and uncurling my toes.

"How was rehearsal?"

"Exhausting. Painful. My feet are killing me, especially my toes."

He pats his lap. "Put them up here."

I shake my head. "They've been in sweaty pointe shoes all day. They're gross and stinky."

"I don't care. Give them to me."

I turn, placing my feet in his lap, and he takes one in his hands. "Which part hurts?"

"Every part."

Luca squeezes, using his thumbs to massage the ball of my foot. "How does that feel?"

I swallow hard. "Really good."

I close my eyes and he moves his thumbs in circular motions up and down the soles of my feet.

"How was your day?"

"Rehearsal was fine, but I need to tell you about something that happened when I was leaving."

"I'm listening."

"I was approached by an FBI agent."

Luca's thumbs slow for a moment and then resume their previous rhythm. "What did he want?"

"Special Agent Reynolds told me that you were responsible for the Bellini and Moretti murders and that I was endangering myself by being with you."

"What did you say to him?"

"That you were a family friend who was helping me through a very difficult time."

"Are you sure that's what you said?"

He doesn't trust me. And I'm going to need to change that.

"Yes, Luca. I swear that's all I said. You can ask Sal. He'll confirm that I didn't talk to him for long at all. I walked away."

"How do I know that I can trust you?"

"You don't. But first of all, I'm telling you about them coming to me. Secondly, by protecting you, I'm protecting our future children. In time, you'll learn to trust me."

Isn't that similar to what he told me?

"Do you believe the agent? That you're in danger by being with me?"

"I believe my family and I are in more danger by *not* being with you."

"You're a Bellini. I know you'd never work with the feds."

I would never work with the feds but not because of any kind of loyalty I feel toward Luca and his family. It simply doesn't fit into my plans for killing all of the Rossini men.

12

LUCA ROSSINI

THIS IS THE THIRD NIGHT IN A ROW THAT EMILIA HAS soaked in the tub before bedtime. She did it the previous two nights because her feet were tormenting her after some difficult rehearsals, but the aroma in the air smells different tonight. Floral. Sweet. Sexy.

She's preparing herself for me.

I'm sitting in bed reading, the radio softly playing in the background, when she opens the bathroom door and stops inside the doorway. She's wrapped in a towel and her wet hair is in a bun on top of her head. Her face is freshly washed without a bit of makeup, and she's still a damn beauty.

Dog-earing the corner of the page, I close my book and place it on top of the nightstand at the bedside. I sit there unmoving and she stands, frozen, tightly gripping the bath towel wrapped around her. Deciding that I should make the first move, I pull back the covers on her side of the bed. An invitation.

There's reluctance in her eyes, but she pushes through it and comes to bed. She drops the towel on the floor and quickly slides in beside me, pulling the damn covers up to her chin.

Emilia doesn't throw herself at me like other women. Hell, she doesn't want me at all. And damn, if that doesn't make me desire her a hundred times more than I already do.

I'll wait for her patiently… because I already know that she's mine. Even if she hasn't yet realized it.

She closes her eyes and trembles beneath my touch when I reach beneath the covers and trace my fingertips along her ribs, narrow waist, and curved hip. "You're shaking."

She opens her eyes and looks at me.

"I'm afraid," she whispers, her voice barely audible.

"You shouldn't be. I'm not going to hurt you."

Her throat bobs when she swallows. "With the way it felt last time, I can't imagine it not hurting."

"Tonight will be different. You'll like it."

She shakes her head, tightly gripping the sheet at her chin. "I won't like it."

"How can you be so sure?"

"Because you're not—" She looks down and fidgets with the sheet.

"Because I'm not what?"

"You're not Nic."

I hear his name on her lips, and I'm instantly enraged.

Will it always be the three of us in this bed? Will I always be competing with a dead man? Or will she eventually forget about Moretti and be able to live the life we were intended to live together?

Throwing the covers back, I get out of bed and go into the bathroom, slamming the door behind me. A few thoughts enter my mind at the same time. One, grabbing Emilia and pulling her to the edge of the bed, shoving my cock into her pussy without warning or preparation. Two, fucking her raw until she cries and begs me to stop. Three, flipping her over facedown to deliver options one and two.

A punishment fuck. That seems like fair treatment for her after saying his name to me when I'm trying to show her tenderness—a tenderness that I don't owe her.

Fucking that pretty little face of hers into the mattress would make me feel a whole lot better. But it would also prove—in her mind—that I am the monster she believes me to be.

No, I won't fuck her face into the mattress tonight. I have something much better in mind.

Despite how much she thinks she's going to hate what's about to happen between us, I'm going to make her enjoy it. Love it. Want more of it. More of me. I'm going to consume her daily thoughts. She won't be able to get me out of her head because I'm going to be there, front and center, erasing any thoughts she might have about Moretti.

With my plan firmly in place, I return to bed—our battlefield. The place where she will fight me and slowly surrender as I conquer her body.

"You can leave the light on if you like."

She leans over and twists the switch. "I prefer the dark."

In the darkness, she doesn't have to look at me. But she can't escape feeling me.

"Forget what you had with him. Let me give you what you deserve."

No response. But I'm not discouraged. I know how this is going to go.

I've never been a man who cared anything about the pleasure of a woman, so this will be new territory. I'm going to have to pay careful attention to Emilia's cues and try to decipher what they mean.

I'm not fond of slow music, but it'll help me set the pace for what I'm about to do. And I smile in the dark when a slow Rod Stewart song begins to play on the radio.

"I Don't Want To Talk About It." I know the song well because my bedroom was next to my little sister's when I lived at home, and she played the damn thing at least a hundred times a day.

Emilia sucks in air when I move toward her. She's clearly frightened of me, and she has every right to be. I've only shown her brutality when it comes to sex. Now it's time to show her tenderness.

I consider the ways a man might put a woman at ease. Kisses. Soft, slow kisses. And gentle caresses.

Foreplay.

I turn on my side, facing Emilia, and reach out to her in the dark. Finding her hip, I pull her toward me. When I grip her body, I'm reminded of how small this woman is. My large outstretched palm easily wraps around her hip bone.

How in the world will this woman ever be able to birth babies with tiny hips like these?

I recall her mother and grandmother, both small women. Their petite frames didn't prevent either of them from birthing multiple children, so I guess I shouldn't worry about that.

When we're lying face-to-face, I press my forehead to hers and give her a moment to adjust to the close proximity of our bodies. Give her time to see that tonight is going to be different.

That *I'm* going to be different.

I cup the side of her face with my hand, my fingertips flirting with the nape of her neck. Her breath is rapid against my mouth, and I take a moment to consider how she's no longer a virgin, but she still possesses the innocence of one.

I curl my fingers around her nape and lean in, intending to press a soft kiss against her lips, but she turns away. I'm not surprised she doesn't allow me to kiss her. I don't expect her to. At least not with this attempt.

Moving my lips, I drag them along her jawline until I reach her neck just below her ear. Opening my mouth, my tongue caresses her silky-smooth skin as I work my way toward the bend of her shoulder.

I listen intently for any sign of arousal. Increased breathing? Moaning? Sighing? But I get nothing out of her. She isn't going to make this easy for me. I can see that right now.

Lightly, I knead the muscles in her back while my hand makes its way down her spine. The curve of her lower back is where I stop advancing instead of gripping her ass and pulling her against my hard cock.

I make a second attempt at kissing her, and she denies me once more. And again, I'm not surprised. I fully expect her to play hard to get.

Moving to the other side of her neck, I nuzzle my nose against her skin and inhale. Whether she realizes it or not, she prepared herself for this—for me—tonight. That means something.

"You smell so good."

No reply.

My hand abandons the curve of her lower spine and grips the side of her hip, encouraging her to roll to her back, which she does without hesitation.

Flattening my hand against her stomach, I slowly move it in a downward circular motion until the tips of my fingers lightly graze the top of her pubic bone. And that's when I hear an almost nonexistent gasp from her mouth.

Finally, some kind of reaction out of her.

Wrapping my hand around the back of one of her thighs, I bend it at the knee, spreading her legs apart. I wait a moment to see if she'll close them, and I'm pleasantly surprised when she doesn't.

Sliding my flattened palm down her stomach, I cup my fingers around the apex between her thighs. I begin by stroking her front to back and back to front, rubbing her so gently that I'm certain she can barely feel my touch. It's just a tease really, to show her that my fingers do have the talent and inclination to pleasure her.

She widens the part between her legs and slightly lifts her pelvis in an upward direction. I smile against her neck as I kiss it because I can feel her softening to my touch. Bending to my will. Lowering those walls that have been keeping me out.

Although small, this is my first real victory with Emilia.

I go in for the kiss, my third attempt, and this time I don't give her the opportunity to turn away. I suck her bottom lip, gently holding it hostage with the suction of my mouth for a moment before releasing.

A second victory. Sort of.

My hand rewards her with increased friction and her breath deepens, accompanied by a barely-there moan. I'm dying for some kind of verbal reassurance, but words could break the spell she's under, and I'm not yet willing to risk it. I want her to be completely absorbed by the sensations she's experiencing. The sensations *I'm* giving her.

These small victories are encouraging, so I decide to seize a deeper kiss. A kiss that will lead to everything else I desire from her.

All it takes is a simple brush of my tongue against the seam of her lips, and she opens fully for me. Being inside her this way for the first time makes me aware of every nerve-ending in my body. Because they're all on fire.

I've never felt inclined to kiss at length because I've seen it as a weakness—an unnecessary act that women want and only weak men give in to. But as I kiss Emilia, I find myself enjoying the intimacy of it between us. Kissing her is like coming home after being away for a very long time.

Emilia Bellini. She tastes like everything I've ever wanted.

Tangling one of my legs around hers, I spread her beneath me, pinning her against the bed. I continue petting her, one of my fingers straying away from the others and finding its way inside her hot, wet cleft where it easily slips and slides through her slickness.

It was only moments ago that Emilia was rejecting my kisses. Now, she can't kiss me fast enough or hard enough as my fingers play her like a lovely instrument in a seductive orchestra.

I too can't kiss her hard enough, can't hold her tightly enough, can't touch enough of her body. In this moment, my entire world is limited to this woman and the touch of her lips on my mine, the feel of my hand between her legs. Anything beyond these things, beyond her, doesn't exist. It's only the two of us in this world as I obey the writhing desire that is burning inside me.

She stops kissing me and breathes heavily against my mouth. "Luca—"

I revel in the breathless whisper of my name on her lips because I know what it means. I know the pleasure that's building inside of her.

"Just breathe and let it happen. It'll be the best feeling you've ever had."

She grips the back of my neck and tenses, holding me

tightly with our foreheads pressed together. She shudders, her body fracturing beneath me as she comes apart. A broken whimper leaves her mouth, and I swear that making her come is the best trophy I've ever won.

She relaxes and releases her grip on my neck, her minty breath remaining heavy against my mouth. And I can't resist kissing her in her aftermath of ecstasy.

"Don't stop. I want the rest. Give me everything. Show me what else there is."

I have her. I finally have her. And I'll burn the world down to keep her.

"I'll give you anything you want, Emilia."

Moving to kneel between her legs, I push my boxers down mine. When I'm bare, I lower my body to hers. My heart pounds and my breath trembles as I settle my hips between her parted thighs, my length pressing against her. Unexpectedly, Emilia hooks one of her legs around me and moves her hips, adjusting the alignment of my erection until my tip is perfectly placed for entering.

Fuck, I think I'm actually nervous about being with her this time.

Why?

I don't know why.

Yes, I do.

I was high on coke the first time we were together. And I know what that shit does to my level of confidence. One little white line and I turn into fucking Superman. I'm invincible and incredible at everything I do. It's one of the reasons I love the shit so much, but I'm not stupid. I know that it's my own personal perception of myself and not everyone else's.

Our first time together could have truly been terrible, and I wouldn't know it. That's why this time needs to be perfect. To make up for any inadequacies that might have happened the first time.

For a brief second, I feel light-headed, a large volume of blood rushing to my dick all at once. Cocaine or not, I'm confident that I've never been fuller or harder.

My hand follows the length of her arm until it finds her hand. I push my fingers through hers, intertwining them into a clasp and resting them on the bed beside her head. I squeeze gently, and she does the same as I kiss her and slowly push into her, inch by inch, until I'm fully sheathed inside her.

I devour her soft moan against my mouth and smile when her other leg hooks around my waist, the soles of her feet running down the muscles of my calves.

Pulling back, I slowly advance again and again, every thrust intentional. Emilia wraps her free arm around my shoulders and holds me tightly, kissing me as I move in and out of her.

Our kissing is slower now. Gentler. And damn, I make a realization. We are not fucking. This is making love.

Lovemaking. Is that even possible when two people aren't in love? I don't know, but either way, I'm enjoying this new-to-me kind of sex.

This—I need *this*. *Her*. Emilia. The life we're going to have together. The babies we're going to make. All of it.

I'm inside her, on top of her, around her. I'm everywhere and she can't escape me.

She moans my name, and I know that in that moment, I'm her everything all at once.

We are fused, two hearts beating as one, and I promise myself—and her—that it will always be like this between us.

She bites my lip, making me growl into her mouth. And then I feel her breaking apart beneath me again as I continue to move. Her climax prompts my own, and I find my release inside her. I'm not quite ready for this to be over so I remain inside her for a moment, gradually becoming soft and eventually sliding out of her. She whimpers at the loss, and I place a kiss against her mouth.

Moving off of her, I lie on my back in the middle of the king-size bed. I don't scoot to my side because I want to be near her. Even if it's only the brushing of our shoulders, it satisfies my need to be touching her.

At some point "So Into You" by Atlanta Rhythm Section has begun to play on the radio, and I tap my toe against the mattress, keeping beat with the music.

"Musician?"

I chuckle. "No. My father would've killed me before having a son who played a musical instrument."

"Why?"

"His opinion is that an interest in music and art makes a man soft."

"What about ballet?"

She's got to be kidding me.

"Ballet is fine for a woman but not a man."

"My dance partner is very manly."

What the fuck? "You have a male dance partner?"

"Yes. His name is Peter and he's not soft."

"Peter's peter had better not be anything but soft around you."

She bursts into laughter. "It doesn't matter. I'm not interested in Peter's peter."

"I won't have my wife being handled by another man."

"I'm not your wife."

"But you're going to be."

"Only if I get pregnant."

"It's going to happen, Emilia."

"And what if it doesn't?"

I sit up and place my hand on her stomach. "There will be a baby inside you soon. I'm certain of it."

"You can't know that for sure."

"I do know."

"How? Do you have a crystal ball?"

"It will happen because it's what I want. And I always get what I want."

"What if I become pregnant and it's a girl?"

"We must have a boy first. A girl can come later."

"It took years for my mother to have a boy. So long that my parents had given up on a son and accepted they would only have girls."

"My mother had all boys with the exception of my one sister. We will have boys too."

"We will have what God gives us."

"Well, it's difficult to argue with that."

She places her hand on top of mine. "I think we should do it again."

"Because you want to increase the odds of conceiving?"

"Of course. I have a lot on the line here. I need a son as badly as you need one."

"Then my hand between your legs won't be required?"

"It's not required, but it was quite nice."

"You liked it?"

Her hand skims up my arm, reaching my shoulder. "I liked everything about tonight."

This is the girl who said she wouldn't like it because I wasn't him. This is the girl who used the word *dreadful* to describe our first sexual encounter, and I'm certain she meant it. Now, she tells me she liked everything.

What a turnaround this is.

I'm not sure which is sexier, her beauty or her submission.

"You came *twice*." Two times. As experienced as I am, it takes me a while to pull off a second one.

"I wouldn't be mad if you made it three times."

Ah, someone's just being greedy now.

I wanted to punish Emilia by making her enjoy sex with me, but I don't think she's the least bit tormented by how much she liked it. Not exactly what I had planned but it works for me.

"Why settle for three?"

13

EMILIA BELLINI

I HATE LUCA ROSSINI. BUT I LOVE THE WAY HE TOUCHED me last night. I enjoyed it enough to let him give me four orgasms before we went to sleep and then another this morning after we woke. I was even the one who initiated sex before he got out of bed to shower.

Something is wrong with me. Terribly wrong.

Luca Rossini is a monster. A monster with hands that bring me the most intense pleasure I've ever experienced. I wasn't expecting that after our dreadful first encounter.

"Make him believe that you enjoy the sex," my mother said.

"Make the most out of his appetite for sex," she also said.

I was supposed to be pretending, and I was in the beginning, but then something unexpected happened. Luca wanted to pleasure me. He was determined to do so. I saw it in his eyes. And then I felt it.

"Is everything okay with you today?" Peter asks.

"Yeah. Of course."

"You seem a bit distracted."

"Sorry. I didn't get a lot of sleep last night."

I'm typically asleep by ten when I have rehearsal the

next day but not last night. Luca and I had barely even gotten started at ten o'clock. The sex and the lengthy in-between conversations went on for hours. We didn't fall asleep until after two, and then he had to get up at six for an early meeting.

We had a busy night and morning.

"I'm planning to practice my fouetté this weekend."

"I can come over and help you."

I could actually use Peter's help, but I know having him over isn't an option. I can never mix my life at the dance company with my life as a Bellini. Or Rossini. And let's be honest. I can't trust Luca to behave. He's already told me that he doesn't like my male dance partner putting his hands on me.

Luca would threaten Peter if he ever came face-to-face with him. I don't doubt that for a second, and I can't take that kind of risk.

"That's so nice of you to offer, but we're going to our house in the Hamptons after rehearsal on Friday. Just a quick little weekend getaway."

"That sounds like fun. Maybe another time then?"

"For sure."

Today's rehearsal is mostly a bust because I'm unable to concentrate on what I'm supposed to be doing. I'm relieved when five o'clock comes, and then I see the black Cadillac at the curb waiting for me, its driver ready to take me back to Luca. But I'm not ready to go back to him. I need a breather. And to talk to someone. Someone who isn't genetically tied to me.

Elena.

Sal doesn't question me when I give him Elena's address. He simply nods and pulls away, driving in that direction.

My life as Luca's betrothed hasn't turned out as I

expected. I imagined myself his prisoner with little to no contact with my friends and family. But the truth is that Luca has given me the freedom to come and go as I please. He treats me as though this is a real relationship.

I can tell that he isn't happy about my job at the dance company, but he didn't demand that I quit. I think that's only because he expects the *problem* to fix itself when —if—I become pregnant, hence the reason he hasn't given me any ultimatums about it. It's a smart move on his part.

He is turning out to be very different from the idea I had in my mind, but he's still the man who killed those who meant the world to me. Nothing will never change that.

Elena opens the door and squeals when she sees me. Throwing our arms around each other, we spin in the hallway of her apartment building. "Emilia! How… how are you here?"

"I'll explain if you let me in."

"Oh yeah. Get your skinny little ballerina ass in here and tell me everything."

Nic was my best friend, but Elena has always been my best girlfriend. I've known her my entire life because her father was Papà's consigliere, or right-hand man. He managed to escape the wedding day massacre because he was away on business for my family. Had his flight not been delayed, he would have met the same fate as the other Bellini men on that day.

Elena goes to the cabinet and takes out two glasses. "We need wine."

"Yes, wine, please. A lot of it."

She pours two reds, passing one to me before she curls into the corner of her sofa. "I've been so worried about you."

"I can't believe I've only been with him for a week. It feels like so much longer."

"Is he the cruel bastard that I suspect he is? Has he been horrible to you?"

Luca is like two different people inside the same body. He has a vile side with a cruel streak, and that part of him wants to hurt me. But then there's also another half of him who wants to protect me. It's confusing.

"The first night was awful. He told me he wouldn't marry me unless I proved my fertility to him by getting pregnant… so *that* began on night one. And it wasn't pleasant at all. It was nothing like what I had imagined it to be." But then, of course, I had always imagined it being with Nic.

"He can't do that. It's not the way. You'll be dishonored if you aren't married."

"Luca Rossini doesn't care about tradition or my honor."

"And you went along with it because you had no other choice?"

I nod. "I was angry when he told me what I had to do. And you know how I am. I couldn't lie down and let him have me without fighting him in some kind of way. I provoked him and took jabs at his manhood. And he made me sorry for it. He was brutal, and it was awful the first time."

"That must have been terrible. I want to go kill him for you right now."

Funny she should mention killing. "My mother and grandmother want me to kill Luca and all of the Rossini men after I give him a son. A son who will be heir to the Rossini and Bellini empires."

Elena grins. "And you'll be the mother of the boy. That's a brilliant plan."

"Giving him an heir means getting pregnant, which obviously means having sex."

"Which is unfortunate but necessary."

Nothing about last night or this morning was unfortunate.

"Mamma told me to pretend that I enjoy the sex. She says I must be a dutiful fiancée until I become a dutiful wife."

"As much as I hate it for you, I think that's good advice."

"Last night was our second time. And I was pretending to enjoy it. And—"

I bite my bottom lip, suppressing my smile because I don't want Elena to think I'm some kind of sicko.

"And?"

"You can't judge me for what I'm about to tell you."

"I understand you're doing this because you have no other choice. I would never judge any of your actions."

I'm about to blow Elena's mind. "I liked it."

"You liked what?"

"Sex with Luca."

"Oh… *ohhh*."

"You're judging me."

"I'm not judging you. I'm… thinking."

I need to explain. Defend myself.

"I thought it was going to be awful like the first time, but it wasn't. He was gentle and took great care in ensuring that I enjoyed everything he was doing."

"Why do you think he was so different from one time to the next?"

"He didn't know I was a virgin. He thought I had given myself to Nic, and that really pissed him off since he sees me as his property. And then I made him even madder because I used Nic to provoke him."

"I see."

"Last night was good. Sooo good." I bite my bottom lip again, but this time I'm unsuccessful at preventing a grin. "And this morning too."

"Define sooo good."

"He gave me four orgasms last night."

"And this morning?"

"Only one. He was in a hurry."

"*Only one orgasm* she says." Elena laughs. "Do you know how lucky you are? No man has ever given me an orgasm."

"Not even Roberto?"

"Especially not Roberto."

"Wow. I would have expected more out of him."

"As did I. But back to you and Luca."

"The man who murdered my fiancé is giving me orgasms. And I like it. I want more of them. And I want more of his devil dick. I'm enchanted by it. How sick is that?"

"Is it possible that you see Luca Rossini as something more?"

"As in what?"

"He's been your betrothed forever. Even if you didn't know him, his name has been in your head all this time. Maybe somewhere deep inside you feel like he's something to you instead of nothing." Elena shrugs. "I don't know. I was just throwing that out there as a possible explanation."

"I don't guess the idea is completely far-fetched. But even if there was some truth to it, he would have ended any feelings I had for him when he murdered my loved ones."

"Orgasms don't require affection."

"Obviously."

In his bed, I'm able to forget who he is. And I become his. Slowly, I feel him possessing me.

"You have to marry this asshole and give him a baby. You might as well get some perks out of it. If it's orgasms and millions of dollars, then so be it."

Orgasms and millions. I could do worse.

"Have you ever seen Luca?"

"Once, but it was through a crowd and at a distance in a disco."

"He is—" I try to think of the right word, but only one comes to mind. "Beautiful."

"At least he's good-looking. You could have gotten stuck with somebody who looks like Joey Fiore."

That guy gives me the creeps. "Totally."

"How long is your leash?"

"Luca lets me do as I please."

"Then go out with me tonight."

I just left an eight-hour rehearsal, and my feet are killing me. "Look at me. I'm a total mess."

"You can get ready here and wear something of mine."

I haven't been out in so long. I miss the party scene. "Where are you thinking of going?"

"Beat's."

Gosh, I love Beat's. I haven't been in months.

"Okay. I'm in."

Luca is sitting in bed reading when I open the bedroom door. He looks up from his book and places it on his lap. "It's after midnight."

"I didn't mean to stay out so late." I really didn't, but Elena and I were having so much fun. Tonight was the first time in weeks that I didn't feel like I was drowning in sorrow.

"I'm told that you visited your friend Elena, and then the two of you went to a disco?"

How does he know that? Did Sal call him? Or is he having me followed?

"We did."

"Did you have a good time?"

"Yes. It felt like old times."

"But these aren't old times. They're new times."

"I've not forgotten."

He uses his finger to beckon me. When I reach the side of the bed, he scoots over and I sit on the edge next to him.

He tucks a wild strand of hair behind my ear and searches my face. "We've discussed this, Emilia. You know that there are people out there who would hurt you simply to hurt me."

"But we aren't married. As far as they know, I'm no one to you."

"I went to a lot of trouble to claim you as mine, and people have taken notice. For that reason alone, they are very aware of how special you are to me. Many of them would like nothing more than to take you from me."

He's simultaneously scolding me while also making me feel like the most important woman in the world to him. It's annoying and sexy, but mostly sexy.

"You have to think about these things now. You could already be carrying my son, and I need you to be safe at all times."

I breathe in deeply and release the breath slowly. "I'm not carrying your son."

"You got your period?"

"Yes. This afternoon."

If he's disappointed, it doesn't show on his face. "Okay. That gives us a point of reference for calculating your fertile time next month."

"I don't know how to do that—calculate my fertile time."

"My mother can explain it to you."

I can't talk to Viviana about having sex with her son.

"I'd be more comfortable asking my mother."

"That's understandable."

He folds down the corner of his book and places it on the nightstand. Reaching for my hand, he tugs. "Come here."

He guides me to sit on his lap, straddling him. His hands cradle my face, and he pulls me close for a kiss.

"It's going to happen next month. You'll see that I'm right."

"And what if it doesn't? Are you going to toss me aside and find another Mafia princess to marry?"

"You will have my son inside of you by the end of next month. I'm certain."

He isn't answering my question.

"Tell me, Luca. Will you cast me aside after ruining me?"

"There's no point in having that conversation right now. No good can come from it."

He'll do it. I can tell by the words that he isn't saying. And that means the pressure is on.

I have to get pregnant. There is no other option.

14

LUCA ROSSINI

"Miracles" by Jefferson Starship. I hear it somewhere in the house, and I'm certain it must be Emilia playing it. None of my men would be listening to that kind of music.

I follow the sound and locate Emilia in the sunroom at the back of the house.

A leotard. Ballet slippers. Hair in a bun. Wearing the full ballerina getup, minus the tutu, she's standing on the toes of one foot, rotating round and round like one of those dolls inside a child's jewelry box.

Damn, it looks painful. I can't imagine the strength it must take to do something like that.

My betrothed is mesmerizing to watch. And sexy as hell.

She lowers herself from her toes and stands on both feet. Panting, she rests her hands on her hips.

"That was truly amazing."

She twists and looks at me over her shoulder. "How long have you been standing there?"

"Not long. What is that spin thing called?"

"A French fouetté. I mastered it years ago, but I have to do a series of them at the end of act 3. By that point, my legs are exhausted, so I'm having a hard time sticking it."

"Is there anything I can do to help?"

Her head tilts. "You'd do that?"

"Help you? Of course."

"You don't think it would make you soft?"

"I wouldn't put on tights for you, but yeah, I would help you if you needed me."

She giggles. "That's a kind offer, but I just have to keep doing it over and over to build endurance in my muscles."

"I didn't realize how much strength you had in your legs until now."

"I'm small but mighty."

"I see that. Do you mind if I hang around for a while and watch you practice?"

"I don't mind."

Strong. Graceful. Talented. Skilled. Beautiful. Emilia is all of those things and so much more.

I watch her for a while and see her becoming frustrated with herself. "I think you could benefit from a break."

"I could benefit from more practice."

I go to her and place my hands on her shoulders. "You can't build endurance in one day. You have practice every weekday for the next six or seven weeks. Don't worry. You'll build the strength required during that time."

She lifts her arm, using her forearm to wipe the sweat from her brow. "You're probably right."

I wink at her and smile. "I'm always right."

"You're always arrogant."

I chuckle because Emilia's honesty entertains me. I love how she's just that way. With her, there's none of those stroke-my-ego games like with other women. She simply tells it like it is.

"Call it a day and do something with me?"

"Like what?"

"I don't know. Anything you want."

"Anything?"

"Your choice… within reason."

"Okay. I want to go to the movies and see *Pretty Baby*. Is that within reason?"

"What's it about?"

"A whorehouse in New Orleans. You should enjoy that."

She wants to see a movie about a whorehouse? Sounds good to me. "Who am I to turn that down?"

TECHNICALLY, *PRETTY BABY* IS A MOVIE ABOUT A whorehouse in New Orleans, but it was not the kind of whorehouse movie I was expecting to see.

"What did you think of the movie?"

"I didn't like it." I didn't like it at all.

"You didn't? I thought it was really good. What did you not like about it?"

"The main character was a twelve-year-old child whose virginity was auctioned off to the highest bidder. It was disgusting. And her relationship with the photographer was repulsive."

Emilia stops walking, and I turn back to look at her. "What?"

She looks at me, saying nothing. Looking puzzled.

"What is it?"

"Don't you have dealings in the pornography industry?"

This girl. Did her mother not teach her that she shouldn't poke her nose around in family business?

"Don't ask me questions like that."

"Why not?"

"Because I will never tell you anything about family business."

"My father often talked with my mother about family business. I'm guessing Marco does with Viviana as well."

"They may discuss some things, but I can promise you that porn production isn't one of them."

Like my mother, Emilia will learn to pretend that pornography doesn't fund her many shopping sprees or luxury vacations.

"I overheard my father talking about it one time. He said your family is heavily involved in it. I was just curious about your role where that's concerned."

Well, she already knows. "I don't have a role in it. Someone else handles it."

"Have you ever gone to a set and watched?"

"A few times but it was a long time ago."

"Have you ever been with one of the girls you film?"

"Yeah, when I was much younger."

She disapproves. I see it in the crinkle of her upper lip.

"Those girls you film are someone's daughters. How would you feel if some sleazeball did that to your daughter?"

"I would kill any man who tries to make my daughter a porn star."

"You always talk about sons. It's odd to hear you say anything about a daughter."

"I want daughters too."

"Will you arrange marriages for them?"

"Absolutely."

"I'm curious. At what age would you give our daughter to a husband?"

I think about that for a moment and recall what

Alessandro told me. *One day when you have a daughter of your own, you'll understand why I had to do this for Emilia.*

"I think thirty-five seems reasonable."

Emilia chuckles. "Thirty-five? Not eighteen?"

"I'm not giving my daughter away when she's eighteen. That's way too young."

"Oh, so maybe you understand a little better now why my father wasn't ready to give me to you three years ago?"

"Perhaps." I hate admitting that.

"I needed that time with my family. I wasn't ready for this then."

"Are you ready for this now?"

"I'd better be."

"I'd been waiting for you a long time. I didn't want to give you the extra three years, but I knew it was what you needed. I wanted you to be happy."

"Thank you for waiting."

I've been waiting for my queen.

And now I have her.

15

EMILIA BELLINI

MY MOM IS COMING DOWN THE STAIRCASE AS I ENTER THE house. No one is as graceful as she is. When I was a child, I always thought she floated like a butterfly instead of walking like normal people.

"Emilia? This is a surprise."

I can't tell if she means my visit is a good surprise or a bad one. You can't always tell with her.

"I called several times, but no one answered the phone."

"That's because I had to let Maria go."

Maria has been with this family for over twenty years. She helped raise me and my siblings.

"Why did you let her go?"

"Your fiancé has taken our assets. I must spend wisely… at least until we get everything back."

There are a lot of other ways she could have said that, but I don't mistake that she chose to use one that implies that I am responsible for our family's lost fortune.

And it makes me feel like shit.

"Where did Maria go?"

"I don't know."

"You didn't ask her if she had a place to live?"

"She was our housekeeper, Emilia. So no, I didn't ask."

Maria wasn't only our housekeeper. She was a second mother to me, and at certain times, a first.

"Why have you brought a bag with you?"

"I'm staying here for a few days."

"Why?"

I walk toward the staircase. "If you'll give me a minute to get inside and put my things away, I'll explain everything to you."

"I assume Nonna needs to be present for whatever we discuss?"

"Definitely."

"And your sisters?"

"Gemma and Micaela. Not Issy."

"Isabella was very upset about not being included in the last conversation."

"Do you think I was wrong for making her leave?"

"The subject matter was a tough one, but she's a Bellini girl. She needs to be conditioned sooner rather than later about the things we must do to survive."

"Sex and murder. Do you really think a twelve-year-old girl should be included in that kind of conversation?"

"Any other twelve-year-old girl? No. But a Bellini girl? Yes."

"I don't think it's right, but she can be part of the conversation if it's what you want."

I don't agree with Mamma. Making Issy a part of this is wrong. No girl her age should hear the things we're about to discuss. But who am I to argue with our mother? Per Nonna's request, Mamma is matriarch of this family.

I place my suitcase on the floor and look around my bedroom. It hasn't even been two weeks since I last slept in this bed, but it feels like a million years ago after everything that has happened this week.

My life is so different now. *I'm* different. I feel like I've aged ten years in the last ten days.

A month ago, I was a nice Catholic girl who was obedient to God. And now? I'm a sex-loving fallen woman who is plotting multiple murders. And for what? Revenge and money.

Luca Rossini has changed me. And I hate him for it.

My family has already gathered in the living room when I enter.

"Welcome home."

"Thank you, Nonna. I'm happy to be back."

"How long are you staying?"

"Only a few days."

"I know you haven't been gone for very long, but you somehow look different," Gemma says.

"I *am* different." I'm not the same Emilia who left this house ten days ago.

"Why has Luca let you come home?" my mother asks.

"Nothing exciting. I simply started my period, which means I'm of no use to him for a few days."

My mother clicks her tongue. "Oh. Well, that's disappointing."

I've only been gone ten days. What did she expect?

"There was no way for it to happen. The timing was off."

"I understand."

"I need you to teach me how to predict which days I can get pregnant."

"It's pretty simple. Just count fourteen days after the first day of your period, and then include the two days before and the two days after. You should ovulate sometime within that five-day window. It's the opposite if you are trying to avoid pregnancy. You would count an extra day before and after and avoid sex during the seven-day window."

"That's it?"

"That's it if you have regular periods about every twenty-eight days or so." My mother clears her throat. "Another thing. Your mucus down there will be different. It becomes stretchy and clear."

Oh my God. My mother is teaching me about *mucus down there*. That's not at all uncomfortable to hear.

"And your body temperature will rise anywhere from a half degree to a whole degree. You'll have to take it every morning before you get out of bed to detect a change."

"Do you believe in this method?"

"I had five planned children instead of fifteen unplanned. I believe in it."

"What about you, Nonna?"

"I don't know anything about it. But I do know that when your mother decided she was ready to be pregnant, she would be the next month."

I hope this works for me.

I really, really, really need this to work.

"Is the sex as bad as it was the first time?"

Erotic ecstasy. Sexual bliss. Sensual euphoria. Take your pick.

"I close my eyes and tolerate it."

"Oh, Em. I'm so sorry this is happening to you. I would take your place if I could," Gemma says.

I think about that for a moment, and I'm surprised by the feelings it stirs. "This is my duty. No one else's."

When I get home, I want him to look into my eyes, caress my cheek… and tell me to take off my panties.

"Everything is riding on this baby. You must give it your all, or we will lose everything."

"I know, Mamma. I'm going to do whatever it takes to give him the son he wants so badly."

My life has never been my own to live. I've always been a piece in this game, but it's time to begin making my own moves.

"I know how I'm going to kill Luca."

"Tell us."

"He's a cocaine addict."

My mother gasps and places her hands together, covering her mouth. "This is wonderful news. Are you thinking overdose?"

"Something like that."

"An overdose would be perfect. Cocaine is a bad habit he picked up before you came into his life. It'll appear as though he died by his own hand. No one will suspect a thing."

"I think it could work."

"I know you don't think so, but you were bred for this life. I've always known that you were destined for greatness, and I wasn't wrong. Everyone is going to know who Emilia Bellini Rossini is."

Emilia Bellini Rossini.

What about Emilia Bellini Moretti? Where did she go? What happened to that girl?

She didn't want this life. She didn't choose it. It chose her. And now she has no choice but to become the *femme fatale* Luca Rossini has made her.

16

LUCA ROSSINI

WALKING BY THE DINING ROOM, I STOP AND LOOK AT THE table. There's a pair of white candles with burned black wicks, obviously once taller than they are now, placed in front of two plates. One is partially eaten, the other is untouched.

Looks like beef and cheese manicotti, one of my favorite dishes. I'd bet anything that it's a Bellini family recipe.

It's barely eleven, and the house is quiet and dark. Has Emilia gone to bed already? Or did she leave and go back to the Bellini mansion?

I open the bedroom door, and I'm relieved when I see the outline of her body on the bed.

"Emilia?"

Nothing.

I strip down to my boxers and slide into bed. Gliding to the middle, I reach for her hip and grip it. "Emilia."

She stirs, twisting to look back at me over her shoulder, and says nothing.

"I'm home."

"I see that." She turns back and settles into position on her side, her back turned to me. "Good night."

"It's been three days. Don't you want to see me?"

"I did. That's why I came home early and cooked dinner for you. And then sat here by myself and ate alone."

"I didn't know."

"You would have known if you'd bothered to call home."

"I couldn't call. There was a situation. A dangerous one."

The mattress bounces when she tosses and turns over to face me. "Are you all right?"

"I'm fine, but one of my men was killed tonight."

"Who? And by whom? What happened?"

I reach out in the dark and cup the side of her face. "I don't want to worry you about such things."

"Tell me, Luca. I want to know."

"It was Rossini family business."

"I don't want us to run this empire the way our parents and grandparents have. I want to be told what's going on."

"And I want you to be burden-free just as our mothers and grandmothers were."

"I'm strong. I can handle whatever comes."

"I know you can, but that's not what I want for my wife."

"Will you at least tell me if you were in danger tonight?"

"If I was, would you care?"

It takes one, two, three heartbeats before she answers. "I would care very much."

"Why? Because my death would free you from this arrangement?"

"It's a waste of time to talk about what-if situations.

I'm not free. I'm yours, and I'm at your mercy. We both know that. And we also both know how pleased you are about that."

"I am pleased by it." And I'm beginning to suspect that she might not hate being mine nearly as much as she lets on.

"Did you learn anything while you were with your family?"

"My mother taught me how to use my period to predict my fertile days."

"That'll be helpful."

"It's not one hundred percent accurate, so we shouldn't limit ourselves to only doing it during the five-day window."

"We should do it on other days too?"

"Our chances of being successful would improve if we did it more days."

"What about every day?"

"Every day would increase the odds of success."

Hmm. I think someone may have an obsession with my newly discovered sexual talents.

"What if I fuck you every night and again every morning? And then maybe on my lunch break?"

"Are you making fun of me?"

I am, one hundred percent.

"I would not dare make fun of you when it comes to sex."

"You are." She rolls over, turning her back on me again. "Fuck you, Luca Rossini. I hate you."

Ah, shit. I've pissed off the princess.

"Come on… I was kidding, Em."

"You don't get to call me Em. Only my friends and family who love me get to call me by that name."

"I was only having a little fun. Don't be mad at me."

"You know what, Luca? There is only a very brief time each month when my body is capable of getting pregnant, and I don't know when that small slice of time will be. I'm trying to cover all the bases because everyone will blame me if it doesn't happen. No one will blame you. I know how this works. I'll be the one who is labeled infertile, and you'll get to move on to the next girl when I'm not able to give you a son."

The increased pitch of her voice is an indicator of the pressure she's feeling.

"Turn over."

"No."

"Turn over and face me."

She doesn't say anything, and she also doesn't move a muscle.

"Now, Emilia."

Still nothing.

"You're so fucking stubborn," I murmur as I grip her hip and force her to roll to her back. "Is your period over?"

"Yes."

Gripping her panties at each hip, I drag them down her legs.

"No. I don't want to."

"Yes, you do."

"I don't."

"Why not?"

"Because I'm mad at you."

"But you wanted it before you were mad?" She doesn't answer me, and that's when I know I have her. "Go on. Admit it."

"I'm not admitting anything."

"You wanted to fuck before I teased you. I know you did."

Her only response is a long sigh.

I push her nightgown up and kiss her bare stomach, dragging my tongue side-to-side across her pubic bone. "Do you get tingles between your legs when I kiss you here?"

Rapid breaths. Tilting pelvis. I'll take that as a yes, but I want to hear her admit it.

"Answer me or it stops."

"Yes, Luca. I get tingles when you kiss me there."

Good girl.

I move my face lower and open my mouth, breathing heavily between her legs but not touching her. She pants and lifts her hips from the bed, grazing my stubbled chin.

"Is your pussy throbbing?"

"Yes."

"Tell me what you want, and I'll do it."

"I don't know. No one has ever done that to me."

There it is—the proof I desperately wanted to hear. Moretti never tasted what belongs to me. Another first that I get to give her.

"Don't worry, Emilia. I'm going to give you everything you don't know how to ask for."

17

EMILIA BELLINI

IT'S TEN O'CLOCK, AND I'VE NOT HEARD A WORD FROM Luca. Again. This little habit of his is beginning to annoy the shit out of me.

Going in search of Sal, I find him in the billiards room with the other resident Rossini soldiers.

"Do you know where Luca is?"

Sal looks up from his hand of cards. "I dropped him and the guys off at Fever."

"Fever? What is that?"

"A disco."

"How long ago?"

"I just got back from taking them."

"Did he tell you when to come back?"

"No. He'll call when he's ready to be picked up."

Luca Rossini is crazy if he thinks I'm going to sit here, night after night, while he goes out partying with his pals. And whoever else.

"I'm going out. I'll need you to drive me in about forty minutes."

"Yes, Miss Bellini."

I phone Elena and breathe a sigh of relief when she answers. It's Thursday night. I'm lucky she hasn't already gone out for the evening. "Get your ass ready. We're going out."

"I started getting ready thirty minutes ago."

"Are you meeting up with someone?"

"Natala. We're going to Beat's."

Beat's doesn't work for me. "Change of plans. The two of you are going with me to Fever."

"Awesome. What time?"

"I'll be there in an hour. And I need to borrow your gold minidress."

I don't have Elena's boobs, but I think I can pull it off.

"What are you up to?"

"I'll tell you on the way."

An hour and a half later, I'm wearing Elena's skimpiest sequin dress and the three of us are navigating our way through the crowd inside the disco club. The place is packed.

I search for Luca, but he's nowhere to be seen. Something tells me that he wouldn't be sitting out in the open for just anyone to see.

"I'm going to the bar and ask where Luca is."

"Do you think they'll tell you?"

"They will when they find out who I am."

I push my way through the crowd to the bar and hold up my hand when the bartender looks my way.

"What can I get you?"

"I'm looking for Luca Rossini."

He laughs. "You and every other woman in this club."

"I'm Emilia Bellini. His fiancée."

"Sure, you are."

I take out a hundred-dollar bill and hold it in front of the bartender. "I need to see my fiancé. Where is he?"

He takes the bill from my hand and points to a room at the top of the stairs. "VIP room."

I should have known.

"Thank you."

"I didn't tell you anything, got it?"

"Understood."

Elena and Natala are on the dance floor with a couple of guys, so I forgo stopping by to tell them I'm going upstairs. I don't think they really care anyway.

A burly huge man uses his arm to block me. "Sorry. Can't let you go up there."

"I'm Emilia Bellini. Luca Rossini is my fiancé."

"This one's telling the truth. This woman will soon be my brother's wife."

I turn at the sound of the voice and see a guy who clearly must be Luca's brother. They could almost pass for twins.

"See? I'm not lying."

The man steps aside and allows both of us to pass.

"I'm sorry we weren't officially introduced the night your family brought you to my parents' house. I'm Stephan."

I have absolutely no memory of seeing this guy at the Rossini compound. But that's no surprise. I was out of my mind with fear and anxiety.

"I'm Emilia."

He smiles. "Yeah, I know who you are."

We ascend the winding staircase, Luca's brother leading me.

"Is he expecting you?"

"No. He has no idea I'm here." I'm sure he thinks I'm at home in bed.

"That's what I thought."

"He's probably going to be pretty pissed off about me coming."

"Probably. And I'm thrilled to be the one who got you in. I can't wait to see his face when he sees you here."

"Do you need to prepare me for what I'm about to walk in to?"

"You had the guts to show up here uninvited. I have a feeling that you're more than capable of handling what you're about to see."

Shit. I don't like the way that sounds.

Stephan opens the door, and I walk into the dimly lit room. There are tables lining each side of the large space and every one of them is surrounded by people.

"Last table on the left," Stephan says.

"Thanks."

I walk the length of the room, and my eyes roam for Luca as I approach his table. And then I see him, surrounded by his guys. He doesn't notice me, and I take the brief moment to observe him in this environment.

A whiskey in one hand.

A burning cigar between his index and middle finger, half smoked.

Several thin white lines on the table waiting to be snorted.

One of the guys at this table leans over and sucks the white powder up his nose. When he finishes, he holds out the rolled bill to Luca.

I stop, frozen in place, and my heart sinks when he takes the bill from his friend.

We agreed, Luca. You told me you wouldn't do cocaine while we were trying to conceive. You promised me you would stop because you wanted your son to be healthy. But you lied.

I should have known I couldn't trust an addict to stop.

My sinking heart is thrown a preserver when Luca passes the bill to the next guy without partaking. Completely unaware that I'm here and watching, he kept his promise to me. That means something to me.

"Chickening out?"

"I don't chicken out."

Stephan chuckles. "No, I bet you don't."

I'm almost to the table when a pretty blonde in a very short dress plants herself in Luca's lap and presses a kiss to his mouth. I stop again, frozen, and I'm not sure how to label the feeling in my gut. But betrayal feels like a good start.

This was a mistake. I shouldn't have come here.

"Who is that woman?"

"Angelica."

"Is Luca in a relationship with her?"

"I think that's a question Luca should answer."

The woman stops kissing him and over her shoulder, his eyes lift and meet mine.

"Fuck this. I'm out of here."

I hear Luca call out my name, and I walk faster, almost sprinting, and I rush down the staircase. Weaving through the crowd, I find Elena and Natala on the dance floor where I left them earlier with the same pair of guys.

"I need to get out of here."

Elena stops dancing. "Why? What happened?"

I shake my head. "I found him with another woman."

"Ah, no way. Are you sure?"

There was no mistaking that. "She was sitting on his lap and they kissed."

I can't believe I was stupid enough to believe him when he said he wouldn't be with anyone else.

"I want to get out of here."

Elena grabs my hand. "Let's go to the bathroom and talk about this first."

With hesitancy, I follow Elena and Natala to the bathroom, and they huddle me in the corner away from all of the drunk clubbers.

"I don't know what you could possibly think there is to discuss."

"Running out of here right now makes you look like you care," Elena says.

"I do care. That bastard is still fucking around with other women. He could give me a venereal disease."

"Running away makes it look as though you're hurt because he's with another woman."

I think I am hurt.

"Do you want to give him that kind of satisfaction?"

"No."

"You need to go out there and let him see you having the time of your life. Find a man to dance with. Give that Rossini fucker a healthy dose of his own medicine."

"Yeah. I can be with someone else too if he wants to play that game."

"That's our girl."

The three of us hit the floor and easily find three men who are eager to dance with us. The guy I partner with certainly doesn't compare to Luca, but then again, not many men do.

He leans down so his mouth is near my ear. "What's your name?"

"Emilia."

"I'm Brian. I've never seen you in here before."

"It's my first time at this club."

"I hope it won't be your last."

I smile and shrug. "I guess we'll see."

We move to "Stayin' Alive" and about halfway through

the song, Brian grips my waist and pulls me closer, his mouth against my ear again. "I can't believe you're dancing with me."

"Why not?"

"Because you're the most beautiful girl in this place."

Hmm. I wonder how many times a night he uses that line.

"That's a very sweet thing to say. Thank you."

"I'm saying it because it's true."

Brian grips my hand and spins me out and then back in. He's not a bad dancer for an amateur.

"Do you live around here?"

Opening my mouth to answer, I don't get the chance because Luca forces his way between us and pushes Brian backward.

I shove Luca's chest, but he doesn't budge. "What the hell do you think you're doing?"

Brian regains his footing and advances on Luca. "Not cool, dude."

Luca reaches inside his jacket and pulls out a Glock, pointing it directly at Brian's forehead. "Put your hands on my fiancée again, and I will kill you."

"Are you crazy? You can't pull out a gun in the middle of a club."

There's deadly intent in the way Luca is staring at Brian. A challenge. He's daring him to make a wrong move. And I'm afraid of what he may do.

Stepping between them, I grasp Luca's face. "Look at me."

His eyes remain locked on Brian.

I pull downward on his face. "Luca. Look at me."

He hesitates a moment but finally obeys, his eyes meeting mine.

"Put the gun away."

Luca looks back at Brian and then finally lowers his arm, returning his gun to its holster.

"Get him out of here."

Two men loop their arms through Brian's. He looks from one to the other and then at me. "What the hell is this?"

Luca says nothing, watching as they lead Brian away.

"Where are they taking him? What are they going to do?"

"They'll take him out back and show him why he shouldn't have put his hands on you."

"No, Luca. Please don't hurt him. We were only dancing. He didn't know."

"He didn't know but you did. The lesson isn't his. It's yours."

"I've learned… I've learned. You don't have to hurt him."

"It wouldn't be much of a lesson if I didn't carry through with the teaching."

I slap Luca's face with every bit of my might. "I hate you. You're a monster."

"Yes, I am, and you shouldn't forget that anytime soon."

"I dance with a guy and he gets beat up, but it's okay for you to make out with some whore on your lap? Did I get that right?"

Luca grips my upper arm, dragging me across the club. I'm suddenly frightened because I don't know where he's taking me or what he's going to do to me once we get there.

"Let go of me."

His only reply is to tug me harder. Painfully.

I want to scream for help, but no one would hear me if

I did. I could make a scene, but that wouldn't work either. People would assume I was high and freaking out.

I'm fucked. No two ways about it.

Luca leads me up the stairs to a private room on the VIP level, pulling the door closed with a hard thud when we're inside. He advances toward me and I back away, eventually hitting the wall.

With his hands on his hips, he stares me down. "I didn't ask her to sit on my lap, and I sure as hell didn't ask her to kiss me."

"That didn't look like the case from where I was standing."

"I told her to stop and get up."

She looked very comfortable with what she was doing. "Have you been seeing her?"

"Yes, but it's over."

"Since when?"

"Since you."

"I don't believe that." I shove at his chest and he doesn't budge. "I asked you to not sleep with anyone while we're trying to have a baby. You're putting my safety and the baby's at risk by being with other women."

I shove harder at his chest and he grips my wrists, pulling me against him. "Listen very carefully to what I'm about to say. I don't answer to you, princess. Not in any way. If I want another woman in my bed, then I'll have another woman in my bed. But I haven't touched Angelica, and I haven't touched any other woman since you. If I had, I'd tell you so myself."

"Why should I believe you?"

"Because I have no reason to lie to you."

I can't come up with any kind of argument for that.

"I'm not a man who will beg and plead for your trust." He presses me against the wall and pulls up my dress. "Believe me or don't. It's your choice, but I'm still going to fuck you and you're still going to give me a son."

I push my fingers into his hair and grip it tightly, tugging and making him hiss.

"I hate you."

He smiles and chuckles. "You wish you hated me."

His mouth crashes against mine, and his tongue pushes its way into my mouth. I turn my face away, fighting and pushing at his shoulders. My dress bunched at my waist, I press my thighs together when he grasps my panties and drags them down my legs.

"You also wish you didn't want me to fuck you against this wall right now."

My flat palms come down hard against his chest. "I don't."

"Liar. Let's see if I'm right." He shoves his hand between my legs, one of his fingers gliding through my slick center. "That's exactly what I thought I'd find waiting for me."

His heart is full of darkness, and I hate myself for still wanting every inch of him.

Luca unfastens his pants and dips his hand inside his boxers, pulling out his cock. He lifts my feet off the floor, and my legs instantly wrap around his torso as though they have a mind of their own, as though they don't need to hear the command from my brain.

Wrapping my arms around his shoulders tightly, I suck air in through my clenched teeth when he slides inside me.

"Fuuuck," he groans against my ear.

He grips the underside of my thighs, his fingertips digging into my flesh as he anchors me against the wall and roughly slams into me over and over. My elbows resting on his shoulders, I grip the top of his hair as he bounces me up and down his dick. I'm certain my body will be covered in fresh purple bruises tomorrow.

"You are mine in a way that no one will ever understand."

The door, which Luca obviously didn't lock, opens, and the club's music fills the small space we're in with "Radar Love" by Golden Earring. The room is dimly lit except for the lights flashing through the cracked door, so I can't make out who our intruder is.

I don't think Luca's aware of our audience. But if he is, it doesn't faze him because his thrusts don't let up.

The silhouette of the person in the doorway belongs to a woman—that much I can tell. And then she opens the door wider and her eyes meet mine. The blonde who was sitting on Luca's lap kissing him.

She sees him fucking me, and I'm surprised when she doesn't turn away and leave. Instead, she watches. It might be cruel, but I'm glad she's seeing us. I want her to fully understand that I am the reason it's over between them.

"Oh fuck, I'm going to come," Luca growls.

The blonde. She's still standing there.

She wants to watch? Let's give her a great finale to this show.

"Fuck me harder, Luca." I close my eyes and tighten my legs around him, my feet digging into his ass. "Give me your son. Put him inside me. Right now."

He pounds harder, and I grip his shoulders as he delivers the final few thrusts. And then he stills, holding me in place against the wall with his cock still inside.

I open my eyes and he kisses my mouth. "I'm taking you home."

Looking over his shoulder, I find the door closed and the blonde gone.

"Okay, but I want to do that again."

18

LUCA ROSSINI

EMILIA STRETCHES AND INHALES DEEPLY, A WEAK MOAN expelling from her throat as she exhales. "I need to get up."

"So do I."

She smiles and giggles. "That's not the kind of *need to get up* I'm talking about."

I stretch and groan as I exhale. "I'm pretty sure it is."

"No. I need to be at mass before nine."

I lift my head and look over at the clock on the nightstand. "It's 7:53. I need to be inside you before 7:54."

"I don't have time. I need thirty minutes to get ready, and then it's a twenty-minute drive. I'll be late if I don't get up right now."

She rolls over to get out of bed, and I grab her waist, pulling her back into bed. "How about I make you late now so you'll be late later?"

Wagging my brows, I wait for a response to my witty comment.

"Mm-hmm. I see what you did there with that. You're very clever."

"It's the first day of your fertile window. Don't you think you should stay in so we can get to work?"

"None of the signs are there. I don't think it's time yet."

"What are the signs?"

"My temperature will increase a little and my—"

She stops, and I wait for the rest of the sentence, but nothing comes out.

"Your temperature will rise and your… what?"

"Oh God." She grins and takes her pillow from beneath her head, placing it over her face.

"Tell me."

She groans. "My vaginal discharge will become clear and stretchy."

"Ohhh. Well, I need to check that." I reach out, sliding my hand between her legs, but she grips my wrist and pushes my hand away.

"We don't have time."

"What if it happens while you're at mass and we miss our opportunity?"

"I don't think the window of opportunity opens and closes that quickly."

Taking her pillow, I toss it to the foot of the bed and crawl over her, pressing kisses to the side of her neck. "Don't go. Let's do this instead."

Her head tilts, offering me full access to her neck. "You are terrible for my eternal life. Since I met you, I've missed every Sunday mass, we commit a mortal sin every day, usually multiple times, and I haven't been to confession once."

"True but I give you orgasms. Many of them. And I don't hear you complaining about that."

"No. I don't have any complaints about those."

"Stay and I'll give you orgasms."

"Oh my God. You are the devil."

"Never claimed otherwise."

She stays.

We fuck all morning.

And I give her three orgasms.

I lie on my back and place my palm against my stomach, rubbing it in a circle. "I'm starving. Believe it or not, it doesn't matter how much pussy you eat. It never fills you up."

She wants to grin. I can see it. And she almost does when the corners of her mouth slightly tug upward. "You are awful."

"That's not what you said while I was feasting between your legs."

Shocking this good little Catholic girl is so much fun. Although I'm beginning to question just how *good* she really is. She gives in to temptation very easily.

"How does an omelet sound?"

"I could eat four right now."

"How about you start with one, and I'll cook you another if you're still hungry?"

"Sounds good."

Sleeping in on Saturday and Sunday. Watching Emilia cook a late breakfast after I've spent all morning inside her. This is how I want all of our weekends to be. At least until our first little one arrives and steals this time away from us.

Emilia slides an enormous omelet from a skillet onto the plate in front of me. "I didn't say how big the one would be."

"It's enormous."

"You said you were starving."

"And you took me at my word."

"I'm learning to do that with you."

This isn't the first time Emilia has cooked for me, but it is the first time I've eaten what she prepared. And I'm delighted to learn that she can cook well. Or at least she can cook great omelets.

"This is very good."

"I'm glad you like it."

"The manicotti looked delicious."

"It was. Too bad you missed it."

"I don't plan on missing meals with you if I can help it, but I need you to be understanding when circumstances keep me away from home."

"I'm understanding when it's family and business-related, but don't expect me to be complaisant when you're in a club drinking whiskey, smoking cigars, and having women throw themselves on your lap and kissing you while I'm sitting at home waiting for you."

"Spoken like a true wife. I like it."

"A wife is what you expect me to be, so you shouldn't be surprised when I act like one."

Actually, I am a little surprised. But not disappointed. Not disappointed at all. "All right. Point taken."

"I hope so."

"This relationship is still very new for both of us, and it will be for a while. We'll adjust, and it'll become easier after we know each other."

"I guess."

I return to eating but Emilia doesn't. And that's when I notice that she's barely touched her food. "Everything okay?"

She lowers her fork to the table and leans back in the chair, looking at me. "I want to talk about that woman from last night."

Why? Is she jealous?

I don't know, but I want to find out.

"Do you think any good can come from having a conversation about her?"

"Did you think any good could come from talking about Nic?"

Okay. She's got me there. "What do you want to know about her?"

"Her name? How you met? When you met? I want to know everything."

"Her name is Angelica. Her father is a soldier for my family, and I've known her my entire life."

"How long have you dated her?"

"Dated?" I chuckle. "I've never dated Angelica."

"Then what kind of relationship did you have?"

"We fucked when I felt like it. That's the kind of relationship we had."

One of Emilia's brows lifts. "That may be all it is to you, but that's not all it is to her."

"How would you know?"

Emilia crosses her arms. "She watched us last night."

"What do you mean *she watched us*?"

"That room you took me to… she stood in the doorway and watched you fuck me against the wall."

Last night, I was sucked into the moment when Emilia told me to fuck her harder, but then she told me to give her my son—put him inside her right then—and I fucking lost it.

I wanted to obey this woman like she was my master and I, her servant.

"I had no idea Angelica watched."

"It hurt her to see us like that. I could tell."

"She says she loves me."

"You don't love her?"

"Fuck no." I've never loved a woman. At least not that way.

"Were you faithful to her?"

"We were never a couple. There was no commitment of any kind, so there was nothing to be faithful to."

"Have you ever been faithful to any woman?"

"I've never had to be."

"Will you be faithful to me?"

"Do you want me to be faithful to you?"

"For now, yes."

I don't like that answer.

"You say *for now* as though our fidelity to each other will be up for discussion at a later time. It won't be. I'll never allow you to be with someone else. I'll kill any man who touches you."

"After last night, I believe you."

"Because you're mine. I'm the only man who will ever have you."

"You've made me your possession, a shiny toy you don't want other boys to play with. But I'm not an object, Luca. I want to love a man with the deepest depths of my soul and have that same kind of love returned to me. I want to be ravished in the most loving and tender way until all I'm able to feel is unbearable pleasure. Don't you want something like that?"

"I do. I want it with you."

"You've killed so many people I love. And then while the women in my family and I were at our most vulnerable, you took everything from us. You're making me marry you… but only after you've disgraced me and forced me into a pregnancy outside of wedlock. How could—"

How could I ever love you? She doesn't complete the sentence, but I hear it loud and clear.

I thought she was beginning to come around. Now, I don't know.

"I'm hoping you can come to feel some kind of fondness for me. If not that, at least some kind of devotion?"

"Would that be enough for you? To go through life married to someone who didn't love you?"

"I don't know. I've never loved a woman and wanted her love in return."

"Do you ever wonder what your life would have been like if you'd been born into an ordinary family?"

"No, because I'm not a fan of ordinary."

"I'm not the only pawn in this game. You've been one as well. Surely, you recognize that?"

I was never going to be anyone's rung on a ladder. "I figured out at a very early age that my father was going to use me as a stepping-stone for his ambitions, so I trumped him and made my own aspirations bigger than his."

"Look at what they've done to us. They've made us their Frankensteins whom they use to gain money and power."

"Frankenstein turned on his creator."

This girl is beautiful and brave and strong and broken all at once. I can't remember ever having a more real and honest conversation with anyone. Real and honest… that's something I've been missing in my life.

Nicolò Moretti was willing to burn the world down to protect the one person he cared about. And I understand it now—why he looked me in the eye and told me that he would never give Emilia up, and the only way I would ever have her was if he was dead.

So he is.

That's a man I understand. And damn, I respect him for it.

"I don't want to do to our children what has been done to us. Promise me that we won't."

I understand Emilia's aversion to arranged marriages, but they are often used for prosperity and peace. "We have no way of knowing what the future holds. Don't ask me to make that kind of promise to you right now. Because I can't."

"I'm telling you now that I won't go along with it."

You will, Emilia, if I say you will. But that's not an argument I wish to have at present.

"There's no reason to argue about the marriage of a child who doesn't exist yet. Can we agree to table this conversation until a decision needs to be made?"

"Happily."

Emilia picks up her coffee cup and takes a drink. "This is cold."

She takes my cup and hers to the sink, pouring the contents of both down the drain, and returns to the table with hot coffee.

"My parents want us to come over for dinner. They'd like to get to know their daughter-in-law."

"Seems a little premature. I would have expected them to want a positive pregnancy test before they invest their time in getting to know me."

Damn. If this girl thinks it, she says it.

"A pregnancy is *my* condition for marriage. Not theirs."

She's bringing her coffee to her mouth for a drink and stops midair. "They don't know we're trying?"

"No. My mother would have my ass if she knew I'd taken you before marriage." That is if she didn't keel over from a heart attack.

"Well, finally. Someone in this family has some respect for honor and the old ways."

While I understand why, I don't like that Emilia feels

dishonored by me. "After we're married, I think you will find yourself very surprised by all the ways I will honor you."

"I look forward to being surprised."

I have so many wonderful things in store for us. She has no idea. And I look forward to making her fall in love with me.

19

EMILIA BELLINI

Viviana asked me to come to the Rossini compound early and help prepare tonight's meal. The women coming together to cook Sunday dinner has always been a weekly ritual in the Bellini household, but we haven't prepared a family meal since our men were killed. I miss that time with my family.

An invitation into the Rossini kitchen to cook with Viviana, Luca's sister, Giada, and their grandmother Zorah is a big deal. They wouldn't do so if they didn't see me as part of their family.

Luca's mother stops what she's doing when I enter the kitchen and comes to me, kissing both sides of my face. "Look, Zee Zee. Luca's beautiful girl has come to cook tonight's meal with us."

His grandmother comes to me and takes my hands. Beginning at my face, she eyes me from head to toe, paying special attention to my midsection. "She has a pretty face, but how is a girl this small going to birth fat, healthy sons for Luca?"

Oh, no, she didn't.

Viviana laughs. "Oh, Zee Zee. Her mother is the exact same size and had five children without any complications. Don't worry. Emilia will be able to birth plenty of fat, healthy babies."

I'm not nearly as amused as Viviana by *Zee Zee's* critical assessment of me.

"Should I call you Zee Zee since I am going to be part of the family soon?"

"If you'd like."

I've only been here a few minutes, but I see no reason to not go ahead and shake shit up early. "If everything goes as Luca plans, our first fat, healthy baby should arrive sometime in April."

The smile leaves Viviana's face, and I can almost see the calculations going on in her mind. "You're pregnant?"

"We're trying." I scan the kitchen counter. "How may I help with dinner?"

Viviana looks at Zorah and then back at me. "What do you mean you're trying?"

"Luca's trying to get me pregnant. I thought he would have told you since proving my fertility is one of his stipulations for marriage."

"Luciano Davide Rossini," she hisses through her teeth and then looks at me. "Have you chosen a date for the wedding? Done any of the planning?"

"He told me to plan it, but I don't see the point because he says he won't marry me unless I become pregnant."

"Oh, no. This will not do at all. You must be married immediately. Luca's son cannot be conceived outside of wedlock."

I was dreading this Rossini family meal, but this couldn't be working out better for me. And now that I have Viviana on my side, I can't stop here.

"It could be a little late for that. It's… *my time* and we've been *trying*. A lot."

"Holy shit," Giada says, dropping an egg on the counter and breaking it.

"Being labeled a bastard could weaken your son's standing among the five families. Do you understand what that could mean?"

This couldn't be working out better.

"I'm very aware, but Luca insisted on doing it this way. And as you know, I'm not in a position where I can refuse him."

"No one can know about this."

"My family already knows."

Viviana flattens her palm over her forehead. "Oh God. This is awful."

"I'm sorry, but I had to tell them."

"Of course, you did. This isn't your fault. No one blames you. The fault is Luca's."

Time to play the pity card. "I don't want my family to be shamed. They've been through enough already."

"I won't let that happen. I'll take care of this with my son. You'll be married as soon as possible, and neither of our families will be shamed."

Finally, someone is helping me.

I'm not eager to marry Luca, but I am motivated to secure my place as a Rossini. Taking his name brings me one step closer to my end goal. But marriage isn't enough. I need his spawn inside of me. And I have the next five nights to get it there.

"Giada, I need you to take over. There's a discussion that my son and I need to have."

"We came separately, so Luca's not here yet."

"He will be when I call and tell him to get his ass over here pronto."

Viviana and Zee Zee leave the kitchen, both mad as hell. I'd give anything to be a fly on the wall whenever the two of them corner Luca. I hope they give it to him good.

"So what's for dinner?"

"Chicken scaloppine."

"That sounds good. What can I do to help?"

"The bell peppers and onions need to be sliced. Can you do that?"

"Sure. Thin strips?" That's how my family likes them.

"Yeah, but leave the onions wide enough for Enzo to pick around. He's still finicky."

"Oh, I understand. My little brother, Giovanni, was the same way."

"I'm glad you came tonight."

"I'm glad I was invited to come early and help out. I love being in the kitchen with family." Although I would prefer to be with my own.

"I'm happy you're becoming one of us. It sucks being the only girl. My brothers are jerks."

"Well, I know one who is."

"It's all an act. Luca likes you. He likes you a lot, actually."

Oh, this visit is proving to be very advantageous for me. "How do you know Luca likes me?"

"I've heard him say some things."

Luca talks about me? "What does he say?"

"What kind of sister would I be if I ratted out my brother?"

"Well, you and I are going to be sisters soon. And sisters tell each other everything."

Giada smiles. "You're a smooth one, but I'm smooth too."

I shrug and laugh. "Hey, it was worth a shot."

"Yeah, it was."

Giada goes to the refrigerator and takes out another egg. "Okay. If I repeat what I heard, you can't tell him I said anything."

"I would never."

"He was upset about the way your first night together went. He came to see Mamma about it."

Well, that corroborates what Viviana said about him being upset.

Giada breaks into a huge grin. "He wanted her advice on how to win your heart."

Win my heart? Viviana didn't tell me anything about that.

"When was this?"

"The day after he took you home with him."

He wants to win my heart, yet he's forcing me to prove my ability to conceive. Those two things don't go together at all.

I'm so confused.

Does he want me to love him? Or does he want me only for procreation?

Which one is it?

Giada and I talk as we cook dinner and like Viviana, she turns out to be a very likable person. And informative. I'm finding it impossible to hate her.

We set the table, and I become nervous when Viviana and Luca come into the dining room. I avoid his eyes because I'm afraid of what I'll see there.

He pulls out a chair for me and leans down, placing his mouth close to my ear. "Someone got me in trouble."

I sit, saying nothing in reply, and he takes the seat next to me.

"We have a lot to talk about when we get home tonight."

Shit.

Luca doesn't speak to me at dinner or in the car on the way home, which only manages to build the tension I'm feeling. The entire ride is a blur as I imagine all the things he's going to say, and possibly do, to me when we get home.

Sal parks in the garage, and I sit in the car unmoving as Luca opens the door and gets out.

"Come on, Emilia. Time to pay the piper."

I enjoyed getting Luca in trouble with his mother, but now I'm the one in trouble, and I'm not having quite as much fun.

I slide across the seat and get out. I follow Luca into the house, then upstairs to the bedroom, and I jolt when he closes the bedroom door.

"Not so brave now, are you?"

If he becomes physically violent with me, who's going to stop him? No one. There's not one single person in this house tonight who will help me.

I should beg for mercy or say that I'm sorry, but I can't bring myself to do either.

"Do whatever you're going to do to me, and get it over with."

"What should I do to you?"

I shrug and shake my head, too frightened to say anything—and certainly not willing to offer any ideas.

"I have an idea about what I want to do to you." He comes toward me, and my heart thumps wildly in my chest as I brace for the worst.

He shoves me down on the bed and crawls over me, pinning my arms above my head. "Would you like to hear what I'm going to do to you?"

I close my eyes and shake my head. "No. Just do it."

"I think I'll whisper it in your ear." His mouth hovers over my ear, his warm breath sending chills down my body.

"I'm going to marry you. Buy a dress, choose the date, and then tell me when and where to show up."

"After we know I'm pregnant?"

"As soon as possible. No baby required."

I'm going to be Mrs. Luca Rossini, one step closer to my end goal. But I must have his son before I can end this.

Good thing I don't mind doing what it takes to get that baby inside of me.

"I think I'll whisper something in your ear now."

"Okay," he says, dipping his head and placing his ear next to my mouth.

Catching his earlobe between my lips, I suck and release. "I still want you to give me your son."

"That's not all you want me to give you, is it, pretty princess?"

"I want that, too."

He releases my wrists and moves down my body. "Then I shall give you both."

20

LUCA ROSSINI

Emilia is something else.

I tell her that I'm going to marry her whether she's pregnant or not, and the baby-making efforts don't stop. She's been even more diligent the last few days. And while I'm not opposed to fucking her every morning and night, I'm in agony because I'm craving some blow like crazy.

Whiskey and cigarettes aren't cutting it anymore.

I promised her I wouldn't use during her fertility window, but cocaine is all I can think about. Even more than sex. It's been too long, and I have to have it. I can't go any longer without it.

I reach into my nightstand drawer and take out the bag of cocaine, slipping it into my pocket, when Emilia goes into the bathroom to get ready for bed.

"I'm going to be out late tonight," I call out.

"Where are you going?"

"Vinny's. He's having a poker game at his place."

"When will you be back?"

"Whenever we're done playing."

"How long is that going to be?"

"I don't know."

She comes out of the bathroom wearing a sexy red nightgown. It must be new because I don't remember seeing her in it. "Tonight could be the night. We really shouldn't skip it."

"Relax, Emilia. I'm going to marry you if you aren't pregnant."

"I know, but I'm eager to give you a son."

"And you will. I have no doubt about it."

She comes to me and reaches out, holding my face and kissing my lips. "Stay with me tonight. Please."

It's tempting.

But the coke in my pocket is more tempting.

I grasp her wrists and pull her hands away, pressing a kiss to one of her palms. "I've gotta go. The guys are waiting for me."

"We aren't even married yet, and you're already bored with me."

"No. Absolutely not."

"To me, it feels like you are."

"I'm not bored with you. I swear."

She looks so sad. I hate doing this to her.

"Will you wake me when you get home?"

"Yes."

"Don't be gone too long, okay?"

I'm trying to not become annoyed with Emilia. I know she wants me to stay because she's trying to give me a son, but going this many days without coke has put me on edge. I'm highly irritable right now and barely hanging on by a thread. I can't be near her right now.

I need to get high so I can get my head right.

I kiss the side of her face. "I'll be back before you know it."

Lie. I already know that I won't be back before morning.

She steps away, crossing her arms, wrapping them around herself. "All right."

She's mad. Or hurt. I'm not sure which. But if I stay, she's only going to be madder or more hurt. And I don't want that.

The music is loud and the smoke is thick when I enter Vinny's house.

"Fuck, you showed. I wasn't sure you would," Monte says.

Vinny laughs. "Hell, I thought we were going to have to send out a search party for you because you've been so far up your betrothed's ass."

"Not her ass. That way won't get her pregnant."

"Damn, Luca. You're not even married yet."

"Close enough. She's going to be my wife in two weeks."

Monte shuffles the cards, and I take the cocaine out of my pocket. My hands tremble as I shake a portion out on the table.

"What does your new ball and chain say about your coke habit?"

"Fuck you. I don't have a coke habit."

"Sure, you don't." Vinny laughs. "I don't either."

"Does she do it with you?" Monte asks.

"No fucking way. I'd never let Emilia do cocaine."

"You let me do it with you, and the sex we had afterward was unbelievable. Don't you remember how good it was?"

Angelica. Who the fuck invited her to this poker game?

"I didn't care if you did cocaine because I knew you were never going to be my wife or the mother of my children. Emilia is, and for that reason, I will never allow her health or safety to be at risk."

"Then I guess you'll never experience coke sex with her. That's too bad. I know how much you enjoy it."

"With Emilia, I don't need coke."

"Right. That's why you're here snorting a rail instead of being at home with her."

Angelica takes the straw from my hand and leans down, snorting the blow I just prepared. When she finishes, she places the straw on the table beside my baggie. "You know how much I love coke sex. I'm ready and willing whenever you decide you want it again."

"You'll have to do it with someone else. You and I are finished."

"We'll see."

I lean in and grip Angelica's chin. "We were over the instant Emilia became mine. I need you to be very clear about that because I won't have you causing problems between us again. Do you understand?"

"Oh, did I cause problems between you and your little princess?"

I know Angelica well, and that underlying grin on her face tells me that she has no intentions of giving up so easily. She still wants me. She's being very clear about it, but the feeling isn't mutual.

Starting over, I prepare another rail of blow. I inhale deeply, taking every granule of the powder up my nose. The euphoria hits soon after, and I'm fucking elated. I've been craving it for too many days.

Flipping my cards over, I smile when I see the four of a kind in my hand, all queens, and I think about Emilia at home.

My queen.

Is there anything more splendid than your queen who patiently waits for you?

Is there anything more precious than your queen who submits entirely to you?

Is there anything more lovely than your queen who wants to please you?

No. There's nothing more breathtaking than the relationship between a king and his queen. Except a king and queen and their full house.

21

EMILIA BELLINI

FOR SOMEONE TO WIN, SOMEONE HAS TO LOSE. AND I don't plan on losing.

"This isn't a good idea," my mother says.

"I don't care. He skipped out on the last day of my fertility window. It could mean the difference in being pregnant or not, and I want this to be over with as soon as possible."

I say the words, and although they're true, they aren't the whole truth. I'm hurt that he didn't come home last night or this morning without so much as a phone call.

"He's going to be furious when he comes home tonight and finds you gone."

It'll serve him right. And a little taste of his own medicine will do him some good. "The bastard won't be madder than I am right now."

"It isn't the same thing and you know it."

"But it should be the same. My feelings shouldn't be less important because I'm a woman."

I'm sick of being told that I must do this or that and it's my place to smile and keep my mouth shut about it.

"Luca Rossini has been raised to do as he pleases without concern for anyone else."

She's got that right.

"He will continue to do as he pleases for as long as I allow him to get away with it. That's why I left."

"I'm afraid you aren't going to accomplish what you hope for."

She's never going to support me in this, so there's no need to continue this conversation.

"I'm tired and my toes are killing me. I'm going upstairs to soak in the tub."

"And what do I say when he calls or shows up here?"

"Say whatever you like. I really don't care."

I have about five minutes of peace before Mamma comes into the bathroom. "He's on the phone."

"I don't care."

"I have to tell him something."

"Tell him to fuck off."

"Emilia… you know I can't do that."

"If you make me get out of this tub and go to the phone, that's what I'm going to say to him."

"Fine. I'll make up something to tell him."

"Whatever you want to do."

I settle into the water and a dense layer of bubbles covers my shoulders. I place my hand on my stomach and think about what could possibly be going on inside me right now.

The beginning of a miracle?

Nothing?

I wish I could know what's happening in there right now. It seems like such a long time before I'll be certain if anything I've done this week was worthwhile.

I groan inwardly when I hear Mamma coming into my bathroom again.

"I told him I asked you to come by after rehearsal. He agreed to let you stay over."

"Wonderful. I have his permission to spend time with my family."

"What is wrong with you? I'd think you'd be happy for the separation from him."

"I am. It's not that."

"Then what is it?"

He stayed out all night. I have no idea what he was doing, or who he was doing it with, but I strongly suspect cocaine was involved. And maybe Angelica.

Thinking about it makes me feel ill.

"I feel like I've lost the upper hand."

"That's what being with a Mafia leader is. Lots of ups and downs. Lots of give and take, but for the woman, definitely more give than take."

"It's not right. I shouldn't have to give more than him. And right now, I've given everything."

I've lost so much and what has he lost?

Nothing.

"As women, it's our plight."

It isn't going to be my plight.

I'm going to have the upper hand. Luca Rossini is going to love me. He's going to want my heart and soul. And when I'm finished with him, he won't be able to bear living without my love.

But he'll never have it.

I'm practicing my fouetté when Mamma comes into the studio. "Luca is on the phone."

"Tell him I'm practicing and can't talk right now."

"He isn't going to continue to settle for talking to me

and not you."

"I don't care what he settles for."

My mother sighs. "You're going to cause some big problems by doing this."

"It wouldn't be the first time I caused problems, now would it?"

"I warned you when you chose Nicolò over Luca that there would be trouble. You didn't listen to me then, but I'm hoping you'll listen to me now."

"You've just been dying to say I told you so."

"You chose the weaker man, and now you're paying for it."

"Luca chose to be a monster. Nic chose differently, but that doesn't make him the weaker man."

"It does in this life."

Mamma was lucky. She fell in love with a boss. I didn't.

I prepare to repeat my fouetté. "Tell him I'm in my ballet studio practicing for the production, and I don't want to be disturbed."

"I'll tell him, but don't be surprised when he comes over here and drags you back to his house by your hair."

"Let him try."

I'M STEPPING OUT OF THE SHOWER WHEN ISSY KNOCKS on the bathroom door. "Your fiancé is on the phone, and he wants to talk to you. He said now."

This is getting old. "Tell him I'm getting ready to go to mass, and I don't want to be late."

"I don't want to tell him that. He already sounds pissed off."

"I don't care if he's pissed off."

"You should care. He's not a very nice man. He could do bad things to you."

He's already done bad things to me, and I survived. "I'm not afraid of him."

"Well, I am. So what should I say to him?"

"I told you. I'm getting ready to go to mass, and I don't want to be late."

"Come on, Em. I can't say that."

"Then hang up on him. I don't care."

"Are you kidding? That would be even worse. I don't want him to be mad at me."

"Then tell him whatever you like."

"Fine."

Issy groans as she leaves and then returns a few minutes later. "I told him you were getting ready for mass because that's not a lie. He said for you to call him when you get back from church."

I chuckle to myself. "Yeah, right. I'm really going to do that."

He left me hanging all night and then the next day too. He'll get no less than forty-eight hours of retaliation if he wants to play this game with me.

"Thank you, Issy."

Being back in church feels good. I've been away for too long. Committed too many sins without confession, and yet I can't bring myself to visit Father Michael.

How would I begin? What would I say?

Leaving the church, I pretend that I don't see the black Cadillac across the street with Sal and Luca inside. I pretend that I don't know he's here to check up on me. I also pretend that his car isn't following us home.

While I'm eager to hash this out, I'm also a little frightened because he's come for me. Luca and I haven't learned how to fight with each other yet. It's a skill that takes practice. And I think I'm about to get some good experience.

Mamma parks the car in the garage, and I'm the last to get out. When I do, he's standing there waiting for me.

"Emilia?" Mamma says.

"I require some privacy with my fiancée," Luca says.

"It's fine. Everyone go inside."

"Are you sure?" Gemma asks.

I wonder what my sister thinks she's going to do against Luca that I can't.

"I'm sure."

Luca waits until my family is inside the house to begin this fight, and I'm grateful.

"You've been gone two days."

"I'm aware."

"Why aren't you taking my calls?"

"Why did you leave me at home all alone without so much as a phone call?"

"Come on, Emilia. You knew where I was."

"You told me you would be back when the poker game was over. You were gone almost twenty-four hours by the time I left. Are you seriously going to try and tell me that you were at Vinny's all that time?"

"No."

"Where were you the rest of the time? And what were you doing?" And with whom?

"The guys and I played poker all night, and then I went to work the next morning."

"Was *she* there?" He knows who I mean. There's no need to say the whore's name.

"Yes."

"I knew it." He was in the same place with her all night. Without me. "You fucked her, didn't you?"

"No, but if I had wanted to fuck her, I would have."

Luca places his hands on his hips and shakes his head. "We've had this conversation already, and I'm growing tired of it."

"Well, I'm not. I need to talk about this."

"Okay. Talk away then."

"Did she try to fuck you?"

He sighs as though I'm boring him to death. "She always tries."

I bet she does.

"You weren't tempted?"

"No. Why would I be when I have you?"

"Did you do cocaine?"

"Yes."

Something else I already knew.

"Was that the real reason you left me and went to Vinny's?"

"Yes, but I kept my promise to you. I stayed clean for days. That's a big deal."

"It's not a big deal if you aren't addicted."

"Fuck, Emilia. I'm *nottt* addicted. How many times do I have to tell you?"

Saying it doesn't make it true.

"You knew when you left that you weren't coming home. You lied to me, and according to you, you have no reason to lie to me. So which is it?"

"I lied because I didn't want to upset you."

"But you did upset me." You hurt me.

"I didn't mean to. I swear. And I'm sorry."

Trust can make something or destroy it. He's broken my trust and it's destroying any progress we've made with each other.

"I'm not ready to go back with you."

"It's cute that you think you have a choice."

"I'm not going."

"Stop being silly and get in the car."

"I'm not."

"You are, princess. I will throw you over my shoulder and stuff you in the back seat of the car if I have to."

"That's what you'll have to do because I'm not going voluntarily."

"I don't want to force you, but I will."

Dammit. I'm fast but not when I'm wearing three-inch pumps. There's no way I can outrun him in these shoes.

I kick out of one and then the other.

"Emilia… don't make me come after you."

I don't reply. Instead, I take off running for the front door. And I'm almost there when Luca's arms wrap around my waist, lifting me from the ground and hoisting me over his shoulder.

I beat my fists against his upper back, but he's unfazed by my physical attack. "Put me down, you big putz."

"Nope. You're coming home."

He carries me across the yard, and Sal opens the door to the back seat.

"Traitor," I tell Sal.

He shrugs. "Sorry, Miss Bellini. He's my boss."

"Well, he's not *my* boss."

Luca roughly tosses me into the back seat and crawls in behind me. "I'm not *your* boss, you say?"

I lift my chin in defiance. "No, you aren't."

Luca reaches for the door handle but doesn't pull it closed. "I need a private moment with Miss Bellini. Take a walk, and I'll let you know when we're ready to leave."

"Yes, sir."

He shuts the door, and I slide across the seat to get away from him. "What are you going to do to me?"

He removes his jacket and places it on top of the seat in front of him. "What do you think I should do to you?"

"Let me go inside my house."

He glances at our mansion and then back to me. "The Bellini compound is beautiful, but it's not where you live anymore. Your home is where my home is. Never forget that again."

Your home is where my home is. Those would be the sweetest words I've ever heard if they were the words of a man who loves me.

"Hmm... you need to be taught a lesson. How shall I do that?"

I look at him, saying nothing. And then I feel this incredible anger come over me, and I can't keep my mouth shut. "You are the one who lied to me and then left me alone for a whole day without any kind of communication —all so you could get high behind my back. You really think *I'm* the one who needs to learn the lesson?"

He smiles. "There it is—that fire I love seeing in your eyes."

His words are gasoline on my *fire*.

"You want fire? I'll show you some motherfucking fire."

Balling my fists, I advance on him, growling as I beat my clenched hands against his chest. "I hate you so much, Luca Rossini."

He only allows me to hit him a few times before he grips my wrists and pushes me down on the seat. "Careful, Emilia. You're beginning to reveal your true feelings for me."

I squirm beneath him, pulling on my arms. "Shut up."

He clicks his tongue. "You wouldn't be angry about me leaving you if you truly hated me."

I shake my head. "You don't know what you're talking about."

"Oh, I think I do... Emilia."

Luca's voice is deep and sultry when he says my name,

making chills shoot down my spine. His stare is intent as though he's trying to see something deep inside my soul. I don't think he's blinked once.

"Are you done being sassy?"

"No."

His mouth comes down on mine, and I turn away as an act of defiance, ripping my lips away from his.

"You're angry with me because I didn't come home and dick you. Admit it."

I turn away from him and stare at the back of the driver's seat in front of me. "You don't know what you're talking about."

With my dress shoved up to my waist, he grabs the back of my thigh and bends my knee, wrapping my leg around his hip. Rocking back and forth, he thrusts between my legs, and I hate myself when I realize how badly I want him inside me.

"Look at me, Emilia."

Without any thought, I instantly obey him.

Dammit.

"You're getting wet right now, aren't you?"

I want to deny it, but I look into those green eyes staring back at me and I can tell him nothing but the truth. "Yes."

Releasing one of my wrists, his hand follows the length of my arm, ribs, and waist, stopping when he slides it between my legs. Pushing my panties aside, he glides a single finger through my center. "Mmm. You never disappoint me, angel."

He knows I want him. The proof is at his fingertips, so there's no point in trying to deny it.

I tug my bound arm, still pinned over my head, and he releases it. With both of my hands now free, they move to his broad shoulders and down his powerful back where the muscles are taut, chiseled, and defined beneath my exploring palms.

The longer he kisses me and rubs me with his fingers, the less I care about our fight. The less I care about how mad I've been the last two days. I turn off my brain and put an end to my angry thoughts. At least for now.

It's been too many days since he was inside me. My body craves him. I want to feel the weight and warmth of him on top of me. I want to be stretched by him.

And I'm not waiting any longer.

Bringing my hands around, my trembling fingers tug at the button on his pants, and then I lower the zipper. I pant into his mouth as I dip my hand inside and grasp his cock, pulling it out of his pants.

"You want it right here? Right now? Like this?"

I already know the windows are tinted so dark that no one can see in.

"Yes. Right here, right now, just like this."

"Fuck, I love the way you hate me."

He grips my knee and pushes it up, parting my legs and bringing us closer together. Pushing my hand between us, I hook my finger through the crotch of my panties and hold it aside while he positions himself to enter me.

With his mouth against mine, I devour his moan when he sinks into me. My body aches from the stretching but also throbs for more. So much more.

He moves inside me slowly and deeply, allowing me to feel every thrust from tip to base before he pulls back and fills me all over again. My free hand reaches for the back of his neck, and I hold on to him as we kiss and move together, our bodies slick with my arousal.

With our noses touching and our mouths sharing the same air, I close my eyes and wait for what's coming. And then it happens—the pulsating waves and earth-shattering release.

Luca grips my thigh, his fingers digging into my flesh. His entire body tenses and he shudders. "Uh. Uhh. Fuck."

Both of us relax, and I let go of the crotch of my panties. And we just lie there for a moment, him still inside me.

And then his hand finds mine. Looking down, I watch as he intertwines our fingers together.

His hands. They've done so many terrible things, and yet they pleasure me. But above all else, they protect me. These hands would kill to keep me safe. Of that, I'm certain.

He says my name and my eyes move to his.

"I want us to love each other with the deepest depths of our souls. With a little time, I truly believe we can get there, and a day will come when our children and grand-children will ask us over and over to tell them the story of how we met and fell in love."

Who is this man? And what has he done with Luca Rossini?

I don't know, but I want more of him.

"I'm ready for you to take me home now."

22

LUCA ROSSINI

I ENTER THE BALLET STUDIO AND WALK THE CENTER AISLE toward the stage. Men in tights—they're everywhere. That shit blows my mind because I can't understand what kind of man would wear something like that and be okay with it.

"Sir, you can't be in here."

I turn to the man's voice I hear behind me. "I'm here to pick up my fiancée. Emilia Bellini."

Confusion spreads over the man's face. "Oh. I guess I misunderstood. I thought you died."

"You're not confused. Her first one died. Lucky for me, right?"

The man looks at me, the wrinkle in his brow deepening. "I'll tell Emilia you're here."

I take a seat on the back row and wait. It's only a few minutes before one of the men on stage makes an announcement.

"Thank you, everyone, for your hard work today. Rehearsal was great. Everything is coming together. Go home, rest, soak your feet, and be back here at nine in the morning."

It isn't long until I see my girl walking out with one of the male dancers, and her eyes widen when she sees me standing at the exit. Judging by her expression, she had no idea that I was here and waiting for her.

"Surprise."

"What are you doing here?"

"I came to pick up my fiancée and take her to dinner."

Emilia slow blinks and curls her lips around her teeth, confirming my suspicion. This guy doesn't know anything about me. I'd bet none of the dancers do.

She shrugs. "It was a tough rehearsal today, and I'm a mess."

"We can keep it casual unless you want to go home to shower and then go out."

"I'm fine with something quick and easy."

She turns to the guy standing beside her and gestures to me. "This is Luca."

I hold out my hand. "I'm her fiancé."

He shakes my hand, and I give him a nice *firm* grip. I'm pleased when a slight grimace forms on his face. "Yeah, I caught that. I'm Peter."

So this is Peter?

"Good to meet you."

I release his hand and put my arm around Emilia. "Are you ready to go, baby?"

She looks up at me and narrows her eyes. "I'm ready."

I glide my hand down her arm and lace my fingers through hers, clasping our hands tightly so she can't jerk it away as we walk to the car.

"What in the world possessed you to come to the dance company?"

"I had business on this side of town, and I thought it

would be a nice surprise to stop by and take you out to dinner."

"It's a very nice surprise. And unexpected."

"What do you feel like having tonight?"

"Pizza?"

"Sounds good to me."

"There's a great little pizza joint a few blocks from here. It's usually pretty quiet."

"We'll go anywhere you want. Your choice."

The restaurant is dark, most of the lighting coming from lit candles inside red glass globes on the tables. The place isn't crowded, so it's easy to hear the soft music playing overhead.

"Has Peter ever brought you here?"

"I've never gone out with Peter."

Hearing that makes me happy.

"He'd like to though. Has he ever asked you out?"

"Not on a date, but he offers to share cab rides."

"Yeah, I bet he would like to give you a ride."

"Well, I'm pretty sure you ended any further offers."

"Good. He needs to know that you're mine."

I should have put an engagement ring on Emilia's finger. People outside of the five families don't know that she's mine.

"You're so damn jealous and possessive. Surely, you must know that if I liked someone, I'd never act upon it."

"Because I'd kill him?"

She nods. "Umm… most definitely."

"Do you like someone?"

"If I did, I wouldn't tell you. But no. There's no one."

I believe her. "I'm glad to hear that."

"You Are So Beautiful" by Joe Cocker begins playing, and I can't resist reaching across the table and cupping my hand around Emilia's. "Not exactly as I would have imagined it, but I think this is our first date."

"Is that what this is? A first date?"

"It feels like it could be."

"We're going to be married soon. I guess we should at least go out on a date first."

She rubs her thumb over my knuckles and looks down. "Luca, you're bleeding."

I shrug, shaking my head. "It's nothing."

"It doesn't look like nothing to me."

"Just a little business I had to take care of."

"What happened?"

"Rossini business."

"I don't like being in the dark about what's happening."

"I am a dominant man who leads and takes charge of Rossini business because to do anything else would be a betrayal of my true nature. This is who I am. I can handle it, and I'm never going to burden you with it."

She wraps her hand around mine. "I know, but I worry about you. I want you to be safe."

"I'm always careful."

But I may have gotten a little sloppy tonight.

Looking at the entrance and then back at her, I bring her hand to my lips and press a kiss there. "I need you to listen to me carefully. I'm about to be arrested. The police are coming through the front door right now, and they're going to take me away. I need you to go to my parents' house and tell my father."

"Luca! Why are you being arrested?"

"Listen to me, princess. My father and our attorney will take care of this. I don't want you to worry about a thing."

"But I am worried."

"Don't come to the jail. I don't want you to see me in there." And I don't want anyone to see you and make the connection while I'm on the inside unable to protect you.

"How long will you be gone?"

Standing, I lean across the table and press a kiss to her lips. "I'm not sure."

Turning, I place my hands behind my back because I don't want Emilia to see them force me to submit. It feels like I get to keep a little bit of my dignity if I do it this way.

"Go, Emilia. I don't want you to stay and see this."

The officer cuffs me. "Luciano Rossini. You have the right to remain silent…"

23

EMILIA BELLINI

Thirty-three days later

MY PERFORMANCE HAS BEEN FLAWLESS EVERY NIGHT THIS week, but I think tonight, the final show, was my best out of the entire production. But it should be. With Luca being in jail for the last month, I've had nothing to do but practice.

More than a month without him.

I've missed that jerk.

And I'm ready for him to come home.

Annette, one of the younger ballerinas, comes by and hugs my shoulders. "Great performance tonight."

"Ah, thanks. You were great too."

"We're going out for drinks. Do you wanna come?"

I have nothing but an empty house to go home to, so why not? "Sure. Sounds like fun."

I change out of my costume and into regular clothes. Not exactly going-out-for-drinks attire but it'll work.

My hair is wavy when I take it out of the bun. It's a little wild and unruly when I shake it, but I like it. Plus, I'm not in the mood to mess with it. It's not as though I have anyone to impress.

"Hey, Em. Some guy is waiting for you outside with roses. I told him you'd be out in a few minutes."

Although still in jail, I guess Luca was able to pull off sending roses to me. His mom probably took care of it, but I'm still eager to see how the card is signed. I'm hoping for a "miss you" or "can't wait to see you."

I come out of my dressing room, and I'm delighted to see the armful of red roses, but then I see who's holding them and I'm thrilled.

He puts the roses down and I run to him, throwing myself into his open arms. "Oh my God. You're here."

He squeezes me tightly. "I made it, ballerina girl."

I lean back and place my hands on each side of his face, pressing a kiss against his mouth. "When did you get out?"

"This afternoon."

I kiss him again. "You didn't call me or come home."

"It was your final performance. I wanted to show up here and surprise you."

"You certainly have."

"The production was great. You were magnificent."

"You watched it?"

"Of course, I watched it."

I can't believe he got out of jail and chose to come to my production instead of all the other things I would have imagined him doing first.

"Thank you for coming. It really means a lot to me." More than he knows.

Luca squeezes me again, this time growling against my ear. "I want you to come home with me."

"I'm supposed to go out for drinks with the other dancers, but I'll tell them that I can't."

"Damn right you can't go with them. After being apart for a month, I need you beneath me right now."

"Okay, okay. I get it."

I understand his need. Because I need the same thing.

I see Peter down the hall talking with one of the other dancers. "Hey, Peter. I'm going to pass on drinks tonight."

"No way. You have to come out with us."

Luca pulls me against him. "Sorry. She's all mine tonight and every other night. You're done putting your hands and lips on her."

I laugh and smile at Peter, but I'm dying on the inside.

Slipping my hand into Luca's, we walk toward the exit. "Did you really have to say that to him?"

"His hands were all over you. He *kissed* you. My fiancée. So yeah, I had to say that."

"Calm down. It was all an act. Part of the performance."

"I don't give a fuck if it's an act or not. I'll kill him if he puts his hands on you again."

"You're such a jealous asshole."

"Yes, I am, and I'm also a jealous asshole who's about to take you home and make up for being apart the last thirty-three days."

We get into the back seat of the car, and Luca pulls me to the center of the seat next to him.

"Eyes forward, Sal. Don't even think about looking back here."

"Yes, sir."

"And turn the radio up."

"Gypsies, Tramps, and Thieves" by Cher fills the car as Sal pulls away from the curb onto the street. It's Saturday night, and traffic is stop and go, stop and go. It's going to take a while, much longer than I'd like, to get home.

"I missed you, Luca."

"I missed you too. You can't imagine how much. I thought about you day and night."

His searing hot lips touch the side of my neck, and as though I'm steel and he's the magnet, I lean into him for more. Turning my head, I grasp the back of his hair and pull him closer to kiss me.

I twist and climb on top of him, straddling him. He sucks air between his clenched teeth, but it's not his usual sexy hiss.

"What's wrong?"

He shakes his head. "I have broken ribs."

I move to get off of him, but he holds me in place. "Why do you have broken ribs?"

"I may have been in a fight or two while I was on the inside."

If he's admitting to one or two then it was probably more like four or five.

"I thought the guards were supposed to stop things like that."

"Don't worry. The other guys look way worse than me."

"I don't care about the other guys."

"Ah, forget about it."

Luca wraps his arms around me, and I kiss his mouth, gradually moving my lips across his stubbled jaw toward his neck. His whiskers are stiff and abrasive against my skin, just the way I like it.

The ride home is nothing but thirty minutes of fore-play, and I'm buzzing from the top of my head to the bottom of my feet by the time we get home.

Luca opens the door before the car comes to a full stop.

"Upstairs. Now," he growls against my ear.

"You don't have to tell me twice."

We reach the bedroom, and an unwelcome thought

occurs to me. "I know you're eager. I am, too, but I've been dancing for over two hours under some extremely warm stage lights."

"And?"

He isn't going to want to hear this. "I need to shower."

"Oh no, no, no, you don't need to shower."

"Oh yes, yes, yes, I do. Trust me on this."

Luca goes to the stereo and turns it on, twisting the dial until he finds a song he likes.

"I don't know why women think they need to be freshly bathed to fuck. Men love it when you smell like a woman. A real woman. Not floral soap."

"Right now, I stink. That can't possibly be appealing to you."

Luca growls beneath his breath. "I've waited thirty-three days for you. I guess I can wait ten more minutes."

"Fifteen," I say.

"*Fifteen?*" He looks at me and growls again. "All right."

Twisting my hair up, I shower in record speed. I can't remember ever taking a shower so fast in my life. Or brushing my teeth.

Opening the bedroom door, I find Luca stretched out on his side of the bed. He's stripped away every stitch of clothing and is lying there shameless and naked. Fully erect.

"I've missed this bed."

"I bet you have."

"More than the bed, I missed my bedmate."

"I can clearly see how much."

"Did my bedmate miss me as well?"

He wants reassurance? I'll give it to him. "I missed you more than I thought I could."

"I didn't know I was going to be so lonely without you."

Me either.

He gets up and meets me in the open floor space of our bedroom. "When I Need You" by Leo Sayer is playing softly, and he wraps his arm around my waist, holding our naked bodies close as we sway back and forth. Slowly rocking, we look at each other, forgetting that anyone else in the world exists.

He pulls us close, our foreheads touching. Despite the removal of his clothing, his familiar cologne still lingers on his skin and in the surrounding air, cocooning me with his smell. His arms squeeze my frame, reminding me that I am his.

"I just need to hold you like this for a minute."

"You can hold me like this as long as you like."

I feel like the sexiest woman alive when Luca stares at me with those beautiful green eyes. And I feel protected inside his embrace

Thirty-three days apart.

Something about that makes me nervous. Puts me on edge. Maybe because I know how desperate he is to have me beneath him again. And it frightens me a little.

A switch flips, and his demeanor instantly changes. So does the energy surrounding us. In that same instant, his mouth presses against the side of my neck and begins moving lower. I tense when he reaches the bend between my neck and shoulder as if he's going to bite me because his kisses are so damn hard.

"I've missed this so much."

"I've missed it, too."

Luca kisses me deeply and moves his hand to my ass, squeezing one cheek as he guides me backward to the bed. When the back of my knees hit the frame, I sit on the bed and move back, lying in the center of the bed.

I know Luca, and I know he needs to be in control. At

least this time. So I lie still, waiting for him to decide how this is going to go.

His heavy body moves on top of me, and he pushes my thighs apart with his knees, spreading me wide. Reaching between us, he touches my center.

"Fuck. Always ready for me."

He's right. I am ready for him.

Gripping his length, he wiggles the plump head of his cock up and down a few times through my slick center and then squeezes into my tight opening left undisturbed for more than a month. He groans as he fills me inch by inch, stretching me, until he has sunk all the way inside me. It isn't possible to be more physically connected than we are right now.

Slow at first, he gradually builds up until he's pounding me hard, each thrust scooting me across the bed. Every thrust is harder and faster than the previous one. He's fucking me like a man who hasn't had sex in years rather than thirty-three days. The sound of his vigorous exertion is heavy against my ear, drowning out the music in the room.

I lie on my back, letting Luca take me the way he wants to take me. Dominating. Raw. Possessive. I ache from the rough treatment, but it feels so good that I don't want him to stop.

His face burrows against my neck, and he writhes on top of me, his sweaty chest rubbing against mine. His cock twitches inside me, and he groans loudly, so damn loudly. I'm sure that every soldier in the house downstairs can hear him climaxing. But he doesn't care. And I don't either.

He kisses my neck and makes his way along my jaw until he reaches my lips again.

"I'm not sure if I'll be able to get enough of you tonight."

"You can have me as many times as you like."

Luca is responsible for all of my throbbing ripples of pleasure and earth-shattering releases. It doesn't matter if we make love or he fucks me raw. He is the one who dominates me. The one always in control.

IT'S REMARKABLE HOW EASILY A PERSON CAN SLIP INTO A habit.

It took a little time, but I eventually came to accept sharing a bed with Luca. And then just when I had gotten used to him being by my side every night, he was gone. Gone for thirty-three days and nights. There wasn't one single night that I didn't long for him to be next to me again.

And now he is.

He's lying on his side looking at me, his head propped on his bent arm. The other arm is outstretched, his fingers lazily tracing circles around the rose-colored flesh of my breast.

"While we were apart, I couldn't stop thinking about these."

I'm surprised to hear him say that. I didn't think he was too enthused by them. "I thought they were *disappointing* to you."

He chuckles. "I lied."

"They're small. I know."

He stretches toward me and places a kiss against the soft round flesh. "They're perfect and I love them."

I push my fingers into the back of his hair, playing with

it. It's much longer than it was the last time I saw him. "You need a haircut."

"I know." He reaches up and runs his fingers through the top. "I'll take care of it tomorrow."

He smooths the top of his hair and then returns to tracing shapes on my skin.

"You missed our wedding."

"Can you believe that? I waited all this time to marry you, and then I missed the fucking wedding." He chuckles. "You have to admit that the irony of the situation is superb."

I haven't been amused by the irony. Not even a little. "We can't wait. It needs to be rescheduled as soon as possible. Next weekend if we can pull it together."

Luca looks up at me, one brow lifting. "You're *that* eager, huh?"

I bite my bottom lip, but I can't contain my smile. "I'm *that* pregnant."

Luca stops tracing his fingers along my skin, and a huge smile spreads over his face. "Are you sure?"

I nod. "The doctor confirmed it."

"A baby. I can't believe it." Luca moves his hand to my lower stomach and spreads his fingers. "When will he be here?"

"The doctor said April."

"Does anyone else know?"

"Mamma, Nonna, and my sisters."

"You didn't tell my mother?"

Viviana would have a heart attack. "I think it would be better for her to hear the news after the wedding."

"I agree. We both need me to be alive so I can marry you."

Luca moves over on top of me and presses his forehead against my belly. "My son is inside you right now, developing and growing. Becoming the next Rossini heir." He looks up at me, his chin resting on my abdomen. "Thank you for giving me this child."

My son. He never mentions a word about a daughter.

"I know you want a boy, but you should be prepared. This baby has a fifty percent chance of being a girl."

"We will have girls one day, as many as you want, but this one is a boy. I already know it. I feel it in my gut."

"I wish you wouldn't be so absolute about a boy. It'll only cause disappointment if it's a girl."

"I won't be disappointed."

I'm not sure if he means he won't be disappointed with a girl or won't be disappointed because he is that convinced that our baby is a boy. I'm afraid to ask him to clarify because I will be mad as hell if he ever tells me that a girl would be a letdown to him.

He crawls up my body until we're face-to-face and strokes his finger down my cheek. "You're more than I ever hoped for."

Luca Rossini is becoming someone different to me. I struggle with the way he makes me feel inside, and I'm beginning to lose the battle. Slowly, he's possessing me. And as hard as I try, I can't stop it from happening.

Luca presses a quick kiss to my lips and slides to the edge of the bed. "Get up and get dressed. I want to go out and celebrate."

"Your release from jail?"

"My freedom. Our wedding. The baby. Everything. I'm a happy man, and I have a lot to celebrate."

"You and I can celebrate the baby privately, but you can't tell your friends about it. We have to keep that to ourselves for now."

"I understand the consequences. I'm not going to tell anyone and risk my son's foothold with the five families."

"Where are we going?"

"Fever. It's Saturday night, so that's where everyone will be."

Ugh. I don't want to go back to that place. "I had a terrible time the last time I was there."

"You didn't seem to be having a terrible time when you were getting fucked against the wall."

"That's not the part I disliked."

"We'll be celebrating this time, not fighting, and we'll be there together. Big difference."

"Okay, but just so you know, I'm not going to put up with Angelica's shit if she's there."

"I don't think I'm the only jealous person in this relationship."

"I'm not jealous." What a damn lie. I'm a hundred percent jealous.

"I don't need you to admit it. I can clearly see it for myself, and I'm flattered."

I could argue, but I see no point in it. Especially when it would be a lie.

"Wear something sexy. I want to show off my beautiful bride to the guys."

An hour later, Luca is a little bit irritated with me because I took so long to get ready, but there is no way in hell I'm going to this club not looking my best. Not when there's a possibility of Angelica being there.

Stephan smiles when he sees Luca and I approaching their table. "Look who escaped from the big house."

"Hell yeah. Boss is back," Monte says.

Luca and his brother Stephan clasp hands and pull each other in for a hug. "They thought they had me, but they couldn't make anything stick."

"That's good, bro. I'm happy to see you out. How long were you in for?"

"Thirty-three motherfucking days."

"I know you are ready to party," Monte says.

"You have no idea."

"I have something that is going to fix you right up." Vinny pulls out a bag of cocaine and taps some out on the table. And my stomach drops to my feet. "This is some good shit. You're going to love it."

I push my hand inside of Luca's and tug. "Come dance with me?"

He watches him prepare the line. "I don't feel like dancing."

Vinny looks up at me. "Do you want to do a rail?"

Luca grabs the front of his shirt and twists it. "I will put a bullet between your fucking eyes if you ever give cocaine to her. Do you understand me?"

Stephan slaps Luca on the back. "Be cool, bro. Vinny didn't mean any harm."

"I'm sorry, Luca. I meant no disrespect."

I put my hand to his face and force him to look at me. "You haven't done drugs in thirty-three days. Now would be the perfect time to stop."

Luca smiles and then chuckles. "You think I didn't do coke while I was in jail?"

"How could you?"

"Baby, that's not how jail works. I still had access to the things I wanted."

"Let him get high if he wants. I'll dance with you," Stephan says.

I don't give a damn about dancing. I wanted to distract Luca so he wouldn't get high. Because I believed that he had been clean for over a month, and I wanted to keep him that way.

Stephan takes my hand from Luca's, leading me down the winding staircase to the dance floor. He looks back over his shoulder when we reach the bottom. "My brother is a jackass. He doesn't deserve you."

"Dancing Queen" is playing, and I'm surprised when Stephan leads me in a New York hustle. "Someone besides me knows how to dance."

"Just an amateur next to you."

"Don't sell yourself short. You're very good."

"I take that as a compliment coming from a professional ballerina."

I look to my left and see Brian, the guy I danced with the last time I was at this club. He's dancing with a girl, and the smile fades from his face when he makes eye contact with me. I feel horrible.

The music is loud, so I have to shout. "I'm so sorry, Brian. I didn't know that was going to happen."

He looks at Stephan. "If you know what's good for you, you'll get the fuck away from her right now. She's engaged to a maniac. He put a gun in my face and then had his friends beat the shit out of me because I danced with her."

"What's your name?" Stephan asks.

"Brian."

Stephan reaches into his jacket and takes out his Glock. "See this, Brian? I'll blow that motherfucker's head off if he comes over here and tries to fuck with me."

Brian freezes and glares at the Glock. "This one has a gun, too?"

His eyes widen when Luca approaches and taps Stephan on the shoulder. "I'm cutting in, motherfucker."

"Listen, Brian. Some crazy shit is about to go down here. You got my back?" Stephan says.

"Fuck." Brian takes a step back and holds up his hands. "I don't want any part of this. I'm out of here."

Stephan bursts into laughter and returns his gun to its

holster. "Did you see that motherfucker's face? I think he shit his pants."

"That was an awful thing to do to him."

"Come on, I was just fucking with him for a little fun. You have to admit it's pretty funny."

Luca is always so serious and Stephan… isn't.

I'm trying to not smile, but I can't help myself. "Poor Brian. I bet he never comes back to this club."

"Dancing Queen" ends and "I Go Crazy" by Paul Davis comes on. Luca reaches for my hand, pulling me close. "Thank you for dancing with Emilia, but I'm here now."

"And just like that, I'm dismissed." Stephan nods at me. "Just so you know, I'm happy to dance with you anytime this stupid fool chooses cocaine over you."

Luca shoves his brother's shoulder. "Get the fuck out of here and stop trying to start shit between Emilia and me."

"You can get pissed off if you want, bro, but you know I'm telling the truth."

Stephan leaves, but his words remain behind in my head. He isn't wrong. Luca chose drugs over me because that's what addicts do. It isn't the first time he's done it, and I'm certain it won't be the last.

"What's wrong?"

I shake my head. "Nothing."

Luca stiffens. "He got in your head, didn't he?"

"Well, what he said isn't wrong."

Luca exhales heavily. "You know how damn happy I am about the baby and about us. I wanted to celebrate."

I don't know why I tried to stop him. That's not part of the plan. "You should celebrate."

"You aren't mad?"

"I'm pregnant. Nothing's holding you back now. Snort as much cocaine as you want."

"Fuck, you are mad at me."

"You know what? You should continue to do whatever you like, Luca. I'm learning that you're really good at that."

"Come on, Emilia. Don't be this way."

"You wanted to get high and you did. End of story. There's nothing to discuss."

"We haven't been together in over a month. I don't want to spend our first night back together fighting."

"And I didn't want to spend it with you high, but I didn't get a choice, did I?"

"I don't want to fight." He puts his arms around me and pulls me close. "Dance with me. Let me hold you and our baby, and the three of us will have our first dance together."

I may be mad as hell and not ready to get over this anytime soon, but that makes me melt into a puddle on the floor.

Wrapping my arms around his shoulders, I hold him tightly. "You have us. We're yours."

24

LUCA ROSSINI

MY GROOMSMEN AND I WAIT FOR OUR CUE TO TAKE OUR places at the front of the chapel. I smile when I remember Emilia saying that she would pray the church didn't go up in flames when I set foot inside.

"Today is a glorious day, son. You finally get to officially claim your Bellini princess."

"My Bellini princess—" I can't say the words without grinning like a fool. "Who already carries my child in her belly."

My father's eyes widen. "A child? Already? Are you sure?"

"Her doctor confirmed it."

"Congratulations, son. This is wonderful news. Does your mother know?"

I'd be dead if she did. "No. We're going to tell her after the wedding."

"She's going to be thrilled."

"She'll be thrilled as long as Emilia has a wedding ring on her finger."

"Viv wasn't happy when she found out that you'd taken Emilia before marriage, but she's going to forget all about that when she finds out there is a baby on the way. Emilia isn't very far along, I hope?"

"No one will know that she didn't become pregnant on our wedding night."

"Assure your mother of that when you tell her. You know how she worries."

"I'll make sure she understands."

"A grandchild. I can't believe it."

"A grandson."

"You think so?"

"I do." I don't know how to explain it. It's just something I feel in my core.

"A Rossini boy—that would be wonderful."

"I didn't think it was possible after the start we had, but things are good between Emilia and me. I think we have a chance at being happy together."

"That's because Emilia is your destiny. She always has been."

The wedding planner beckons us with her finger. "Time to take your places."

The time is finally here, and this ceremony will make it official. Emilia and I will be bound to one another until only death can part us. That's exactly the way I want it.

My father, brothers, and I take our designated spots in front of the wedding guests. I rest one hand over the other and breathe steadily as I watch Emilia's bridesmaids walk the aisle, taking their places opposite us. Bellini sisters on one side and Rossini brothers on the other. It's exactly the way I always imagined it.

I look at the faces of our guests and wonder how many of them sitting on the bride's side would like to kill me right now. The majority, I presume, if not all. I bet a few of them have even had discussions about how to make that happen.

With the bridal march playing, Sofia's eldest brother escorts my bride down the aisle. The long train of her dress drags behind her, gliding over the rose petals that have been dropped by two flower girls, both her young Bellini cousins.

I see her and I'm overjoyed. But also regretful because it should be Alessandro giving Emilia to me. Her father walking her down the aisle to be given in marriage is a special moment that I stole from her, and she'll never get that back.

Her dress is white lace from the edge of her collarbone all the way down to her feet. With her lace veil mostly concealing her face, she's the perfect image of what a virginal Catholic bride should look like. But I wish I could see her face. Or at least her eyes. Maybe then I could see how she's feeling as she comes forward to join herself with me forever.

I want Emilia to be happy… happy with me. That's what I've always wanted for her, and I'm going to work every day to make that a reality.

"Sofia Bellini, do you consent and gladly give your daughter Emilia to Luca Rossini?" the priest asks.

"I do." Sofia says the words, but her tone is less than convincing.

Sofia's brother, Riccardo, briefly whispers something in her ear before passing her hand to me.

"Be good to her, Rossini. She deserves that."

"She's going to be treated like a queen."

"I guess we'll see, won't we?"

I lift the veil from her face, and our eyes meet for the first time. To my surprise and joy, she smiles.

"You look beautiful."

Her voice is soft and low. "Thank you. You don't look so bad yourself."

Taking a deep breath, my fingers close around Emilia's. Exhilaration pumps wildly through my veins because this day has finally come. I have her, and I'll never let her go.

But it isn't that simple. I have work to do if I'm to convince her that she wants to be mine.

I want Emilia to love me.

As husband and wife, we will share a sacred bond. My loyalty to her will be unwavering. The trust I place in her will be like none I've ever given before.

This isn't a normal relationship at all. It's anything but ordinary.

It's everything.

We are allies. We are consorts. We are one.

My allegiance belongs to Emilia Bellini Rossini.

I would kill for her.

I would die for her.

There's no one in the world she can trust more than me. Her husband.

The ceremony begins, a Catholic wedding mass because it's what she wants. Me? I would have been fine without all the singing and reading and praying and kneeling. It all seems unnecessary to me. Let's say some vows, exchange some rings, kiss, and call ourselves husband and wife.

And eventually we do.

"You may now exchange a kiss," the priest says.

I'm tempted to sweep her backward and kiss the hell out of her, but she asked me not to. She wants this public kiss to appear as though it's our first. As though we don't share a bed every night. As though she isn't already carrying my child in her belly.

I find it entertaining that my bride wants to play the part of the innocent Catholic virgin when I know her to be a sexy-as-hell vixen who enjoys being fucked against the wall in a disco club.

"Only a small kiss. You promised," she whispers when I lick my lips.

"I haven't forgotten."

I reach for her face and cradle the sides before placing the softest, most innocent-looking kiss against her lips. "It's done. You're finally my wife, Mrs. Rossini."

"I am."

I don't know who all we've prayed to during our wedding mass, but one thing is for sure. Our marriage is official.

I help Emilia with her dress and veil as we get into the black limo waiting for us at the curb outside the chapel.

"Did you notice that the church didn't go up in flames with me in it?"

She smiles and giggles. "I was so sure it would."

"See? I'm not the devil after all."

"I'm not so sure I'm convinced of that."

"Maybe I'll convince you in time." I reach into my jacket and remove the ring box in my pocket. "Your devil-husband has something for you."

I open the box and take out the newly forged ruby ring identical to the ones worn by Mom and Zee Zee. "This ring signifies your place within the family. One look at this on your finger and anyone from our world will know exactly who you are."

I take her right hand, sliding the ring on her middle finger, and then I kiss it. "You are my queen."

She looks at the ring on her finger. "Your queen," she whispers.

I've waited so long for her, and now she's mine. She doesn't know it yet, but I'm going to do whatever it takes to make her happy.

25

EMILIA ROSSINI

"Ah, alas, my daughter is a Rossini." She clicks her tongue. "A *dreaded* Rossini."

"Not just a Rossini wife. A Rossini *queen*." I lift my hand, showing my mother the ring Luca placed on my finger. "He says that anyone from our world who sees it on my hand will know exactly who I am."

My mother takes my hand and inspects the ring. "It's identical to Viviana's and Zorah's. This is very significant because the only way he would have given this to you is if you mean something special to him."

I hold out my hand, looking at the ring. "I wasn't expecting this."

"I don't want to know everything you had to do in order to make him believe you're worthy of this ring. Whatever it is, you've done an excellent job."

Is my pregnancy not the first clue? "You know what I'm doing to make him happy."

"I do, darling, and it makes me sick to think about it. I'm so sorry. I can't imagine what it must feel like for you when you lie with him."

It feels pretty damn good, actually. "I somehow manage to get through it."

"Just like you somehow got through the wedding ceremony today. You did very well. I myself almost believed that you are a happy bride."

"The kiss appeared as though nothing more has ever passed between us?"

"It was very convincing."

"He did exactly as I asked."

"Don't give him too much credit. It's not in his best interests to flaunt your physical relationship in front of the five families."

I shrug. "I know."

"Never forget that Luca Rossini will always choose to do what benefits him most. You will never come first in his life."

Maybe not but our son will. I already see how much Luca wants him. How much he loves him. And I am our son's mother. Some portion of his love for our child will extend to me. How can it not when our son will be half me?

"The upside to this is that you're pregnant. You've done the work, so now you won't have to have sex with him anymore."

Umm… no, that's not going to work for Luca. "I'm his wife. He's going to expect sex from me."

My mother rolls her eyes. "Tell him it could hurt the baby. He won't know any different. He'll go get sex somewhere else, and you'll be left in peace."

I don't want Luca to go get sex somewhere else.

"I hadn't thought of that. I'm sure he won't touch me if he believes that it could harm *our little Rossini prince*."

The wedding planner waves, motioning for me to join

her and Luca by the dance floor. "I've got to go. Susan needs me. We'll talk later."

"Come, Emilia. It's time for the first dance," she says.

Luca holds out his hand and leads me on to the dance floor. "What song did you choose for our first dance?"

"'You Needed Me.'"

"Hmm. Don't know that one, but the title sounds fitting. Because I do need you."

It's not exactly my kind of music, but the song is becoming very popular at weddings. And since nothing about our marriage is typical, I thought it would be nice to have something that is traditional. "In an odd way, this song is very fitting for us."

We sway to the music as our guests look on. "How have you felt today?"

"Didn't sleep last night. Sick this morning. Tired all day. And my feet are killing me."

"Do I need to take you up to the suite?"

We can't leave our wedding reception. "We have so much to do: the toasts and speeches, dinner, cake cutting. We can't leave yet."

"Doing those things won't make us any more married than we are right now."

"I know, but everyone expects it."

"To hell with what everyone expects. Stress isn't good for you or the baby. I don't want you to overdo it."

"There will be plenty of time to rest later."

"Promise you'll tell me if it becomes too much for you. I won't hesitate to take you to the suite. To hell with what the guests think."

"I'll tell you. I promise."

Our guests clap when the song ends, and we take our places at the bride and groom's table. I'm not upset about getting to sit down for a while.

"Take your shoes off and give me your feet. I'll rub them during the speeches."

"You are not rubbing my feet at our wedding reception."

"I'll do it under the table. No one will see me."

"How about I take you up on a foot rub later?"

His brow lifts. "Well, that could be a problem since I'm going to be rubbing something other than your feet later."

Luca likes to talk dirty, and I enjoy pushing him to take it to the next level. "Tell me what you'll be rubbing later. And how."

"I would love to, but my father is about to make his toast."

"All right. Later then."

"Definitely."

Marco steps on to the riser where the band is playing and takes center stage where a mic on a stand awaits. "Thank you for coming to celebrate this wonderful occasion, the joining of my son Luca with his beloved Emilia."

I think *beloved* is a stretch.

"This has been a union that we've been looking forward to for many years. To give you an idea of how long, I'm going to share a story with you. Alessandro and Sofia invited our family over for dinner one night. Luca and Emilia were playing in her room, and things got quiet, a little too quiet, which is typically an indication of trouble. Sofia and Viv went to check on the children and found Emilia wearing one of her white dresses, and she had taken a pillowcase from the bed and turned it into a veil. The flowers she was carrying had been swiped from one of Sofia's floral arrangements." Marco laughs. "Emilia's teddy bear had married them, and we missed the whole ceremony."

Our guests erupt into laughter and small fragments

from the past begin to move to the forefront of my mind. One piece joins to another piece until the fragments become bigger.

"I remember our pretend wedding."

"I thought you had no memory of me at all."

"I didn't think I did, but hearing your father talk about it makes little pieces of the past come back to me."

"What do you remember about it?"

"Most of what he described. And I kissed you on the mouth."

Luca nods. "You did."

"You didn't want to play wedding because you were older. You thought it was stupid, but you gave in and let me have my way because you didn't want me to cry."

"Yes. That's exactly how it happened."

"And now we are married."

"By a priest this time. Not a teddy bear."

"And it isn't pretend. Our marriage is real."

Toasts, speeches, dinner, cake cutting, dancing. It's after ten, and there's no sign of the reception letting up anytime soon. There's far too much alcohol left for anyone to leave.

"I think I've had enough. I'm ready to go to the suite."

"That's all you have to say."

"I need to say goodbye to my family before we go. I won't get another opportunity since we're catching an early flight in the morning."

"Meet back here?"

"Sounds good."

My mother is dancing with Luigi Gaspari, patriarch of the Gaspari family. And they look as though they aren't having too shabby of a time.

"I'm sorry to interrupt, but Luca and I are leaving. I wanted to say bye."

"Would you excuse me for a moment?"

"Absolutely. Congratulations on your marriage, young lady."

"Thank you."

"Why are you leaving? It's still early."

"I'm tired and we have an early flight." Plus, I already know that I'm going to be nauseated when I wake up. It's a recipe for a miserable morning.

"Are you sure it's a good idea to travel in your condition?"

"I'm barely pregnant. It's fine."

"I'm your mother. I worry."

"You don't have to worry. Luca will take care of me." There are a lot of uncertainties in my life, but that isn't one of them.

"Only because he wants to take care of his son who happens to be inside of you. Never forget that."

"Either way, he'll keep me safe. You don't have to worry."

My mother puts her arms around me and squeezes. "I love you, Emilia, and I'm so proud of you for being this family's hero."

I'm not a hero. Not even close. I'm something else entirely.

The captive who longs for her captor.

An angel who craves her devil.

A queen who needs her king.

A woman who wants to consummate her marriage.

My heart pumps wildly as the elevator lifts us to the hotel suite we're staying in tonight. The nervous jitters that I'm feeling are unexpected. I've slept with Luca many times, so I already know there'll be no surprises waiting for me, but there's something more to tonight than simply sex.

Luca is my husband and I am his wife. Tonight consummates our marriage, and it also seals our union. It will bond me to him forever, both in the eyes of God and the five families.

Death will be my only escape.

He unlocks the door and swings it inward, holding it open with his foot. "Not the threshold of our home but it'll do." Scooping me into his arms, he carries me inside the suite and doesn't return my feet to the floor until we're inside the bedroom.

Looking around, I take in the elegance of the room and smile when I see the rose petals on the bed. "This is beautiful. Did you do this?"

"Not me. It was your sisters and cousins."

"What about the chocolate strawberries and champagne?"

"I get to take credit for that."

"It's too bad I can't have champagne."

"I think it would be okay to have a sip during a toast with your new husband."

"I've already had several sips." So many that I had to start fake-drinking while everyone was making toasts so I wouldn't call attention to myself for forgoing alcohol. That would be a dead giveaway about my pregnancy.

"One more won't hurt."

Luca takes the bottle from the ice bucket and opens it with a loud pop. "That one had some power behind it."

He pours two glasses, handing one to me.

"To my wife, Mrs. Rossini, the sexiest woman in the world who was worth two decades of waiting." He hesitates, looking at me with such devotion in his eyes. "Believe me when I say that you are the most important thing in my life. You and our child. Never doubt that for a moment."

"I believe you." And I do. But not because I think Luca loves me. His feelings are a result of a sense of duty.

I drink a sip from the glass, and Luca takes it from me, placing it on the desk. "Turn around."

Gathering the skirt of my dress, I spin on my toes and stop when my back is facing Luca.

"My ballerina bride."

"I'm not much of a ballerina anymore."

Luca's hands move to the back of my dress. Beginning at the top, he pops each button, loosening my dress around my body.

"Are you angry at me for taking your passion away from you?"

"I was at first, but now I get to be a mother instead of a ballerina. How can I be angry about that?"

"Will you train our daughters to dance?"

"I will if they show interest, but I won't push anything on them."

Slowly, my dress sags and slips down my body. When Luca finishes with the last button, he allows it to fall to the floor on its own. I'm instantly lighter.

Standing before him in my white lace undergarments, I reach up to take my veil from my hair.

"Don't. Leave it just a little while longer. I like the way it looks with your lingerie and stockings."

I've never worn anything this sexy in front of him. I must admit that I like the ravenous expression I see on his face. I like his hungry eyes feasting on my body.

"Stay just like that. I want to look at you while I take off my clothes."

Luca simultaneously kicks out of his shoes and loosens his tie. He gives the black fabric a firm yank, tossing it aside, and then moves on to his vest. Piece by piece, he removes his wedding attire until he's only wearing boxers. The outline of his fully erect bulge is very visible beneath the thin fabric of his underwear.

My husband's body is a work of art, as though a skilled artist chiseled each groove, each rise, each fall. I feel so protected when I'm inside his strong arms.

Never taking his eyes off me, he pushes his boxers down, and they fall to the floor. He is all man, from his length to his width. His very proud hard-on is like cupid's arrow pointing directly at me, ready to be launched.

"Take everything off except the garter belt and stockings."

I've never been okay with the thought of a man giving me commands, especially in the bedroom, but my body unexpectedly responds to his instructions as though some kind of primal instinct is being awoken. Something inside me likes hearing him tell me to take off my clothes. My inner perversion likes that my choice is being taken away. I like it because it gives me a reason to not feel ashamed about giving him everything he wants.

He remains where he is, watching me remove my veil, then bustier, and lastly, my panties. His eyes drink me in as though he's trying to etch every inch of my body on his brain.

He inhales deeply and blows the breath out through tight lips. "Damn, I have a sexy wife."

His patience stretched to the max and ready to snap, Luca stalks toward me. We reach for each other at the same time, our mouths coming together for our second kiss as husband and wife. This time, it's the fiery kiss we've both been longing for, and every cell inside my female body responds to it.

My world narrows to the sensation of his tongue dueling mine, his hungry lips sucking and kissing. His taste floods my mouth—whiskey and some other flavor I can't put a name to.

My husband's mouth devours me. My lips. The sides

of my face. My neck. His kisses tell me words that his mouth never has. He wants to possess me, body and soul.

Liquid heat surges between my legs, and I thread my fingers into the back of his hair as we stumble toward the bed. Together, we tumble on top, lying sideways.

My thighs guided open by his knees, his body settles between my legs, the two of us fitting together perfectly like puzzle pieces. Lifting my hips, I rub myself against the physical proof of his arousal and pleasure curls tightly in my lower belly.

His large frame positioned over me, he supports his upper body on his arms, barely allowing any of his weight to press against me. "Are you okay?"

"I'm fine. What we're doing is fine. You aren't going to hurt me or the baby."

"I know. I'm just trying to be gentle with you."

Reaching up, I grip his chin in my hand. "Don't be."

"Fucking you raw doesn't feel right when I know there's a baby inside you."

"You're going to need to get over your fear, or this is going to be a very long pregnancy." For both of us.

"Okay. I'll work on that."

Reaching between us, he guides his hard length to my entrance. Pushing his swollen crown through my impatient center, he slowly sinks until we are perfectly joined as one. It feels so right. He stays that way for a moment, pinning me beneath him, our eyes connected. I smile, and his own lips curve up in response.

It doesn't matter how many times we're together. He always stretches me in the most delicious way, filling me until I feel like I can't take another inch, but I can't remember it ever feeling quite this good. Never this intimate.

Face-to-face. Skin-on-skin. Heart-to-heart.

A husband and wife couldn't be more deeply connected than we are right now.

And it feels so damn good.

I gave myself to Luca in the beginning because I had no other choice, but now I'm giving myself to him because it's what I want. No game play involved.

Pulling back, he rocks into me over and over. He breathes heavily, his open mouth against mine, as he moves his hard length in and out of my tight chamber.

My fingers cradle his cheeks and I stretch upward, kissing him. And he kisses me back, filling my mouth with his tongue. And the two don't waltz. Instead, they tango.

Lifting my hips in sync with his thrusts, the head of his cock perfectly strokes the sensitive bundle of nerves inside me. One plunge builds on the next and the next, gradually strengthening my imminent climax.

There's an internal frenzy as I wait for my release to find me. It's physical, but it's mental too. A quiet desperation. A fear that it might slip away before it has a chance to emerge.

Gripping his hair, I stop kissing him. I simply hold my parted lips against his, panting against his mouth when my release begins.

My orgasm. I am its hostage. And it is my captor.

Wrapped in his protection and devotion, I open my eyes and look into his. Waves of pleasure rush over me, around me, through me. His pace doesn't change as he studies me, watching my mouth become an 'O.' And then I feel him shuddering, coming apart with me, tumbling into the bliss together.

He deepens his final thrusts and his entire body tenses, surrendering to his climax. He pulses inside me, his eyes locked on mine, and the sexiest groan I've ever heard vibrates deep inside his chest.

Our wedding night. It's so much more than I ever dreamed it would be. That it could be.

And so, it's done. I am bound to Luca. I belong to him for as long as we both live.

And for now, that's okay.

26

LUCA ROSSINI

FOR TWENTY YEARS, I'VE CALLED EMILIA MY BETROTHED. For six weeks, I've called her my wife. For thirteen weeks, she's carried my child inside her.

I'm a happy man. So damn happy. I didn't know this was possible.

My parents are throwing a party at their house tonight, a celebration, and the announcement will be made. Everyone within the five families will learn that there's going to be a new heir of the Rossini empire. A child who will be taught our ways from the very beginning. Half Rossini, half Bellini. With those genes, there isn't a chance in hell that he won't be destined for greatness.

Slipping into the shower, I wrap my arms around Emilia from behind and cup her tits in my hands. "These are getting bigger."

"And more tender."

I lessen my grip. "Am I hurting you?"

"No. They're just extra-sensitive these days."

I flick my thumbs over her hard nipples. "I like them."

"As demonstrated by your inability to keep your hands

off them."

"I can't keep my hands off you period."

"I'm aware, but we don't have time for that."

I kiss the side of her neck at the spot she loves, trying to persuade her. "Not even a quickie?"

"Sorry, no. Your parents want us to come to their house early."

"For what?"

"This is our party. We need to be there to greet the guests as they arrive."

I express my frustration in the form of a growl against her neck. "And I'm sure we'll have to stay late."

"You know we will."

"Will you be angry with me if I celebrate by doing a line or two with the guys?"

"Always celebrating," she murmurs beneath her breath. "I don't know why you're even asking. You don't care if I get mad."

"I do care. I don't like it when we fight."

"And I don't like it when you get high. You aren't yourself. You become someone else entirely." She hesitates a moment. "I don't know why you're asking me if I'll be mad. We both know you're going to do it regardless of what I say."

"I've cut back. A lot. You know I have."

She places her hand on top of mine, lacing our fingers, and brings it to her stomach. "Do you feel that?"

It feels like a hard ball inside of her. "Yes."

"That's our child. Don't you want to do better for him?"

Emilia told me she was pregnant, and I believed her, but feeling her growing womb against my hand is tangible confirmation. This child is still small but very real.

I'm going to be a father. There's going to be a tiny little

person who comes out of Emilia's body, a child she and I created together. He's going to call me Dad and depend on me to teach him how to run this empire.

"I'm going to do better for him. I swear. But he isn't here yet. I have time."

Emilia turns in my arms and wraps them around my shoulders. "He isn't here yet, but his mother is."

"I'm not an addict, Emilia." How many times do I have to say this?

"If I asked you to never do it again, would you be able to stop?"

"I could walk away from it and never do it again if that's what I chose to do." But that's not what I want. "There's no reason to stop right now. The baby isn't here yet, and I'm not hurting anyone by doing it."

"You think you're not hurting *anyone* when you do it?"

"Not that I can see."

She searches my eyes for a moment and then says, "Okay. I won't bring it up again."

Emilia releases her hold around my shoulder and steps away, getting out of the shower. It feels like she's surrendering, allowing me to win this debate. She's no longer arguing her point, but I don't want this discussion to end like this.

"Come back."

"Can't. I need to get ready so we're not late for the party."

I said that I was going to quit, and I am. When I say that I'm going to do something, I do it. But I'm going to quit on my own terms, and tonight isn't the time.

Emilia has little to say to me before we leave the house, and that doesn't change in the car on the way to my parents'. I wish the cocaine conversation hadn't come up. It's soured what should be a happy occasion for us.

"Will you at least try to look happy tonight? There are going to be a lot of people from the five families there, and all of them will be judging us."

"I'm happy."

"You don't look happy. You look upset."

"I'm fine."

"You're not fine."

She smiles. "See? Happy."

I know what true happiness looks like on her face, and this isn't it. "Don't lie to me. What's wrong with you?"

"I told you I wasn't going to bring it up again, and I'm not."

"You may not be bringing it up with words, but you're still definitely bringing it up."

She shrugs. "What do you want from me, Luca? I can't and won't pretend to be happy about you doing something that could hurt you."

"I'm always in control."

"Sure, you are."

Damn, she makes me so fucking mad sometimes, so mad that I'd like to put her over my lap and spank her ass until she cries and begs me to stop.

And then I think about all the reasons she wants me to stop using cocaine, and I can't be mad at her. She's afraid for me and has my best interests at heart.

"Don't worry. I'm careful."

She turns to look at me, and the concern I see in her expression is genuine. So damn real. "Your physical safety isn't my only worry."

I'm not at all at ease. I don't like being the reason behind Emilia's distress. I want to be the man who solves her problems, not causes them.

Emilia keeps her distance from me after we arrive at my parents' house. I'm not pleased by that. This party is intended to show the five families the strength we have when we are together. That's impossible to do when she refuses to be by my side.

"Where is Emilia? I haven't seen her since shortly after you arrived," my father says.

"I'm not sure, but she's around somewhere. Probably with her sisters."

"It's time to make the announcement, and your mother is about to burst."

"All right. Give me a minute to find her."

"Bring her to center stage when you do."

I search as I weave through the guests in my parents' house and find Emilia sitting in my mother's private parlor. "What are you doing in here?"

"Thinking."

"About what?"

She sighs. "How much my life has changed the last few months."

"And how much more it's going to change when this baby comes?"

"Definitely."

"This baby is going to be the best thing that has ever happened to either of us."

"I know." She places her hand over her stomach. "And I don't want to raise him without you."

"You won't. I'm going to be here with you every step of the way."

She nods but I see the doubt in her eyes.

"I'm not going to make you any promises right now. You're not in a mindset where you'd believe me anyway, but I'm going to prove it to you."

I hold out my hand. "Come with me. It's time for the announcement."

With her arm looped through mine, I escort her to

center stage. My chest is inflated with pure pride as I bring my beautiful pregnant wife before the members of the five families.

"Thank you for coming tonight. Emilia and I are happy that you are able to be here so you can share in this joyous occasion with us." I look at Emilia and she looks up at me, smiling. The first real smile I've seen from her tonight. "We are thrilled to announce we just found out that we are expecting our first child."

"We're going to be grandparents," my mother shouts from where she's standing among the guests. I should have known she wouldn't be able to contain her happiness without some sort of outburst.

"Half Rossini, half Bellini," my father adds.

Our guests applaud, and I take Emilia's hand in mine when the noise dies down.

"If we are blessed with a son, I would very much like to name him Alessandro after your father. If it pleases you."

Emilia stares at me, tears forming in her lower lids. She nods and two large drops fall down her cheeks. "*If it pleases me?* Are you serious? Of course, it pleases me."

She reaches up, wrapping her arms around my shoulders. Coming up on her tiptoes, she stretches upward and presses a kiss to my mouth. "You have no idea what that means to me."

"You have no idea what *you* mean to me," I whisper against her ear.

Our guests break into applause again. Sounds of congratulations and best wishes overlap.

Emilia's mood improves after our announcement, and I'm relieved when she socializes with our guests. I'm hoping she has forgotten about our fight earlier this evening. Or at least put it out of her mind for the moment.

Monte punches my upper arm. "Fuck, Luca. You're going to be a father."

Vinny slaps me on the back. "That sure as hell happened fast."

"Luca does everything perfectly. It's no surprise that he already has an heir on the way," Stephan says.

No one can know that Emilia was pregnant before we married. Not even the guys. "I guess I got it right on the first try."

"You think it's a boy?" Stephan asks.

Angelica's heels click against the marble tile floor as she approaches. "Luca gets everything he wants. Of course, this baby will be a boy. He'll finally have the Rossini heir he's always wanted.

She takes out a bag of coke and flips it back and forth in her hand. "We have to celebrate the good news. Where can we go hit this?"

I think I may have managed to fix things with Emilia. I can't fuck it up by getting high tonight. The fight we had earlier is still too raw. "None for me. I'm not doing that tonight."

"Sure, you are, Luca. You never say no to cocaine."

"I'm saying no this time."

"Why would you do that?"

Because I've upset my wife, and I want to do better for her.

"Tonight is about announcing Emilia's pregnancy, not getting high."

"Your new wife is giving you the son you've always wanted. That's something to be celebrated."

"He doesn't want to do it. Leave him alone," my brother says.

"He wants it, Steph. He always wants it. Don't be fooled by this act."

She isn't wrong. I haven't gotten high in a few days, and I want it. I want it badly. But I'm trying to resist for Emilia.

"Come with me, guys," she says, beckoning us with her fingers. "No one will see us on the back patio."

Vinny is the first to go after Angelica, followed by Monte.

One quick hit. Emilia will never know.

I take one step, and Stephan grabs my upper arm. "Think about Emilia and your baby. Don't go with her, bro."

"Just one tiny little hit. That'll be it. I swear."

My brother releases my arm. "You're a grown man, and I'm not your keeper. You make your own decisions."

"That is correct. I'm going to be *your* leader. Not the other way around. Don't ever forget that."

"You're going to regret doing this when you have to look Emilia in the eye and you see that you've broken her heart."

"I've already told Emilia I was getting high tonight." I leave off the part about the fight that ensued afterward.

"Maybe you did, but you sure as hell didn't tell her you were getting high with the woman you were fucking before you married her."

"I don't want Angelica."

"I doubt Emilia will see it that way."

"Just keep your mouth shut about this."

My brother shrugs. "Sure, Luca. Whatever."

I catch up with Angelica and the guys on the back patio.

"Luca goes first. This is his celebration," she says.

"Where are we going to do it?"

"Luca knows where we're going to do it."

Angelica opens the bag and pulls down her shirt, shaking some of the coke on her tits.

"Hell yeah. I've never done cocaine tits before," Monte says.

I shouldn't be here doing coke, and I sure as fuck shouldn't be here snorting it off Angelica's tits. "I can't do it that way."

"*I* can do it," Monte says.

"No. This dust is for Luca. He goes first."

"I can't do that anymore."

"We don't have a lot of options out here. This way is fast and easy."

Fast. Easy. And wrong.

"You want to do it and get back to the party before you're missed, don't you?"

"Yeah."

I'll be quick.

I step toward her and close off one of my nostrils, lowering my face to her chest. She laces her fingers through the back of my hair, and I inhale quickly and deeply, vacuuming the powder from her skin.

"Lick the rest off."

"Fuck no."

"Come on, Luca. You didn't get all of it."

"One of them can have the rest. I'm not licking you."

"Umm… Luca."

The euphoria spreads throughout my body, that glorious splendor that I chase way too often.

"Don't talk to me right now."

These fuckers know I don't like to be distracted during the beginning of my high.

"Luca, man?"

Can they not shut the fuck up?

"Vinny, I'm going to shoot your fucking kneecaps off if

you keep talking to me."

"Luca, your wife."

"My wife what?"

I open my eyes and see Emilia standing in front of me.

Fuck. How much of that did she see?

She doesn't say a word. Her only reaction is to turn and walk away, going back into the house.

"Fuck, Luca. You need to go after her."

I do but not without dealing with Angelica first. "Did you know she was out here?"

She shrugs. "Your pretty little wife needed to see what you were willing to do when you thought she wasn't looking."

"You convinced me to do that out here so she would see?"

"It's better she finds out who you really are now before she falls in love with you. I wish someone had given me a similar lesson."

I grasp Angelica's throat and shove her against the house. "You jealous bitch."

"Let go, Luca, before you squeeze too hard," Monte says.

I release my hold and she grabs her throat, coughing and sputtering. "Don't blame me. I didn't make you do anything. All of this was your choice."

Angelica is partially right. I did choose to do this and that's on me, but she owns some of the responsibility as well. She intentionally lured me to a place where she knew Emilia was and arranged for her to see something that must have looked terrible.

Because it was terrible.

And I'm terrible for doing it.

An honorable man doesn't dishonor his wife.

And I've dishonored mine.

27

EMILIA ROSSINI

Luca Rossini saw me naked, and I don't mean without my clothes. I'm talking about being truly bared to your husband and opening yourself up to him completely. Letting him into your thoughts, your fears, your hopes, your dreams.

Suddenly, it's as though I no longer have my husband. In the oddest way, it feels like becoming a widow.

How can I kill him when he's this wonderful? That's what I thought to myself when Luca announced to everyone that if the baby is a boy, he wants to name him Alessandro after Papà.

How can I not kill him when he's such a son of a bitch? That's what I'm thinking right now.

That's the kind of man Luciano Davide Rossini is. One minute he makes me swoon. The next, I want to pump him full of cocaine so he can die doing the thing he loves most.

Trust. It's more than simply believing your husband won't betray you. Real trust is having the heartfelt belief that your partner will make the choice to do the best thing for his wife and child rather than what feels good to him in the moment.

That doesn't describe Luca.

Looking at myself in the bathroom mirror, I lean forward and dab the corners of my eyes with tissue. I must be one of the stupidest people on earth. How could I believe that I was possibly falling in love with that asshole? And even more, how could I believe he was falling in love with me? My mistake. But I'm clear about where things stand now. Luca made sure of that when he buried his face in that whore's chest.

He may not love me, but he's still my husband, and he owes me his loyalty. It's the way.

But we already know that Luca isn't one for honoring the old ways.

I leave the bathroom and go in search of my mother. I find her having what looks like an intense conversation with Luigi Gaspari, the same man she spent quite a bit of time with on the dance floor at my wedding.

"I'm sorry to interrupt, but can I talk to you for a moment?"

"Of course." She turns back to Luigi Gaspari. "Would you excuse me?"

"Absolutely. We'll continue this conversation another time."

I lead Mamma away from the crowd. "What's wrong?" she asks.

"I could kill Luca Rossini."

"You *are* going to kill him."

"No, I want to kill him now. Tonight."

"Why? What did he do?"

"He dishonored me."

"Tonight? In front of the five families?"

"Not in front of everyone, but in front of his friends."

"What did he do?"

"I caught him doing cocaine tits."

"*Cocaine tits*? I've never heard of a such thing. What is it?"

"He was snorting cocaine off a whore's chest. The same whore he was sleeping with while he was betrothed to me."

I replay my words and recognize how they could be perceived by my mother. And that wouldn't be good.

"The point is that he has dishonored me."

"This wouldn't have happened if your father was here. He's taking advantage of having no one to answer to."

"If I knew for sure that this baby was a boy, I'd kill him tonight while he's sleeping."

"Well, there's no way to know what it is so you're stuck with him until the baby is born. And even longer if this one is a girl."

Oh God. What if I'm like my mother and I have girl after girl before I finally have a son? It could be years.

"This baby is a boy. It has to be." Because I can't be stuck with a man who sneaks away and does cocaine tits with his former lover.

Or is she really *former*? I thought so but now I don't know.

"There's an upside to this. Be grateful he's still interested in this girl. He's bothering her tonight instead of you."

That doesn't feel like an upside to me. "You're right."

"In your condition, everyone would understand if you want to leave early. Would you like Tome to drive you home?"

I think that's a great idea. "Yes, I would like that."

I quietly slip away unnoticed, not saying goodbye to anyone. The house is dark and empty when I go inside. All of the men who typically patrol in and around the house are at the party and I'm glad. I want to be alone.

I'm lying in the dark seeing Luca and Angelica over and over in my mind, and the ache I feel proves just how much I don't hate my husband. And I can't stand it.

This wasn't supposed to happen. I wasn't supposed to develop feelings for him. How is it even a possibility when the plan was to kill him? I don't understand.

The door opens and light floods in through the gap, shining on my face. A dark silhouette comes into the room and sits on the bed beside me.

"I need you to get up and get dressed," Luca says.

"No."

"Do it, Emilia. Now."

"Why?"

"No questions."

"Are we in danger?" I don't hear distress in his voice, but that's immediately where my mind goes.

"If I say yes, will you get your ass up and get dressed?"

I turn on my side again. "Sorry. I'm not feeling very cooperative right now."

Luca goes to the chest where my casual clothes are and takes out shorts and a T-shirt, tossing it at me.

"Put this on, or I'll throw you over my shoulder and carry you downstairs in your nightgown, which you won't like very much considering who's down there."

Giving in, I get up and change into the shorts and T-shirt he chose. "Is something wrong?"

"Yes. Something is very wrong."

"Did something bad happen after I left the party?"

"Stop asking questions. You're going to know exactly what's going on in a few minutes."

I follow Luca down the stairs and in our living room I

find Monte, Vinny, Stephan, and a member of my own family—my uncle Riccardo.

And then there's her. The whore.

"No, Luca. You didn't bring that woman here!" I squeeze the words through my clenched teeth. "I hate you. I will hate you forever for bringing her into our home."

"She's here for a reason. I want her to see what you and our baby mean to me so there's never any more confusion about it."

"I know this baby means everything to you. I don't doubt that for a second. But me? I mean nothing to you, and you clearly demonstrated that tonight."

"I had a moment of stupidity and made a terrible mistake. I dishonored you, and I want to right my wrong."

That's not how it works. "You can't undo it. And as hard as I try, I'll never be able to unsee it."

"I can't undo it, but I'm going to show you how truly sorry I am in the only way that makes sense to me."

He takes off his jacket and drops to his knees in front of me.

Luca Rossini is going to beg? Plead? What world is this?

"I'm showing you and everyone in this room what I'm willing to endure in order to earn your forgiveness."

"You think *enduring* a little humiliation on your knees will make me forget?"

My uncle comes forward, and I notice the brass knuckles on his hand. "Alessandro would have been entitled to this, but Luca has asked me to act on his father-in-law's behalf, which I gladly do."

And then it clicks, and I finally understand what all of this is about.

"You are my queen. And God help anyone who disrespects my queen. That includes me." Luca gives my uncle a nod. "Now let's make this right."

The first punch made by my uncle is to the right side of his face, and like one of the scenes from "Rocky," blood spews from his mouth and splatters across the front of my shirt.

He falls on his all fours and shakes his head before regaining his composure and rising to a kneeling position again. "Next."

The following blow lands on the opposite side of his face, and he sways but manages to remain on his knees.

The assault continues, blow after blow. I guess most women would cry and plead for it to stop, but I can't even if I wanted to. Without doubt, my uncle would tell my mother that I asked for mercy on Luca's behalf, and that would cause a hell of a problem. But also, I don't ask because I have my own reasons.

Luca chose to do this for me, and I want to see how far he's willing to go to gain my forgiveness. If I ask my uncle to stop, I'll never know the extent.

Plus, I think he deserves a little pain for dishonoring me so he isn't likely to do it again.

My uncle's hand is busted and bleeding when Luca collapses on the floor, unable to rise to a kneeling position again.

"I think that's plenty."

Uncle Riccardo leans forward, resting his hands on his thighs, catching his breath. "I was beginning to wonder if you were going to let me beat him to death."

"Believe me. I considered it."

I lower myself to my knees and lean over Luca, pushing his wet hair away from his forehead. "We're going to take you upstairs now."

"I can't walk," he mutters through busted, bleeding lips.

"I know."

I look up at Stephan. "Help me get him to the bedroom?"

"We've got him."

Stephan, Vinny, and Monte lift him from the floor and carry him up the stairs. I take a few steps to follow behind them, but I stop when I realize that I'll miss my opportunity to say something to Angelica if I don't do it now.

"That brutal beating you just witnessed… Luca chose that so he could prove where his loyalty lies, which is with me. *Me*—his *wife*. Have you ever known him to do anything like that for a woman?"

"No."

"Do you believe he would ever do that for you?"

"No."

"Luca chose cocaine tonight, not you, and I'm aware of the difference now. Are you?"

"Yes."

"My tolerance for you has run out. Offer your body or your cocaine to my husband one more time and you'll no longer have a nose for snorting that shit because I will have the motherfucker cut off your face and stuffed down your throat. Do we have an understanding?"

She nods. "I understand."

"I'm glad. Now leave my house because you are not welcome here."

I walk with her to the front door and slam it with a thud when she's on the other side. "If I never see her again, it will be too soon."

"You were too kind to her. Your mother would have had that woman beaten until she couldn't lift her head."

My uncle isn't wrong. My mother didn't tolerate women who threw themselves at my father.

"Because she loved him." And she still does.

"Don't you love your husband?"

My uncle's words take me by surprise.

"No." I laugh and shake my head. "Not at all."

"Hmm… I think someone is either lying or delusional."

I can't let my uncle walk out of here believing that I love Luca. "He murdered my family. How could I ever feel anything but murderous hatred for him?"

"I think you don't want to love him. But I also think you can't help yourself."

"You're wrong."

"You don't fool me, Emilia. I saw the pain on your face each time I hit him."

"I don't know what you think you saw, but you're confused if you think it was love."

"You didn't take pleasure in his suffering."

"If I didn't, it only proves that I'm not a monster."

"It means far more than that, and we both know it."

"I'm still in. That hasn't changed."

"Make sure you are. Because your mother won't accept anything less than one hundred percent."

"I'm very aware of what Mamma will not accept."

When my uncle is gone, I go to Luca in our bedroom. He's lying perfectly still on top of the bedding on his side of the bed. Bleeding. Ruining it. And I don't care.

"I need him undressed. And when I'm finished washing him, I'll need help changing the bedding."

"No problem," Stephan says.

Luca groans loudly when his stillness is disturbed to remove his clothes. "Leave me the fuck alone. I'm hurting."

"I have to clean you up."

"Don't bother."

"I'm not going to leave you like this. You have wounds that need cleaning."

A string of profanities leaves his mouth as Stephan and Vinny strip away his clothes, leaving him only in his boxers. That's when I remember his previously broken ribs. They just healed, and I suspect that they're probably fractured again.

"Do your ribs hurt?"

"Every-fucking-thing hurts."

"Everything may hurt right now, but your wife knows where your loyalty lies. That's what is important," Stephan says.

I come to the bed with a large basin filled with warm water and begin by washing his bloody face.

"I was seduced by the cocaine. Not her. It was never her."

"I know."

"I'm committed to you. I always have been. And I'm committed to our child."

His eyes are black, his pupils nearly the size of his green irises. "I know you want to be committed, but I'm afraid you're always going to choose drugs over us."

Stephan leans over Luca and lowers his face to his brother's. "By some miracle, this woman doesn't hate you and want to kill you while you sleep. You've been given this wonderful gift and you're throwing it away? Do you see that you could lose your wife and baby if you don't stop doing this shit?"

"I've got it."

"Are you sure you comprehend the situation?"

"I will lose Emilia and Alessandro if I keep doing it. I follow."

"And you two putzes… don't let me find out that you've given him coke or your time on this earth is over. Zero tolerance."

"No cocaine. Got it," Vinny says.

Luca is an addict whether he admits it or not. I'm not sure he can vow to quit and actually do it. But if he doesn't, he understands what's at risk.

Alessandro and me.

Calling our son by my father's name makes this baby feel even more real. Not a pawn. Not a game move. Not an insurance policy.

Real.

Luca grimaces when I cleanse the wounds on his face. I'm not sure that he doesn't need a few stitches. One of the cuts over his brow is pretty deep, but I know he'd die before going to the emergency room.

When his cuts are clean and no longer bleeding, the guys lift him while I remove the filthy linen beneath him and replace it with clean.

I roll the bedding into a ball. "Hey, Vinny. Can you toss this into the trash on your way out?"

"Sure thing."

"Thanks."

Vinny stops in the doorway of the bedroom and looks back at me. "I'm sorry this happened."

"Me too," Monte adds.

I don't blame Vinny and Monte for any of this. I don't even blame Angelica, although I'm certain she encourages it. Luca is a grown man and makes his own decisions.

Vinny and Monte leave but Stephan sticks around.

"Getting rid of the bedding is a good excuse to decorate this room in something new that you like."

"I'm not sad to see it go. I hated that bedspread." It looked like Luca had picked it out.

"I think you should go with something pink and floral."

"You love antagonizing Luca." I knew it the first time we met, and he took me to the VIP room of Fever without warning Luca. He wanted to see a fight.

"I'm his brother. Nothing gives me more pleasure than annoying him."

"And tonight's beating? Did that give you pleasure?"

"Yes, but not for the reason you might think. My brother made a mistake and finally understood how he was hurting you. He took ownership and did what was necessary to correct his wrongdoing. He made me proud tonight."

"I think you're going to make some lucky girl a very good husband one day."

"Would I make a very good husband for your sister?"

"Gemma?"

He nods. "We danced at your wedding and again tonight."

I'm sorry, Stephan, but my mother isn't looking for a second Rossini son-in-law.

"I think your sister is absolutely beautiful."

"Gemma is beautiful, both inside and out."

"Is she betrothed to anyone?"

"No."

"My father will be choosing a bride for me soon. I'd like to have some say in that."

"I'm sure you would, but your family already has all of the Bellini holdings. You would gain nothing by marrying Gemma. She has no wealth to bring into a marriage."

"I'm not Luca. I don't care about those things. But if my father wants to debate it, I can argue that she and I would have half Rossini, half Bellini children, same as you and Luca. That's something that seems to be pretty important to him."

Calling his grandchildren half Bellini is very important to Marco for some reason.

"I'll talk with Gemma, and if she's open to the match, I'll speak to our mother on your behalf."

"Thank you, Emilia. I appreciate that."

"Thank you for your help tonight. I couldn't have done this without you."

"Is there anything else I can do before I go?"

I shrug. "I don't know of anything at the moment."

"I'm only a phone call away if you need me."

"I'm sure the patrol soldiers will be here soon. I'll have them in the house if I need immediate help."

"I'll call tomorrow and check in on the asshole to see how he's doing."

I adore Stephan's wit. I sort of would love to see him with my sister.

Stephan stops in the doorway, looking back. "I meant what I said before. He doesn't deserve you. But I'm hoping with time, he'll change my mind."

"Maybe he'll surprise us both."

I wash Luca's blood from my body and put on a clean nightgown before slipping into bed beside him.

"I'm sorry, Emilia."

I'm surprised when I hear Luca's voice because I thought he was asleep. Or unconscious.

"How are you not knocked out?"

"It's the cocaine."

"Right." I didn't think about that.

"I'm so damn sorry about the whole thing with Angelica."

"As demonstrated by asking my uncle to beat you half to death."

"Getting my ass kicked isn't enough. I need you to hear me say the words too."

"I believe you."

"I'm going to stop."

"Before the baby comes?"

He hesitates a moment. "Now. Tonight. I'm not doing it again."

"I don't want you to make that kind of promise to me unless you mean to carry through with it."

"I mean it. I'm done with that shit for good."

He's addicted, and he's never had to go without it. "What's going to happen after a few days and you're craving it? Are you going to sneak away and come home with dilated pupils?"

"I'm not going to do that to you or Alessandro."

"I want to believe you." But I don't.

"I'm going to show you instead of giving you empty promises."

I lace my fingers through his. "I know how much you already love this baby. You can do it for him."

"I can do it for you." He squeezes my hand and brings it to his mouth, kissing the top. "But I'm going to need your help. I can't do it alone."

"I'll do anything to help you get through this."

"It's going to get bad. It could turn into too much for you to handle."

"I expect it to be bad, and I can handle it. I'm not delicate."

"Stephan should stay here in case you need him."

"He'll be happy to help. He wants you to get better."

"I don't want to see anyone else while I'm crashing."

"I'll tell everyone you're sick and can't get out of bed. No one in the family will know you're detoxing."

"My brother's right. I don't deserve you. I don't deserve to be this baby's father."

"If you truly believe that, then change. Become a man

who deserves to have me as his wife and Alessandro as his son."

"I am. And I'm going to become the man you would have chosen if you'd been given the choice."

My old life is falling away right before my eyes. He's making me feel something for him.

Would it be so terrible to fall in love with my husband?

28

LUCA ROSSINI

EMILIA RETURNS FROM THE BATHROOM WITH A FRESH, COOL washcloth, wiping the sweat from my face and forehead. "I'm going to turn up the air conditioning."

I grip her wrist. "Don't. You're already shivering."

"It's fine. I can put on more clothes."

"You're pregnant. You shouldn't be chilled."

"And you shouldn't be sweating like this."

"I'm okay." I'm not okay and we both know it.

"What can I do? Tell me and I'll do it."

"It's all part of the process. It'll pass."

When we were trying to conceive, I went four days without cocaine. I used whiskey and cigarettes to push through day three and a little more to get me through day four. That isn't something I told Emilia because it made me feel weak.

And now, day six? Or is it day seven? I can't remember anymore.

I'm in more agony than I was when Riccardo beat me to a bloody pulp. I have no energy, and yet I'm unable to sleep. The last three times I dozed, I dreamt that Emilia and the baby died during childbirth. It was so vivid—and terrifying—in my mind.

"Your mother called earlier."

"What did you tell her?"

"That you have food poisoning. She wanted to come over, but I told her she should stay away."

"Thank you for handling her. And everyone else."

"It's what a wife does for her husband."

"I know this hasn't been easy for you. Thank you for taking care of me."

"We'll make it through this, and you'll be so much stronger when you come out on the other side. A better leader. A better father."

"A better husband."

I plotted and killed so I could have her for myself. Instead of plotting to kill me in return, she chooses to save me. Who does that?

How did I get so lucky to have this woman? I don't deserve her or our child.

"If I cook something for you, do you think you could eat?"

It seems like I would be hungry after going so many days with barely eating anything. "I could try."

"It's been a while. I think you should put something in your stomach, or you'll become weak."

I'm already weak.

"Maybe soup?"

"Does creamy tomato parm sound good?"

"Yeah, if it's not too much trouble."

"It's no trouble at all."

Emilia leaves, and I'm not alone for long before Stephan taps on the door. "Is it okay if I come in?"

"Sure."

He sits in the chair he brought to the bedroom, the one he holds down when Emilia has to step away from me for more than two seconds.

"I'm not suicidal, you know? I can be left alone."

"I know, but you're going through some pretty rough shit. You need to know that you're not alone."

"You sound like her."

"Well, she's a pretty smart girl."

"That, she is."

"Plus, she's not bad to look at. Neither is her sister."

"You like her sister?"

"I don't know, but I'd like to find out if I do."

"Gemma?"

"That's the one. I asked Emilia to see what she can do."

"I'm sure she'll do what she can. My wife likes you."

"I'm waiting for Dad to bring up the topic of marriage any day now. I'd like to be able to choose my own wife."

"Having your wife chosen for you isn't so bad."

"Yeah, not bad for you because you lucked out. I might not be so lucky."

"I am one lucky bastard. That's for sure."

"Do you feel like coming downstairs to eat? It might help you feel better to get out of bed for a while."

I doubt it. "I don't feel like doing anything."

I've never been in a slump like this. It's as though I feel nothing.

Happiness. Joy. Excitement.

I'm empty inside.

I think about the baby, and I can't even get excited about him. I'm hollow and ashamed to tell anyone. I won't admit it because what kind of asshole father can't be happy about the kid that he's done so much to get?

"I'm sure Emilia will bring your dinner up here if you don't feel like going downstairs."

"I think that's better. Maybe I'll feel like coming down for breakfast in the morning."

Stephan leaves when Emilia returns with my soup. As usual, it's tasty. Everything she cooks is delicious, but I don't have an appetite. All I can think about is cocaine. "This is great, but my appetite hasn't returned yet."

"It's okay. Maybe later."

She takes the tray away, and we lie in bed watching television for a while, but the sounds and flashing lights are too much for me. I need a calmer environment. "Maybe I should try reading for a little while."

"That's a great idea. Reading always helps you fall sleep."

It does when I'm not foaming at the mouth for some blow.

Letters blur. Words run together. I drift, thinking about getting high.

I close my book and toss it on the nightstand. "I can't concentrate. I'm going to try to go to sleep."

Emilia closes her book and places it on her nightstand. "Turn over on your stomach. I'm going to give you a massage. Maybe that'll relax you."

I'm so on edge. I don't know if I can stand to be touched right now, but I don't want to tell her that.

She gets up and goes to the radio while I turn over. "You love music. Maybe something soft and slow will be soothing."

I doubt it. "We can try it."

She comes back to bed and sits on my ass, stretching forward to grip my shoulders while "Magnet and Steel" plays. "Relax, Luca. Deep breaths. You're so tense."

"I'm trying, but this is an intense situation for me."

"I know it's hard for you right now, but you're eventually going to be okay. You have to keep thinking about the end result."

That's great advice, but it doesn't stop the overwhelming craving. The hunger inside me feels like it's taking over my mind and body.

Her hands are all over my back, rubbing my skin. And I can't stand it. "I'm sorry, baby, but that's not helping at all. I need you to stop."

"Okay. I'm sorry."

She moves away and lies on her side next to me.

"It's not your fault. It's me. All me."

I turn over and lie on my back, staring at the ceiling and blowing breath through pursed lips.

"Maybe I can take your mind off of it another way?"

She scoots closer and stretches upward, kissing the length of my neck. Her hand slides into the front of my boxers and wraps around my soft cock.

I want her. I always want this girl. But right now, I want cocaine more.

"I can't, Emilia. I want to but I'm in full-blown withdrawal. Sex is the last thing on my mind right now."

"I'm sorry. I don't mean to be insensitive to what you're going through. I'm just trying to distract you any way I can."

"I don't think you're insensitive at all. I appreciate everything you're trying, but I think the only thing that's going to fix this is time." Or cocaine.

"Let's turn off the lights and try to sleep. It's been a really long day. Maybe you can fall asleep if it's dark and quiet."

"We can try that."

I lie on my back staring at the dark above me while I

listen to Emilia breathe. Tapping my fingertips against my chest, I drum "You Really Got Me" by Van Halen between glances at the clock. When I've drummed for at least thirty minutes, I decide that I can't do it anymore. And I can't stay in this bed another minute.

Emilia is in a deep slumber when I leave the bed. I know because the rhythm of her breathing doesn't change when the bed shifts.

She's been sleeping harder the last few weeks. I think the pregnancy takes more out of her than she's willing to admit.

I tiptoe to the closet and take out a pair of jeans and shirt. Slowly, I dress in the dark, hating myself for what I'm about to do to her and our son.

I said that I was done. I told her I was stopping—stopping for her. But the truth is that I can't live without it. I need it as much as I need my next breath.

I go still when I hear her stir.

"Luca?" she whispers.

I don't answer because one, I can't explain why I'm dressed as though I'm going out. Two, if I don't say anything, then maybe she'll go back to sleep.

"Don't… Luca."

Fuck. I'm busted. So fucking busted.

What am I going to say to her?

"Love you… Luca," she murmurs.

I hear those words and realize that she wasn't calling out to me because I woke her. She's saying my name because she's dreaming of me.

Love you… Luca. Fuck. Even if she is only dreaming and doesn't mean it, how can I walk out of here after hearing her say those words?

I undress and return to bed, prepared to drum every

song I can think of if it keeps me from leaving to go get fucked up. And then a different thought comes to mind. The story I'll tell our children when they ask me how I met their mother.

The story will begin like this: Once upon a time, a devil fell in love with an angel.

29

EMILIA ROSSINI

THE ROSSINI COMPOUND IS STUNNING. TENS OF thousands of twinkling lights on the exterior. An enormous live tree making the first floor of the mansion smell like a winter forest. Garland and Christmas collectibles, and red velvet bows everywhere. Viviana really goes all out.

Christmas is going to be different this year without Papà and Giovanni. And Nic. But this year I have Luca and our baby. Sort of. I include the baby because he's been working overtime to make his presence known.

"Look at you."

My mother puts her hands on the sides of my stomach. "My grandchild is growing big and strong."

"Is that a polite way of telling me that I'm getting fat?"

"The baby is growing, and your body is accommodating him. You aren't fat." A line forms across my mother's brow. "Did Luca call you fat?"

"Oh God no." I put my hands on my stomach. "He loves my round belly. He can hardly keep his hands off it."

"Only a few more months to go."

"Luca is going to die if April doesn't hurry up and get here."

My mother laughs. "Good. That'll save you from having to kill him."

We haven't talked in a while about our plan to kill the Rossinis. When we do, there's going to be a problem—a big one—and my mother isn't going to be happy.

I tried, but I can't escape loving him.

And I can't kill the man I love.

"I don't know why Viviana insisted on my attendance at this Christmas party for the Rossinis. I am not a Rossini. I think she did it to piss me off."

I thought Viviana's invitation was a nice gesture. "She wants to include you in the holidays because you're going to share a grandchild."

"This child will bear the Rossini name, and that's all. He is our boy and our boy alone. He will be raised like a Bellini."

Bellinis versus Rossinis. I'm sick to death of hearing about it.

My mother gestures toward Stephan. "I've noticed that one giving a lot of attention to Gemma at these get-togethers."

I'm glad Mamma noticed and is bringing it up. I didn't want to be the one to introduce the idea. "That's Stephan. Marco will be choosing a bride for him soon, and he has expressed interest in Gemma."

Mamma's head jerks toward me. "Marco or Stephan has expressed interest in Gemma?"

"Stephan."

"He told Luca?"

"He actually told both of us. He wants to spend time with her and see if they're compatible."

"But he would gain nothing by marrying her." I hear the suspicion in Mamma's tone.

"Stephan is different. He isn't interested in marrying for money or power." He and Gemma are very much alike in that aspect.

"That's unfortunate for Stephan because money and power is all that his father is interested in."

Money and power. Is it not what most of the men of the five families are interested in?

"Stephan would like to have your permission to spend time with her."

"Is he asking for a date?"

I shrug. "I guess you could call it that."

"That's not going to happen. I'm in the middle of negotiating a betrothal for her."

"Gemma hasn't said a word about a betrothal."

"Because she doesn't know yet."

"Who?"

"The eldest Gaspari grandson."

Ah, this is making sense now. "I wondered why I was seeing you with the Gaspari grandfather at all of the Rossini functions."

"His grandson will be turning twenty-one soon. His betrothal fell through, and he's eager to make a good match for him."

I love my sister, but she would bring nothing to the Gasparis. "Why is he considering Gemma?"

"That's what I'm wanting to talk to you about. The Gasparis want to join us in our mission."

"Our mission?"

"To kill off the Rossini men and take possession of the entire empire."

Gaspari doesn't want to help us out of the goodness of his heart. If that were the case, he would've stepped in when we were at our weakest and pleading for help after our men were killed.

"He must want something in return?"

"Just a fair share."

"What does he consider a fair share?"

"Half."

"Half of the *entire* empire? Bellini and Rossini?"

"Yes."

I've always heard that the Gasparis are a greedy lot. Looks like the hearsay is true.

"For half, what will be his role in the takeover?"

"After you kill Luca and Marco, they will step in and provide us with manpower."

"I'm the one who kills the two most dangerous people in the family, and they'll sweep in for cleanup and take home half the prize plus my sister?"

I don't fucking think so.

"We need allies, Emilia. I'd be a fool to turn down their offer."

"Mamma! Their offer is shit. They're cowards. If they really wanted to help us, they would have before. At the very least, they would now offer to handle the dirty work instead of leaving it for me to do."

My son is entitled to the entire empire, and she wants to give half of it to the Gasparis because they're willing to step in after the leaders are dead? No. If I agreed to this, I'd be robbing my son of his inheritance, and I won't do that.

"No. Absolutely not. We are not doing this."

"I'm head of the Bellini family. I make the decisions and we *are* doing this."

My mother made me a piece in her game, and now she's surprised because I've decided to show up and fucking play? "Then it's a good thing I'm Rossini now."

"Emilia!"

"Being betrothed to Luca wasn't my decision. Marrying him wasn't my decision. Getting pregnant by him wasn't my decision. But by God, this will be my decision and I say no, Mamma. We are not doing this."

"That son of a bitch has gotten to you."

"This has nothing to do with Luca getting to me. We're talking about two legacies created by two powerful families, and the Gasparis are neither of those families."

"Half is better than nothing."

"How do you know they won't take everything? How do you know they'll stop with the men and not kill my son?"

"They won't."

"Any threat against the Rossinis is a threat against my child."

"So you're truly Rossini now?"

"My baby is Rossini. That makes me Rossini whether I want to be or not because I will never rise up against my child."

My mother's eyes widen. "My God. You're in love with him."

It's useless to try and deny it. "What did you think would happen when I was put with him?"

"What about Nicolò?"

"I loved Nic. He was a wonderful man, but I never felt about him the way I feel about Luca. The two loves are entirely different."

"I saw this happening right before my eyes, but I told myself that I was wrong because I didn't want to believe it."

"I'm sorry, Mamma. I know you don't want to hear this."

"I lost my husband and son for nothing, and now you are in love with their killer."

My mother isn't wrong. The Bellini and Moretti men died in vain for decisions I made. The guilt I feel is a worm squirming its way into my core. It's a remorse I'll have to live with for the rest of my life.

"You have become the devil's whore by choice, and your child is his spawn."

I stare at her, stunned, because I can't believe she'd say such a horrible thing to me about my child.

"Oh, Emilia. You stupid girl. You should have stuck to the plan because now a battle is coming. And with the help of the Gasparis, the Bellinis won't lose the next war."

Cold. Numb. Empty. That's what I feel inside as I watch my mother walk away from me.

All of this was my parents' and grandparents' doing. They made a pact to give me to the Rossinis. Put me on a throne next to him. And now she means to take that from me after everything I've done?

How can she be so cruel to me? To the grandchild she's yet to meet?

She throws us away the minute we are of no use to her. I'm not sure why I'm surprised. That's what you do with pawns when they can no longer advance your Mafia game play.

"What's wrong, baby? Why do you look like someone just kicked your puppy?"

Oh God. I can't tell Luca about my mother and the Gasparis without going back to the beginning. I'm going to have to tell him everything.

How I planned on killing his father.

How I planned on killing his brothers.

How I planned on killing him.

I'm not ready to have that conversation. I'm terrified Luca will hate me.

And so I stall.

"It's a no-go on Stephan and Gemma. My mother is in discussion with the Gasparis about a betrothal to the eldest grandson."

"A connection with the Gasparis would be beneficial for your family. It's a good move on your mother's part. So why do you look so sad?"

"I don't want my sister to get stuck with someone she didn't choose."

He pulls me against his chest and squeezes me tightly. "You didn't choose me, and I think we're doing pretty great."

"Yeah, we are."

"Don't worry. It'll work out for both of them, maybe with other people, but they'll be okay."

It's two days until Christmas. I don't want to ruin our first holiday together by confessing all of this shit to Luca, but I'm afraid to wait. The Gasparis could be making plans right now. They could strike at any time, and we must be prepared for what's coming. I can't allow anyone to be hurt because I chose to have the perfect first Christmas rather than address the problem at hand.

"We need to talk."

"Sounds serious. Everything okay?"

"No." My eyes fill with tears. "Everything's not okay. We have a problem."

"Hey, baby. Has someone done something to you?"

"Where can we go talk privately?"

"Mom's parlor. Dad's office. Your choice."

"Viv's parlor."

Every step I take brings me closer to telling Luca the

truth. I feel like I may throw up. Or pass out. I'm not sure which. Maybe both and possibly in that order.

"You're trembling. What's going on?"

"I have some things to tell you. Terrible things. And I don't know how you're going to feel about me after I do."

"Calm down. Everything's going to be okay."

"You are not going to be okay with this."

"Have you fucked someone else?"

"No."

"Do you want to fuck someone else?"

"No."

"Is this baby mine?"

"Yes."

"Are you leaving me?"

"No."

"Those are the only things I wouldn't be okay with so calm down. I don't want you to be upset. It's not good for you or the baby."

"You know how much I hated you in the beginning."

"You were loud and clear about it."

"I didn't want to marry you. I didn't want to have sex with you. I didn't want to have your baby."

"I was aware."

"What you aren't aware of is the plan that my mother and I hatched before she turned me over to you."

"I do love a good plan."

He won't love this one. "As you know, there was no getting around marrying you and giving you a child."

"Ah, my favorite part of the plan."

"This is serious, Luca."

"I know it is, but I'm trying to put you at ease."

"It's not possible for me to be at ease while I tell you this."

"You can't tell me anything that is going to change the way I feel about you."

I'm not so sure about that.

"I was planning to kill you after I had your son. I was going to take back my family's legacy by plucking off each of the Rossini men until my son was the last surviving heir of the Bellini-Rossini empire."

"You're a Bellini, Emilia. I'd be sadly disappointed in you if you hadn't formulated some kind of plan to kill me and take back your family's empire."

"You aren't mad?"

"No, and I'm not at all surprised by your ambition. You have that very special Bellini steel pumping through your veins. With you as his mother and me as his father, can you imagine what kind of cojones this kid is going to have?"

Why am I not surprised by this?

"You haven't asked, but no, I'm not still planning to kill you."

"Oh, I know. You like the orgasms I give you way too much to take me out."

"That's very accurate. But all joking aside, there's more, and you aren't going to be happy about it."

"Let me have it."

"I am no longer my mother's puppet because I'm not Bellini anymore. I am Rossini. You and this baby make me so, and I am joined to you now and forever."

I am a creature who has turned on her creator; therefore, I am a true Frankenstein.

"And your mother isn't happy about it?"

"She is joining forces with the Gaspari family. They say they're coming to take the Rossini-Bellini empire for her."

"In exchange for what?"

"Half."

"Life has been good. There hasn't been a war among the five families in ten years and now those stupid motherfuckers want to step in and rise up against us over a matter that has nothing to do with them?"

"Their threats against this family are also threats against our baby." I place my hands on my round stomach. "You have to protect him, Luca."

"Nothing is going to happen to him. I won't let it."

"You're all I have now. I can't lose you."

"You're not going to lose me or him. The three of us are a family."

Love is a volatile thing.

It begins. It grows. It changes. Sometimes it ends.

It can be easy. It can be hard.

Love can be damaged. It can be mended.

Love can sneak up on you when you least expect it, and it can also disappear without any warning.

Love.

It's what you make it.

And I decide to make it with Luca and our child.

30

LUCA ROSSINI

THE GASPARI FAMILY IS FOOLISH AND WEAK. A BUNCH OF greedy, lazy motherfuckers. Their wealth was accumulated by the great-grandfather. The three living Gasparis have done nothing but piss it away. And now they're trying to jump aboard a ship that they believe is being relieved of its captain and crew. They think they're going to sit back and let someone else do the hard work and then reap the reward in the end.

It's fucking pathetic. But we'd be the fools to give them the advantage by underestimating them. We must be ready if and when they come. Above all else, Emilia and our child must be protected.

"Look at it this way. We get a bigger bedroom."

Emilia walks over to the bed and runs her hand over the silky bedspread. "A very gorgeous bigger bedroom that I'm sure your mother spent a ton of money on when it was decorated by a top interior designer." She looks up at me. "But it's not *our* bedroom."

"I'm sorry. I know how badly you want to stay at our house."

"I do, but I understand why it's safer for us to be here."

Our safety is dependent upon the entire family being in one place, and that place is the Rossini compound. Things become precarious when we're scattered about and splitting our soldiers between two households.

"We obviously don't know how long we'll be here. What will we do about a nursery if we're still living here when the baby comes?"

"The room across the hall is empty."

Emilia laughs. "God, Viv would love that."

"She's over the moon about us living under her roof. I'm not certain that she wouldn't implode if her grandchild got to live here too."

Emilia rests her hand on top of her stomach. "It's nice to have *one* grandmother who is excited about the baby."

"I'm sorry things have gone the way they have with your mom."

"Me too."

"And I'm sorry that our first Christmas Eve together is being spent moving."

"We're together. That's all that matters. But I do have a few concerns about living here."

"Such as?"

"Our bedroom is on the same hall as your brothers' and sister's." One of her brows lifts. "Sound travels."

"They're going to hear us fucking."

"Luca—"

"I'm sorry. We're not going to stop because they can hear us."

"We'll have to be quieter."

"No, we won't."

"The thought of them hearing us is embarrassing. I don't want them to hear me when I... you know."

"You're *sooo* loud when you come."

"I am, I know."

"Then I guess you don't get to come while we live here."

"If I don't get to come, then neither do you."

"We'll bring the stereo from the house. The subwoofers too."

"That's what I thought."

Everyone sleeping in this part of the house will know we're doing it every time they hear loud music coming from our bedroom. Great. Stephan and Dante won't rag on me about that at all.

Fuck it. Who cares? I'm getting laid and they're not.

My mother lightly taps her knuckles against the door. "Getting settled in okay?"

"Yeah, I think so."

It's weird being back in my old bedroom, this time with a pregnant wife.

"Do you need anything?"

Emilia shrugs. "I'm sure we'll come up with some things after we unpack. I feel like we left everything at home."

"Anything you need, just ask. If we don't have it, we'll get it for you."

"That's really sweet, Viv. Thank you."

"Dinner is at six."

"Do you need me to help?"

"Honey, I wouldn't dream of asking you to help cook dinner after the day you've had."

"Another time then?"

"There will be plenty of time for you to help."

My mother leaves, and I close the door behind her. "People popping into my space is going to take some getting used to after living on my own."

"How long has it been since you moved out of here?"

"Four years. Long enough to get used to doing things the way I like them."

"And then I came along and wrecked all of that."

"You didn't wreck anything. But this baby? He's going to flip shit upside down."

"Do you know anything about babies?"

"I'm the oldest of five and I… don't… know… shit… about babies."

"Nothing about that shocks me."

"Do you know anything about babies?"

"I was a girl born into a Catholic Italian family. I know everything about babies. I practically raised Isabella and Giovanni. They were like my own children."

Giovanni Bellini, a boy far too young to die. "I've never told you this, but it wasn't my intention to kill your brother. He was trying to be a hero. It all happened so fast. I didn't mean to. It was an accident."

She nods and a tear rolls down her cheek. "That was my brave boy. He thought he was invincible because Papà had taught him to believe that he was."

"It haunts me, Emilia. Every day. I wish I could take it back."

Emilia grimaces, and a quiet sob is unleashed from her chest. I wrap my arms around her, and she clings to me, her face buried against my chest as she cries.

"I'm so sorry for taking that boy from you. And your father. Even Nicolò. He didn't deserve to die for loving you."

She shakes her head. "Stop. I can't. I can't."

I have to say these things to her. "I was selfish and greedy and pompous. I didn't have a clue about what it was to love someone. But I know now because I love you, Emilia, and I will never hurt you again."

She lifts her head, and her eyes meet mine. "I wanted to hate you. I tried. I tried so damn hard, but I couldn't hate my way out of being in love with you. I love you, Luca. So much."

Embracing her face with my hands, I press a kiss to her lips. "I've been so afraid that you could never love me because of what I did to you and your family."

"I didn't want to love you. I fought against it for so long, but it's no use. I can't *not* love you."

I put my hands around each side of her belly. "I already love this baby."

"I know you do. And I love him, too."

"We're going to be a happy family, aren't we?"

"We're going to be very happy."

Suddenly, I'm bathing in the sunshine of her love. But I learned something a long time ago about love and sunshine. When you're standing in its warm rays, it's difficult to imagine that a storm is on its way.

EMILIA'S EYES ARE CLOSED, HER BREATHING DEEP AND steady. Lying on her side, she's facing me with her hand resting atop her round stomach like a mother protecting her young even in her sleep.

She's a wonderful wife. I'm so lucky to have her.

And she's going to be a wonderful mother. There's no doubt in my mind.

I lie still, studying her features and ponder how many of her traits our child will inherit? Her darker hair? Her deep-caramel eyes instead of my green? Those freckles across her nose?

I can't wait to see who he looks like. But indeed, I must wait. Too long according to what her doctor says.

She inhales deeply and opens her eyes, smiling when she sees me looking at her. "What are you doing?"

"Looking at you while you sleep."

"Well, that's not creepy at all."

"I was looking at your face and wondering if the baby will look like you."

"No. He'll look like you."

"And if the baby is a girl?"

"Still you."

"Why do you feel so strongly that the baby will look like me?"

"Because you're so damn dominant and overpowering in every little thing you do. Why would your genes be any different?"

"I couldn't stop being dominant or overpowering if I tried. It's who I am."

"I know. And I love that about you."

"It's one of many things you love about me, right?"

"Yes, one of many, many, many things."

She reaches out and taps the tip of my nose. "You look older."

"Well, I am a year older than I was when we went to sleep last night."

"Happy birthday."

"Thank you."

"Our first birthday together."

"Yours is next but sorry—" Reaching out, I rub her stomach. "This little one's birthday is the one I'm most looking forward to."

"I know. Me too."

Emilia jolts when three loud smacks land against our closed bedroom door.

"Mom told me to come up and tell you that your

birthday breakfast would be on the table in twenty minutes," Stephan shouts.

Emilia brings her hand to her chest. "Shit, he scared me."

She grew up with all sisters until her little brother came along. I'm sure things were mostly calm around the Bellini house, so she's not used to the brotherly antics Stephan pulls to annoy the shit out of me.

"That's it. I'm going to kill that motherfucker."

"Don't, Luca."

I throw back the covers and dash toward the door, slinging it open. The asshole is standing there grinning. "Did I interrupt your birthday sex?"

He takes off running, and I tackle him in the hallway.

"Good Lord. You're twenty-five, no, twenty-six years old, and you're acting like a child. Stop!"

We roll around on the hallway floor throwing half-strength punches while Emilia squeals for us to stop. She probably thinks we're going to hurt each other.

And we might.

"Boys."

With only a single word from our mother, Stephan and I both instantly still like well-trained dogs hearing their master's command.

Old habit.

"I won't have that foolery in my house."

My brother and I stand, each of us wiping the blood from our noses.

"I was just playing with him, Ma. He's overreacting like he always does."

"I'm not overreacting. You startled my wife. My *pregnant* wife. That's not good for her."

"I'm sorry, Emilia. I didn't mean to scare you."

"It's okay. I'm not mad."

"See? Your mate is perfectly fine, wolf. Calm down."

"You believe I'm overreacting, but that's because you don't understand yet. You will when you have your own wife."

"I'm sure I will be protective if Dad gets me a honey as good-looking as Emilia."

"You can talk about honeys later. I'm sure Zee Zee is taking the biscuits out of the oven, and there'll be another scolding if you don't get down there before the food gets cold."

"We'll be down as soon as we change."

Only a few minutes to spare. We'll need to be quick.

I close the door and push Emilia against it. Going in for a kiss, my mouth lands on the side of her face when she turns her head.

"You have blood trickling from your nose."

"Come on, Emilia."

"Come on, Emilia, *what*?"

"It's just a little blood."

"And it looks gross running out of your nose."

"It's my birthday. I want sex for breakfast," he whispers.

"Well, you're getting biscuits instead. Maybe Zee Zee will put a candle in one."

"Are you seriously going to make me wait for birthday sex?"

"I've learned one thing about being part of this family. You don't keep Zorah Rossini waiting at mealtime. So yes, you'll have to wait for birthday sex."

"You're right. None of us want to face her wrath."

"Don't worry, birthday boy. I have all kinds of birthday surprises for you. We're going somewhere tonight. And before you argue that it isn't safe, I've already made arrangements with some of the soldiers. They're going with us."

"Oh, Emilia. I don't know if that's the best idea."

"It'll be fine."

I'm not a fan of surprises. "What are we doing?"

"That's for me to know and for you to find out."

"Can I at least know where we're going so I can be prepared?"

"Nope."

"One clue?"

"No."

"Man, you are one tough cookie."

"You're going to love it, and that's all you need to know right now."

31

EMILIA ROSSINI

Envying him, I watch Luca inhale an entire dozen raw oysters. "How are they?"

"Very good." He grins. "Too bad you can't have any. I know how much you love them."

I do love them, and I plan to pig out on them after this baby is born.

"I can have cooked oysters."

He licks his bottom lip. "Sorry. Not the same thing."

"They're not, but the charbroiled ones with parmesan are pretty good."

"I can call the waiter over and order some."

"No, it's fine. My pasta is filling me up."

"But pasta's not an aphrodisiac."

"It's not, but I have pregnancy hormones so we're starting on a level playing field."

Luca sighs. "Do you have any idea how badly I want to take you home, to *our* house, and have a night without six of my family members sleeping down the hall?"

I bet I do.

"Then you're going to love the rest of your birthday

present." I remove the hotel room key from my purse, dangling it in front of him. "You don't have to put your hand over my mouth tonight."

A smile spreads across his face. "You got us a room in this hotel?"

"Not a room. A suite."

"I was not expecting this."

"This is a hotel restaurant. Did you think I brought you here only for dinner?"

"I did."

"Well that would have just been cruel."

Luca takes my hand and kisses the top. "I needed this so much. You don't know how much."

"I think I know exactly how much because I need it too."

"Are the soldiers staying here?"

"Only a few rooms away. They can be at our door in a matter of seconds if needed."

"The Gasparis would never strike against us in public."

I'm beginning to wonder if they're ever going to strike at all. "It's been two weeks, and they've done nothing."

"I'm not sure they ever will. They aren't known for aggression. I don't think they'd know how to plan an attack."

If my mother wasn't involved, Luca would have already relieved the human population of the Gasparis, but he's refrained on my account. He says he can't take another parent away from me.

"I don't want to keep living like this. Can't we go home?"

"I wish we could, but that isn't possible until we're sure that they aren't planning something."

"Maybe I can talk to Gemma. I think she would tell me what's happening."

Luca shakes his head. "I don't want you to do that."

"Gemma isn't a threat to us."

Like me, my sister is a pawn for my mother to use.

"You don't know where her true loyalties lie. She could give you fictitious information, so you'll develop a false sense of security."

"My sister would never do that to me."

"Just like your mother would never turn on you and her grandchild?"

As much as I hate it, he makes a valid point. "Right."

"I'm going to get us home, but I need time."

"I know you want to be home as much as I do. I'm trying to be patient." But it's so difficult, especially with my progressing pregnancy.

I want to paint the nursery… in *our* house. Buy a baby crib. Pick out baby bedding.

Do normal things to our home to prepare for our child.

"Speaking of patience. I have none right now. I'm ready to take you upstairs."

"But it's your birthday, and we haven't had dessert yet."

"We'll have one of everything sent up to the room."

"One of everything, huh?"

"If it gets you beneath me quicker. Besides, my real dessert is under that dress that I'm dying to peel off you."

"I don't require bribery, but since you're offering, one of everything works for me."

"Dessert comes after I come. Not before."

"Dessert comes after we both come."

32

LUCA ROSSINI

As soon as we're inside the room, I pull Emilia against me, but she pushes me away. "No."

What the fuck? "What do you mean no?"

"Go to the bed, and I'll be there in a minute, birthday boy."

I'm hard as a rock and I need relief. "I don't want to wait. I want you now."

"You can't have me now. I have a birthday surprise for you, and trust me, you don't want to ruin it by not waiting."

"I hate surprises."

She blows a raspberry. "You won't hate this one. I promise."

"Don't make me wait too long." I can't take it. And I shouldn't have to because it's my birthday.

She winks. "I would *never* make you wait for me too long."

Ohhh, the things I could say in reply to that.

Emilia shoves me. "Go on now."

"I'm taking my clothes off while I wait for you."

She rolls her eyes and murmurs a profanity. "Fine. Take off your clothes."

Yes, I think this is one surprise that I am going to like.

I become more impatient as Emilia stays in the bathroom for far too long. "Come on, baby. I'm ready."

"I'm almost finished."

What the hell is she doing in there?

Finally, she opens the door, only her head peeping out. I instantly see that her long tresses have been slicked back into a bun on top of her head. "Are you ready?"

Naked beneath the sheets, I sit up in bed, ready to fuck my wife. "Baby, I've been ready. I'm painfully waiting on you."

She smiles, and my own expression mimics hers.

"Okay."

She steps out wearing only two things: pink pointe shoes and a stiff pink and gold tutu, her pregnancy belly protruding over the top. I think it's the tutu she wore in *Sleeping Beauty*.

"Fuck," I say, mostly to myself.

"You told me you had fantasized about fucking me in my pointe shoes and tutu. Well, husband, I'm going to make your fantasy a reality."

Best birthday present ever.

"First, I need to warm up. A ballerina always needs to do her stretches."

She gracefully floats across the room and places one hand on the desk. She rises on to her pointes and lifts one of her legs in the air. Grabbing her foot, she pulls it up until her legs make one straight vertical line.

No panties. She's spread wide apart right there for me to look at. And I see everything. Every. Thing.

Fuck.

The air is knocked from my lungs, and I'm unable to speak. All I can do is look at her pussy.

My wife's body is a wonder. So few people have the ability to do what she does, but to put herself in that kind of position while she's almost seven months pregnant? She's a marvel.

She returns her foot to the floor. "I think I'm ready for my performance now."

My cock got hard when she dangled that hotel key in front of me at dinner, but now it's engorged to the point of almost hurting. My balls are tight and aching because I need to get off so badly.

She crawls on to the bed and climbs on top of me. Gripping her hips beneath her tutu, I squeeze the extra bit of soft flesh on her hips that hasn't been there until recently. Her hips and my hands move together as she rotates her pelvis. She grinds against me, sliding her wet pussy up and down my length. Teasing me.

And it's the best tease I've ever had.

Rising on her knees, she reaches between our bodies and glides my cock back and forth through the slickness of her center, coating the tip. And then she slides down my length until every inch is deep inside her, exactly where it belongs, and can go no farther.

Gripping my shoulders, she holds tightly. She moves up and down, her pussy gripping my dick and holding on to it as though it will never let go. My beautiful wife does all the work, letting me simply enjoy sitting back being fucked.

Happy birthday to me.

Emilia releases my shoulders and leans back, placing her hands on my thighs for support. Arching her back, she rolls her hips as she moves up and down, and her soft, slow breaths become quick, shallow pants.

Her chest is poked out and her tits, which have gotten

so much bigger lately, are right in my face. Reaching out, I palm both of them at the same time, rolling her nipples between my thumbs and index fingers. Even pinching them a little bit.

Her hands leave my thighs and she throws her arms around my shoulders, pulling our upper bodies together. My response is to do the same, wrapping my arms around her waist.

Tangled together, she presses her forehead against mine and continues to bounce up and down my dick, showing no signs of fatigue. My strong, beautiful, pregnant wife. Nothing in this world compares to her.

For love, I'd do *any*thing. For her, I'd do *every*thing.

"You are my husband and you own me. I want to own you, too."

Those are the single most erotic, intimate words that Emilia has ever said to me.

"I'm yours. Even the breath in my lungs belongs to you."

Emilia's grip around me tightens, forcing her pregnant belly to press against my stomach. Her movement changes and I feel her body's tight grip around my cock.

And I'm a goner.

Exploding inside her.

Claiming her.

I hold her tight and in place because I don't want to leave my favorite place in the world—inside her. Not yet. I want to treasure this moment with her for a little while longer.

Locking her hands behind my neck, she slumps around me. "Mmm. Satisfying… and exhausting."

Abruptly, she straightens and takes my hand, placing it on top of her belly. "Do you feel that?"

"I do. Wow." My son is already incredibly strong.

She giggles and I feel an ooze of wet warmth leak out of her and drip down my balls. It sort of tickles.

"Oh my goodness. This baby is moving like crazy. He never moves this much."

"He's angry that his slumber was disturbed."

"Well, his mamma is drained and is ready for her dessert."

Placing a quick kiss against my mouth, she moves off me, and my cock immediately aches from the separation. But it won't be our only joining. I intend on being inside my wife many times tonight.

Returning to the bed with the room service menu in hand, she opens it. "I think I'm going to order the char-broiled oysters to go with my dessert buffet."

Chocolate and oysters. "Oh, that sounds appetizing."

"I'm almost seven months pregnant. Don't judge me."

"Order anything you want, baby. I need you to regain your strength."

"Are you planning to exhaust me again?"

"Yes, I am. Many times. But what I really want is for you to ride my dick again."

"You liked that, huh?"

"Fuck yeah, I liked it."

I am a man who is always in control. Letting someone else take over for a while was nice. And who better than my queen?

33

EMILIA ROSSINI

Sitting on the exam table, I study a diagram on the wall. It's of the female anatomy with a baby coming through the birth canal.

How the hell is my body going to be able to do that?

I wonder how big Luca was when he was born. That's something I need to ask Viviana since birth weight could be hereditary.

The door opens, and I turn to be greeted by my doctor. Except it isn't my doctor.

"Gemma! What? How are you here?"

My sister comes to me, wrapping her arms around me.

"I called the doctor's office and pretended to be you. I told them I had forgotten when my next appointment was so I could find out when you were going to be here again. When I got here, I told the nurse you were waiting for me to arrive, and she brought me to your exam room."

"I'm so happy to see you."

I have missed Gemma so much. I've missed all of my family. Even my mother.

"I'm happy to see you too."

Gemma puts her hand on top of my stomach. "I can't believe how much the baby has grown since the last time I saw you."

"It's still too long until he comes. I'm ready to hold him now."

"You believe it's a boy?"

"I say *he* because I've listened to Luca talk nonstop about a boy. I don't care. I just want my baby to be safe and healthy."

"Are you afraid?"

I nod and tears fill my lower lids. "I always thought I'd have Mamma and Nonna there to help me through it."

"Oh, Em. I'm so sorry all of this has happened."

"I can't believe Mamma has turned her back on me and my baby. And even worse, she's declared war against us."

"She's so hellbent on revenge that she can't see how deeply she's hurting each of us." Gemma's eyes become glassy. "She's betrothed me to Andrea Gaspari."

"The last time I spoke to her, she told me she was working on that."

"He's awful, Emilia. A spineless pansy. I can't be married to a man like that."

A spineless pansy won't come to our compound with guns blazing.

"Gemma, I have a baby to think of. Can you tell me anything at all about the plans the Gasparis are making against us?"

"They don't tell me anything, but I've overheard Mamma on the phone. They're trying to plan something, and I get the impression that it isn't coming together very well."

Luca said that they probably didn't know how to prepare for an attack. I think he must be right.

"We've been waiting six weeks and nothing."

"Something is coming. Be prepared."

I believe my sister. And it breaks my heart that my mother would be part of this.

I understand that she is still grieving for my father and brother, but I'm her daughter, and I'm still here. Her grandchild will be here soon, and she doesn't care. She only cares about the moves she'll make in this Mafia game.

"I'm careful. I rarely leave the compound because Luca makes me take an army with me wherever I go."

"Because he loves you."

"He does and I love him. I didn't think I could, but I do. So much. I'm happy with Luca. I truly am."

"I'm happy your marriage has worked out for you."

Gemma smiles, and I know what she's going to ask before she says the words.

"Stephan is well."

She laughs. "I'm that obvious?"

"You are. Definitely."

"Has Marco chosen a bride for him yet?"

She looks nervous as she awaits my answer. "He's looking, but he hasn't found anyone yet."

"I had hoped he would be interested in me."

"Stephan is very interested in you. He asked me to speak to Mamma on his behalf, which I did, but she had other plans in mind for you."

"They're not *my* plans. I don't want to marry Andrea Gaspari. And I don't want to be away from you or be part of a war raging between our houses."

I've thought about this over and over, and all possible conclusions of this war end badly. "What can we do to end this civilly?"

"I don't know because Mamma won't be happy until the Rossini men are dead. Nothing less will do."

"Allies are the only thing keeping her afloat at this point. Without them, she has nothing. She's powerless."

"The Gasparis are broke and desperate. The only reason they offered to help Mamma is so they can get half of the fortune."

I know what the holdup is. "They made the offer when I was still in the picture. Without me to do the killing, it's turned into more than they can handle."

"I think that's it."

Who knows when or if they'll ever act against us? This could go on forever.

"I need to go before I'm missed."

"Will you try to come back for my next appointment so I can see you again?"

"I will if I can pull it off without anyone suspecting."

"Is there anything you'd like me to tell Stephan for you?"

Gemma removes an envelope from her pocket. "You don't have to tell him anything on my behalf. Everything I want to say to him is right here in this letter."

My sister loves Stephan. She must. That's the only reason she would write a letter to him.

"Hopefully, I'll see you in two weeks." She touches my stomach. "And you too, little Alessandro."

I hug my sister, tell her that I love her, and then she's gone. And I don't know for sure when I'll see her again.

And that's when I begin to cry.

34

LUCA ROSSINI

SNAKING MY ARMS AROUND MY BELOVED FROM BEHIND, I pull Emilia against my chest and kiss the side of her face. "How was my little one at your appointment today?"

"Perfect, according to Dr. Morris."

Just as I wanted to hear. "Excellent. And his mamma?"

"I'm good. No problems."

"Should we still expect to meet him in April?"

"That's what Dr. Morris says."

I've never been known for patience. "I want him to be big and strong when he's born, so I guess he should stay in as long as possible so he can get fat."

"Not too fat." She twists inside my embrace and wraps her arms around my shoulders. "These hips of mine aren't made for birthing according to Zee Zee."

"You do everything perfectly. Giving birth will be no different."

"I hope so because I do not want to be cut open."

"You're going to do great. Don't worry."

But she is worried. I see it all over her face. And as her husband, it is my job to reassure her. "You have the most talented doctor in New York City. I've made sure of it."

"I know, and I trust that I'm in very capable hands."

"Is there something else going on?"

"You've come to know me so well."

That's a yes.

She releases me and I step back, leaning against the kitchen counter. "Tell me what's going on."

"I saw Gemma today."

I take in a breath, intending to give Emilia a piece of my mind about doing what I specifically told her not to do, but she puts her hands up to silence me.

"She came to me."

"Where?"

"She tracked me down at the doctor's office because she wanted to see me."

"How the fuck did she get through the soldiers assigned to protect you?"

"It wasn't their fault. She came to the exam room."

Gemma is clearly a very clever girl to have worked that out. And I'm not at all pleased that she so easily gained access to my wife.

"What did she have to say?"

"A few things. And I know you think we can't trust her because you don't know where her loyalties lie, but I know where her heart is, and it isn't with our mother."

I don't understand this trust she has for a sister when her own mother didn't hesitate to declare a war that includes Emilia. "Tell me why you have so much confidence in her."

"First of all, she warned me to be careful because the Gasparis are still making plans to attack us."

"What kind of attack?"

"She doesn't know."

"Baby, that's not new information." And it's not reason to trust her.

Emilia goes to her purse on the counter and takes out an envelope. "She gave me this to give to Stephan."

"A letter?"

"Yes. She told me that everything she wants to say to him is in it. I think it's a declaration of love. But if not that, then possibly a plea for him to marry her."

"Which means she wants out."

"Yes, and if she wants out, then her loyalties aren't with Mamma."

"What about her betrothal to Gaspari?"

"She says he's awful and she won't marry him."

"Stephan is here. Do you want me to have him meet us in the conference room?"

"I do."

After Stephan has read Gemma's letter and had time to absorb it, our entire family comes into the conference room and each takes a seat around the table. When we gather here, it's usually to discuss business that has nothing to do with my wife, mother, or younger siblings. But today's discussion is entirely family business.

I nod at Emilia. "You can start."

Emilia is sitting back in the chair, her hands propped on top of her abdomen. Eight Rossinis are surrounding her, ready to hear what she has to say.

"I saw my sister Gemma this morning. She says the Gasparis are still planning an attack."

My father chuckles. "There's no reason for any of you ladies to worry. We'll be ready when they come."

"I'm not worried. I know I'm safe here. That's not really what this meeting is about." Emilia turns to Stephan.

My brother places the letter on the table. "Gemma sent this to me through Emilia. Her mother has arranged a marriage between her and Andrea Gaspari, which she does not desire."

"I'm sure she doesn't want that. Have you seen him?" Giada makes a gagging sound.

"Gemma seems like a very sweet girl. I hate that for her," my mother says.

"She wants to marry me."

My father is quiet for a moment, and I'm certain he's considering the pros and cons of having Gemma as his daughter-in-law.

He taps his fingers against the table. "Sofia will never agree to a marriage between the two of you, so I can only assume that Gemma means to leave the Bellini household?"

"She says she plans to do so whether we marry or not."

"Then her allegiance doesn't belong to Sofia."

Stephan points at the letter. "Not according to what she says in this."

"Do you want to marry her?"

"We didn't get a lot of time together, but I feel like things would have moved in that direction eventually."

"So you like her then?"

"I do. And I'm aware that I must choose a bride soon. She would be my choice."

A smile spreads across my mother's face. "I think Gemma would make a fine wife for you."

"Another Bellini girl for another son. This is wonderful. I wasn't counting on having a second one in the family."

"Gemma is supposed to come to the doctor's office and meet me at my next prenatal appointment. That could be the safest way to get her out."

"How long until your next appointment?"

"Two weeks."

Stephan shakes his head. "Two weeks is too long. She

could be married off to Andrea Gaspari by then. I want her to be out of their hands as soon as possible."

"I'm sure all phone calls coming into the house are being monitored, so I can't risk calling her. And I'd be too afraid to try and get a message to her through anyone."

"Then I don't have a choice. I'll have to go in and take her."

"I don't think I like that. It sounds very dangerous," my mother says.

"Did you ever consider going in and stealing Emilia?"

"Sure, I did."

Emilia's head jerks around. "You did?"

"Of course, and I wish now that I had." I regret killing all of those men who meant so much to my wife.

"Emilia, I'm going to need you to tell me how to navigate through the house."

"I can do that, but I want to know what kind of plan you have in mind."

"I can't go in hot. I'll do it quietly, so they won't realize she's gone until after we've made our getaway."

"I trust you to keep my sister safe, Stephan. Don't let me down."

"Don't worry. I won't."

STEPHAN IS DECKED OUT IN BLACK FROM HEAD TO TOE. "Your plan is good, bro."

Stephan chuckles. "It's brilliant even if I do say so myself."

"There's only one problem. It doesn't include me."

"That's because I'm doing this alone."

"No, you're not. I'm going with you because you need

someone to cover you. You need me." No one will cover my brother's ass like I will.

"I appreciate your offer, but I'm doing this solo."

"Why, when you don't have to?" There's nothing to prove.

"I want to look back on this years from now and know that Gemma is mine because *I'm* the one who took her. Not my older brother. If you'll stop for a moment and give it a little thought, I think you can see where I'm coming from."

I wouldn't have wanted anyone to help take Emilia. "Okay, I see it."

"This plan is going to go off without a hitch. I'm confident in it, and I wish you would be too."

I actually am. "The next time I see you, you'll have your woman with you."

"Unless she turns me down and tells me to get the fuck out."

"Won't happen. The girl wants you."

"Well, we're about to find out."

35

EMILIA ROSSINI

I TRY TO CONCENTRATE ON THE BOOK IN MY HANDS, BUT it's useless. Every thought in my head right now is about Stephan and Gemma.

Placing my book on my stomach, I turn to Luca. "Do you know what Stephan's plan is?"

"I do."

"Is it a good plan?"

"It's a very good plan."

"Do I want to know what it is?"

Luca stops reading and looks back at me. "No, and even if you did, I wouldn't tell you."

"Why not?"

"Hearing the plan won't calm your nerves."

"Because it's dangerous?"

"Stop, Emilia."

"Sorry. I'm not trying to be a pest, but I'm worried."

"I am as well, but fretting isn't good for you or the baby."

I return to reading, but I'm only a few paragraphs in

when I give up. "I should choose a room for Gemma and change the sheets so they'll be fresh."

"That won't be necessary."

"It's the proper thing to do."

"Stephan is going to sweep in, throw her over his shoulder, and carry her away from that madness. Do you think he won't have her in his room tonight?"

This is my nineteen-year-old *virginal* sister who has never been in love. Unless something has changed since we last discussed it, she hasn't even kissed anyone. "Gemma's not that kind of girl. She's very innocent, even more so than I was. She's not going to be staying in Stephan's room with him."

I don't know what Luca is thinking. Viv isn't going to let hanky-panky go on under her roof between them if they're not married.

"Care to place a wager?"

"What kind of wager?"

"I don't know. If you win, what would you want from me?"

I can only think of one thing. "A full-body massage. With oil and everything for one hour. Not a minute less."

"My hands all over your body for an hour? That sounds like win-win for me."

"What do you want from me?"

Luca chuckles. "I want you to suck my cock. And use lots of tongue and throat. And hands on my balls."

I should have known.

"An hour-long massage versus a one-minute blowjob. You're on."

"Whoa, heeey… I will last way longer than a minute."

"Okay. Two minutes then."

"Come on, Emilia. You're bruising my ego."

"I'm not insulting you. I just know how excited you get

when you're sliding in and out of my warm… wet… slick… mouth."

"You keep talking like that and I'm going to have you on your knees, wager or not."

I shake my head. "I'm pregnant *and* my stomach is in knots. Your cock in my mouth wouldn't be a wise decision right now."

"I was thinking about using sex to distract you… but message received."

"Based on Stephan's plan, how long do you think it'll be before they're here?"

"Baby, I have no idea."

"I'm sorry. I know you don't have a crystal ball."

"Hey, how about I give you a massage now?"

"Without winning the wager?"

"Sure. If it'll take your mind off this and help you to relax."

I'd be nuts to turn down a massage. "The baby oil is under the sink."

With the bottle in hand, he returns from the bathroom. "Take off your nightgown."

"Massage only, mister. I'm not in the mood to fool around."

"I understand."

I lift my nightgown over my head and toss it to the foot of the bed. Still wearing my panties, I crawl on all fours to the middle. "Is this where you want me?"

"Perfect."

"For obvious reasons, I'll have to lie on my side instead of my stomach."

"Your side is good."

He pours some oil into his palms and briskly rubs them together. Beginning at my shoulders, he squeezes and releases my tight muscles. "You're so tense."

"You aren't?"

"I am but I'm not pregnant."

"I'll try to relax."

"Breathe in and out, deep and slow. Maybe that'll help."

Luca inches his way from my shoulders to my lower back and then around my hips to my protruding belly. "He's grown so much this month. I think he's tripled in size the last few weeks."

Everyone has noticed his growth. "He's making himself known to everyone. That's for sure."

"We haven't talked about a girl name."

I'm surprised Luca would bring that up. "I thought you were convinced he was a boy."

"I do think it's a boy, but we should be prepared just in case. Do you have something in mind?"

I don't even have to think about it. "I've always thought Marisa was a pretty name."

"Marisa Rossini. I like that. It's a strong female name." Luca rubs his hand in big circles around my stomach. "Marisa or Alessandro? Which one of you are in there?"

"Whoever's in there is doing flips." I place my hand over Luca's and move it to the spot where I feel the strongest movement. "Do you feel that?"

Luca chuckles behind me. "I do and it's amazing. I can't believe there's a little person inside you."

"He's already so strong just like his dad."

"Don't forget his mom. She's pretty strong, too."

"I can't wait to meet him. Or her."

"Me either."

I close my eyes and enjoy the feel of Luca's hands and fingertips kneading and rubbing my body. I'm not sure how long he's been at it when I doze off. I only know that my heart pounds erratically when he tells me to wake up and get dressed.

"They're here?"

"Yes."

"Both of them?"

"Yes."

"And they're both safe?"

Luca hesitates. "Gemma is unharmed."

"But Stephan isn't?"

"The doctor is on the way."

My heart sinks. "What happened to him?"

"Gunshot."

"Is he going to be all right?"

"I don't know."

"Where are they?"

"Stephan's bedroom."

I yank my nightgown over my head and slip on my robe, tying the belt above my bulging abdomen. Waddling as fast as I can down the hallway, I find Gemma sitting beside Stephan, her hand cupped around his.

"Can I do anything to make it better?"

"Having you here makes it better."

She shakes her head. "I can't believe you came for me."

"How could I not after reading that letter?"

Viv comes into the room. "I need everyone to clear out. Dr. Schroeder is here, and you know how he likes his space."

Gemma leans over Stephan and kisses his forehead. "I'll only be in the hallway if you need me. All you have to do is call out, and I'll come."

"Thank you."

My sister comes out of Stephan's room and falls into

my arms, sobbing, her brave face gone. "Oh, Em. It was awful. I thought we were both going to die."

"Shh… all is well now. You're safe and Stephan is going to be fine."

"He risked his life by coming for me, and now he's lying in there with a gunshot wound. And it's all my fault."

"He knew the risk involved and he still chose to come for you. Because he wants to marry you."

"I can't believe what just happened. The whole thing was like something out of a movie. He saved me. He's my hero."

"How are Micaela and Isabella?"

"They miss you. Both were so jealous because I saw you and we got to talk."

"I miss them so much. How is Nonna?"

"Tired. All of this is taking a toll on her."

"I was afraid of that."

"Mamma is obsessed with revenge. It's poison in her veins and causing her to not think clearly."

"What does Nonna have to say about all of this?"

"She has begged Mamma to not work with the Gasparis. She believes no good can come from it."

"No good can come from it. The Rossini are organized and ready to fight. Mamma and the Gasparis will fail if they challenge us. I don't understand why she can't see that."

"She doesn't understand the war she's starting. And I'm afraid for her."

"The Rossinis are growing impatient. They're ready to end this."

"I was so afraid that they would strike against us first, and I would be caught in the middle."

"They would have if it weren't *my* mother involved. Luca is afraid it will cause problems between us."

"Would it?"

"No. I would never fault Luca for protecting our family."

"You consider yourself one of them."

"I am Rossini. And if you marry Stephan, you will be too. You need to understand that."

"I do."

The doctor emerges from Stephan's bedroom. "Two bullets extracted. No major damage as far as I can see. I'm leaving antibiotics and pain medication. Call me if there's excessive fever or blood loss."

"Well, he has an exceptional bedside manner," I whisper to Viv.

"He doesn't make small talk because he likes to get in and get out as quickly as possible."

"Obviously."

Not making a move, Viv and I stand motionless in the hallway, and Gemma turns back to look at us.

"You're the one he wants, darling. Not us. Go on and see him," Viv says.

Gemma nods. "Thank you."

"I think Gemma should stay with Stephan in his room tonight," Luca says.

"That's probably a good idea. He shouldn't be left alone," Viv says.

From behind, Luca wraps his arms around me and pulls me close, his mouth hovering over my ear. "Gemma is staying in his room tonight, so it looks like I'm getting my cock sucked after all."

"You are such a jackass."

"Maybe so, but I'm a jackass who's getting his cock sucked tonight."

36

LUCA ROSSINI

EMILIA'S BREATHS ARE DEEP AND REGULAR. THE PREGNANCY has really been taking it out of her lately, so her naps are longer, allowing her to fall into a deeper sleep. This means I should have about an hour until she wakes. Long enough to take advantage.

Quietly, I lift the chair in our bedroom and place it at the bedside. When I'm satisfied with its position, I go to the desk and take out my sketchbook.

My *secret* sketchbook.

I open the book to a clean page, and using my favorite charcoal pencil, I begin tracing the outline of Emilia's body on the paper. She's lying on her side, knees slightly bent, hair spilling around her on the pillow. One arm is tucked beneath her head, and the other is resting on the top of her belly. I love the way she's always touching her stomach, even in her sleep.

I trace her delicate small frame and then begin work on her face. Those features... I've drawn them at least a hundred times in the last eight months, all without her knowledge. And I'm getting pretty good at nailing them even if I do say so myself.

Do I enjoy drawing Emilia because she's my wife and the mother of my child and I love her? Yes.

But it's more than that.

With Emilia, everything she does comes from within. She has dark impulses, same as me. It's the Bellini in her blood, just as it's the Rossini in my veins. It's one of the things that makes her so thrilling to watch.

We're both a little fucked up, but together, we are unstoppable.

I glance at the clock every few minutes, doing a countdown in my head. Right now, I anticipate about fifteen minutes until she wakes. It should be safe to work another five minutes. I don't want to push it too close.

Glancing up at her face, I study her features and then return my focus to the page and shade the areas beneath her high cheekbones.

"Fuck, that's all wrong," I mutter to myself beneath my breath.

"Luca? What are you doing?"

My hand becomes motionless, and I hesitate for an instant before looking up at her. Saying nothing. Because I don't know what to say.

I'm caught.

"What are you doing?" she repeats.

Lifting my sketchbook from my lap, I close it. "Just watching you sleep."

"You pulled up a chair at the bedside so you could watch me while I nap?"

"Yeah. I like to watch you sleep."

"You're so weird sometimes."

I shrug. "In my defense, I never said I wasn't."

"What are you reading?"

I look down at my book. "Oh this? It's nothing."

"It doesn't look like nothing."

I shrug again, shaking my head. "Nothing of interest. You'd find it boring."

Emilia sits up and reaches out. "Let me see it."

"I told you, princess. It's nothing of interest."

"Is that a *sketchbook*?"

Dammit. My wife is sometimes, oftentimes, too damn smart for her own good.

"Yes, Emilia. It is a sketchbook."

"You were drawing me while I was asleep?"

"Yes." Because you're my favorite subject.

"I want to see."

"No." That's not going to happen.

"Why will you not show me?"

"Because my drawings aren't good."

"Who told you they weren't good?"

"No one told me. I just know."

"Have you ever shown them to anyone?"

"You know I could never do that."

"Let me guess. Because art makes you *soft*?"

"Exactly." And who would I show them to anyway?

"Contrary to what you've been taught, art doesn't make a man soft, Luca."

"No man in the Rossini family would ever see it that way, so no one can ever know about this little activity of mine."

"I won't tell anyone." She smiles. "If you let me see them."

"My own wife would blackmail me?"

"No, not really, but I am dying to see them."

"I've never shown my drawings to anyone."

"I'm your wife. The mother of your child. I'm not just *anyone*."

Today's drawing isn't my best work. I'm not excited about showing it to her. "I didn't get very far today. You woke up too soon."

"I'm sorry about that." Emilia pats the bed beside her and smiles. "Come sit here and show me what you've done."

Drawing is a hobby. Just something to pass the time. So why am I nervous about showing my own wife?

Sitting beside Emilia on the bed, I open my sketchbook to today's drawing and hand it to her. "It's only partially finished."

"Oh, Luca—" Emilia traces her finger along the curve of her body on the page. "This is beautiful."

She flips the page to my previous drawing from several days ago—Emilia sitting in a tub, her breasts and pregnant abdomen peeking out of the water.

She places her finger over her charcoal breasts and turns to me. "Ah, I'm naked?"

If she doesn't care for the little peep show in this one, then she's probably not going to be thrilled with some of the earlier drawings.

"You're not naked… well, technically, you are naked, but you're covered."

"Not enough." She takes her hand away. "Did you draw this from memory when you sat with me by the tub earlier this week?"

"Yes."

"This is incredible. How do you remember the details?"

"I don't know. I just see it in my head, and I'm somehow able to get it on paper."

Emilia moves to the next drawing—a sketch of her

overlapping hands, the left adorned with her wedding ring. The right, bearing the Rossini ring.

"My God. The detail is amazing."

She flips the page and comes across my favorite—my bride wearing her lace wedding gown and tulle veil. Her expression in the drawing is identical to what I saw on her face that day. I had to draw it so I'd always remember it.

And below the charcoal rendering of my bride are five words.

"My queen. Forever and always," she reads aloud.

"You are my queen, Emilia. Forever and always."

She leans over and places her hand against the side of my face, pressing a soft kiss to my mouth. "And you are my king."

"I'm not sure I've ever heard you admit that."

She smiles. "Well, it has taken me some time to come to a place where I'm willing to admit that. But yes, you are my king, and ours is an overwhelming, never-ending, restless love."

Emilia returns her attention to my sketches, stopping to appreciate each one, complete or not.

"How long have you been drawing?"

"For as long as I can remember."

"You've never taken any kind of art class? Not even when you were in school?"

I can only imagine what Marco Rossini would have said about that. "My dad would have had me killed before he would have allowed me to take a *pussy class*. You know that."

"Art isn't for *pussies*, Luca."

"I know, but it doesn't matter. I'm Mafia. I'm never going to be an artist."

"You are so much more than Mafia. Can't you see that?"

"I aspire to be more, but it can never be."

"It shouldn't be that way. You should be able to create art if it makes you happy. And especially when you're so clearly talented at it."

"I'm afraid it'll have to be our little secret."

"I will always keep all of your secrets."

She turns the page and giggles. "Oh my. This… *this* is an interesting one. I don't recall ever wearing anything like that or posing my body in that position… or doing that to myself with my fingers."

Okay. Not all of my drawings are based upon images I've actually seen. Some of them, particularly the earlier ones, are based upon fantasies I had in my head.

She looks at me, and the question she isn't asking is written all over her face. "Yes, Emilia. I've imagined you that way many, many times. I would love to see you wear something like that, and I'd also love to watch you do that to yourself."

"Really?"

"Yes, really." I'm a man.

She grins and returns to flipping through my sketch-book. "It's a no while I have this enormous belly, but who knows? Maybe after the baby is born, I'll do that for you."

That's not a no. I'll take it.

She closes my book, holding it on her lap. "You're an excellent artist, Luca."

"Sure you aren't just saying that because you're my wife?"

"It's true. You have a crazy, wonderful, natural kind of talent." She flattens her palm over the top of my book. "It can't be taught. This is something that you must feel deep inside."

Because I've never shown my drawings to anyone, I've

never heard opinions about them. I don't know what to say. It feels odd to hear that kind of praise, even from my wife.

"I'm glad you like them."

"I keep learning things about you. Are you ever going to stop surprising me?"

"I hope not."

"I hope not either."

37

EMILIA ROSSINI

Luca wants me to be calm and stress-free for the baby, but then he turns around and does shit like this. "I'm nervous about this trip."

"What part of it is making you nervous?"

"You'll be hours away from me. I could go into labor while you're gone."

"Four hours there, four hours back. What are the odds that you'll go into labor and deliver the baby before I'm home again?"

Eight hours is a long time. It could happen. "I don't know what the odds are, but I'm telling you that I don't have a good feeling about this trip."

"What if I promise to call you when we get there?"

"What good will that do if I'm in labor? A phone call isn't going to stop my contractions."

"I'd know that I need to haul ass on the way back."

That's a terrible idea. "The weatherman is predicting snow. Do you have to make the pickup tonight?"

"Sal is very experienced at driving in snow. It'll be fine."

"I don't want to have this baby while you're on the road."

"You won't. It's three weeks until your due date."

"The doctor said I'm considered full-term now. I could deliver any day."

"Are you having contractions?"

"I had some earlier, but they stopped."

"That's a good thing because we've only been married seven and a half months. You have to hold this baby in for a little longer."

I hope he's kidding. "I have no control over how long I'm able to hold him in. Perhaps you should have thought about that nine months ago when we weren't married, and you were so adamant about me proving my fertility."

"Do you want to hear something funny about that?"

"I'm not in the mood for jokes tonight."

"I'm not going to tell you a joke." Luca grins. "Promise you won't get mad?"

Anytime he says *promise you won't get mad*, I always get mad. "No, I don't promise."

"I lied to you about proving your fertility to me."

"Lied to me how?"

"You never had to prove to me that you could get pregnant. I was going to marry you regardless. I just wanted to fuck you, and I knew that was the only way you'd let me."

"Luciano Davide Rossini."

"You sound like my mother."

Oh my God. I can't believe him.

I clench my fist and slam it against his chest. "Ohhh, you fucking asshole."

"Yeah, I totally am."

"Uh, I hate you so much right now."

"Baby, you've tried like hell to hate me, but you've never been able to."

"But *that*… *that*… was just so wrong. If I didn't want more children, I would kick you as hard as I could in your nuts."

He puts his hands on the sides of my belly. "I lied to you, and for that I'm sorry, but the result of my deception is this beautiful little life growing inside you. I will never be sorry about that."

I want to be mad at him. I do. And I should be.

"I can't be sorry about it either." I reach up, grabbing his jaw and pulling him closer. "But don't do that shit to me again. Lies and deception are the fastest way to make me stop loving you. Do you understand?"

"I understand, love."

I squeeze his cheeks, pushing his lips out, and press a kiss to his puckered mouth. "Good. Now go. The sooner you leave, the sooner you'll be back, and I can be at ease." Because I damn sure won't sleep a wink while he's gone to retrieve these guns from Boston.

"I love you."

"I love you too. And please be careful."

"I'm always careful."

"I know, but I have to say it because it's not just you and me. We have a baby to think of now."

I remember the days when I prayed for the things I have in my life now. A husband I love. Our first child. I couldn't bear to lose either of them.

"Everything I do is for both of you. There's never a time when I'm not thinking of you and this baby."

Stephan opens the door and comes back into the house from the garage. "We've been out here warming this truck up for twenty minutes. Are you coming or what?"

"I'm coming. I'm coming."

Luca kisses me, and I grip the front of his coat, holding

on to him a little longer than I ordinarily would. "I'll be back home before you wake up. "

Something feels off. And I don't know what… until two hours later when the contractions begin.

Going to my sister's room down the hall, I tap lightly on her door. "Gemma? Are you still awake?"

"Yeah, come in."

She sits up and turns on the lamp at her bedside.

"I'm sorry. I don't mean to bother you."

"It's fine. I wasn't asleep. Is everything okay?"

"I don't know. I've started having contractions."

"How long ago?"

"They just started."

"How far apart are they?"

"I think about eight minutes."

"Is that close?"

"Not really but I'm worried that this is the beginning and something will happen before Luca gets back."

"You need to lie down and relax."

"Do you mind if I stay in here with you?"

"Of course not. It'll be like old times."

Gemma tosses back the covers and I climb into bed beside her.

"Aren't you worried about Stephan?"

"Of course, I'm worried. I wish he was here with me instead of out there moving guns in a truck on icy roads in the middle of the night. But that is what Mafia men do. And we sit here worrying. That is what Mafia wives do."

I'm a Mafia wife. Gemma is a Mafia fiancée.

"We're younger versions of Mamma. Both of us. How in the world did that happen?"

"You married a Rossini man, and I'm about to do the same exact thing."

"It's strange how history repeats itself."

I inhale deeply and breathe out slowly when I feel the tightening of my upper abdomen.

"Contraction?"

"Oh yeah."

"What does it feel like?"

Using my fingers, I press against each side of my lower abdomen. "The worst menstrual cramps I've ever had in my life."

Gemma breathes with me and rubs the top of my belly until the pain subsides.

"I wonder how soon Stephan will want to have a baby."

"He's going to be your husband. Ask him."

"I want to spend time with Stephan and get to know him before we have a baby. I'm afraid he'll tell me he wants one right away."

You should know your husband before marriage and pregnancy. That's the way it's supposed to be, and it makes me sad that Luca and I didn't have that special time together. We're going to be parents soon, and I'm still trying to figure out who Luca is.

"Are you going to use birth control?"

"Rhythm method and withdrawal." Gemma holds up her hand and overlaps her middle finger across her index. "Fingers crossed."

Another pain begins and I groan. "Luca will be lucky if I ever have sex with him again."

Hour one: contractions eight minutes apart.

Hour two: contractions seven to eight minutes apart.

Hour three: contractions six to seven minutes apart.

And each hour they're getting harder.

"These are definitely getting closer. The last two weren't quite seven minutes apart."

I'm in labor. It's still very early, but it's labor. And my level of anxiety is rapidly rising.

I want Luca here.

"They've been gone five hours, so that means they're on their way back. Don't worry. Luca is going to make it back in plenty of time to be here when this baby comes."

The next contraction begins, and it's the most painful one I've had. "Ohhh!"

"Breathe, Em. Breathe in deeply and out slowly."

When the contraction ends, I slide to the edge of the bed. "I can't lie like this anymore. I need to get up and walk."

Gemma follows me down the hall and into my bedroom. "Do you think we should wake Viviana and let her know your labor has started?"

"No, I think it's too early for that. It'll be hours before it's time to go to the hospital. We should let everyone sleep. With this being my first, it'll probably take a while."

I can't believe I'm thinking this, but I hope it takes a while. I can't give birth while my husband is on the road doing a job.

Please hurry home, Luca. Please come back to me. I don't want to do this without you.

Hour four: contractions five to six minutes apart.

Hour five: contractions four to five minutes apart.

Gemma rubs my lower back while I lean over the bed. "Your doctor told you to come to the hospital when your pains were five minutes apart."

"I know, but Luca should be back here in an hour. I don't want to go without him."

"Someone will make sure he comes to the hospital as soon as he gets back."

"The contractions aren't that bad. I have plenty of time."

"You're such a liar. I can see how much pain you're having."

I shake my head. "I'm not doing this without him."

"You may not have a choice if your contractions keep getting harder and closer."

"I'll know when we need to go." Surely, I'll know.

"It's not as if he's going to be in the delivery room with you. He'll be out in the waiting room, smoking cigars with all the guys."

I don't know if I believe that. Luca is far more excited than the average father-to-be. I don't see him casually smoking it up while he waits to hear if I've given him a son or daughter.

"He has to be there because I want to be the one to tell him if it's a boy or girl."

"Uh, Em. You're making me so nervous by waiting around."

Viviana appears in the doorway of my bedroom and taps against the frame. "Everything okay in here?"

"Everything is not okay. She's in labor, and she won't go to the hospital because Luca hasn't made it back from the run yet."

"How long have you been having contractions?"

"Since ten o'clock last night."

"Emilia, that's seven hours."

"It hasn't been that bad."

"She's lying. She can hardly breathe through them."

"I think you should go to the hospital."

"But Luca will be back soon. I want him to be there with me."

"You're accomplishing nothing by staying here. This baby doesn't know that its father isn't home yet. It's coming regardless." Viviana shakes her head. "And weeks before we need it to, I might add."

I couldn't care less what the five families think about my baby's date of birth in regard to my wedding day.

"I'll need someone to bring Luca to me as soon as he gets back."

"Absolutely, without delay."

I don't want to go without him. But I also don't want to deliver this baby here without a doctor. "All right. I'll go."

"Where is your bag?"

"Luca put it in the car a few days ago."

"Good. I'll get dressed and wake Marco. He'll want to know that our first grandchild is about to make his debut into the world."

"Sal went with Luca and Stephan."

"Then I'll wake Tony to drive us."

After Gemma helps me change, we find Marco and Viviana waiting for us at the foot of the stairs. "I hear my grandson decided to make his appearance while his father is away?"

"He's trying very hard."

"Don't worry, Emilia. Luca will be here when his son comes into the world."

Everybody keeps saying that, but I'm not so sure. "I hope so."

"Careful now," Marco says, taking my hand and helping me into the back seat of his Lincoln.

"I'm in."

Tony lifts the garage door and gets into the driver's seat. "Which medical center are we going to?"

Bang.

POW. POW. POW.

Thick, sticky red liquid and matter splatters all over the interior of the car. And me.

Tony's brains.

"Down! Everybody down!" Marco yells.

I try to bend over, but my abdomen won't let me lower my head as I should. Physically, it isn't possible, and my only alternative is to slide down onto the floorboard of the back seat.

Marco slams the car door shut and dashes to the garage door controller, striking his hand against the button to close it.

One one-thousand. Two one-thousand. Three-one thousand. Four one-thousand. Five one-thousand. Six one-thousand. It's frightening how many shots can be fired in a matter of only six seconds.

The shots don't stop when the garage closes and it does little to prevent them from reaching us.

"They're going to shoot through the door. We can't stay here. Everyone has to move inside."

I'm not a mother yet, and my child hasn't even had the chance to live.

Collateral damage. That isn't the way I want either of us to die

"Marco, help Emilia. She must go first."

I don't know if she believes I'm more deserving of going first because I'm pregnant, or if I'm easier to get out of the car because of my small size. Maybe I'm a hindrance to her escape with my position on the floor. I don't know and it doesn't matter. I don't have time to think about it because Marco slings open the door, pulling me out of the car and into the safety of the house.

Leaving Viviana and my sister behind.

Marco shoves me at Guido, one of the Rossini soldiers, and I fall into his arms. "Take her. I'm going back for Viv and Gemma."

Gripping the front of Guido's shirt, I press my face against his chest when the next contraction begins. "Ohhh!"

"What's wrong? Have you been shot?"

"No. I'm… in… labor."

"Shit… shit."

"What is happening?" Zee Zee shouts, rushing down the stairs as quickly as her legs will carry her.

Guido grips me beneath my arms, holding me up while Marco, Viviana, and Gemma join the growing crowd of people at the bottom of the stairs.

"Will someone tell me what is happening?" Zee Zee shouts.

"We're being attacked," Marco says.

"By the Gasparis?"

"One would presume."

"How many of them are there?"

"I don't know, but that was at least a dozen guns firing at us at the same time." Marco curses below his breath. "They came tonight because they somehow knew Luca, Stephan, and half of the soldiers from the compound wouldn't be here." Marco shakes his head. "Stupid. I shouldn't have sent so many soldiers on the transport."

Viviana places her hand on Marco's shoulder. "Don't be angry with yourself. You were protecting our sons and the arsenals in the trucks. Where would we be if the Gasparis got their hands on that kind of artillery?"

"Ohhh!" A contraction begins and I grip Guido's shirt again.

"She's in labor?" Zee Zee asks.

"Yes, and she has been for quite some time. She needs to be at the hospital."

"When did it start?"

"Several hours ago."

"Well. It looks as though we're having a baby in the middle of all this chaos."

"No, no, no, I can't give birth to this baby while we're under attack."

"The child doesn't care. It's coming regardless." Zee Zee looks at Guido. "Please carry Emilia to her bedroom."

Guido scoops me up in his arms and climbs the staircase, and every Rossini woman, including my sister, follows him. He jostles me in a less-than-gentle manner with each step he takes.

"You should change into a comfortable nightgown. Preferably one that you don't mind tossing in the trash when all of this is over," Zee Zee says.

"When what's over?"

"After you deliver the baby."

I hope she's kidding. "I can't have this baby at home without a doctor."

"Oh, you can. Trust me."

"We need to call for help," Gemma says.

"Honey, I checked the phone already. They've cut the lines," Viv says.

"I don't want you to worry, child. I've attended many births, and all of my children were born at home. It's a natural process."

"I don't want natural. I want twilight sleep."

Our housekeeper, Laura, comes into the bedroom. "Yes, Mrs. Rossini?"

"We're going to need lots of linens and towels. And any kind of antiseptic we have in the house."

"Yes, ma'am."

Oh God. This is happening. Luca's grandmother is going to be the person who brings this baby into the world. Not the brilliant doctor that Luca insisted upon.

Anything could go wrong and what then?

My life and the life of my baby are in Zee Zee's hands.

In God's hands.

Pray. I need to pray. I need to confess my sins and ask God to forgive me for the wrong I've done.

"Oh, oh. Here comes another contraction."

"Up, child. You need to be upright until you feel the urge to push."

Push? I'm not pushing. I won't push this baby out. I will hold him in until next month if I have to.

Zee Zee takes one hand and Viviana takes the other, pulling me off the bed to a standing position. "Stand, walk, squat. Do whatever feels best to you until the urge comes."

Holding the bed, I bend at my waist and over the mattress when the next pain comes. Oddly, it takes away the pressure I feel in my lower back, which is some relief.

"Come on, Em. Breathe in and out, deep and slow. You can do this," my sister says.

I don't want to do this. Not this way.

Within the hour, my contractions are so close that it feels like there's no break between them. I'm in constant pain.

"I can't do this. I can't do this. I can't do this," I mutter below my breath.

Zee Zee rubs my lower back. "It won't be much longer now, child. You're close."

"I can't do it. I'm not made for this. You said so yourself."

"You were a Bellini then, but you're a Rossini now. And you're going to give Luca a fine son."

The next contraction begins and it's different. The baby feels lower. "I feel pressure down there."

"Do you have an urge to bear down?"

"Yes. God, yes."

"Obey the commands of your body."

"How?"

Zee Zee and Viviana hold me beneath my arms. "Squat and bear down."

What? No. "I don't want to do that."

"Modern doctors put you in a bed, but trust me, girl. This is the easiest way to birth your baby."

Viviana nods. "She's done this many times. She knows what's best, Emilia."

The last thing I want to do is push this baby out, but it's as though my body commands it of me. I have no control when the next contraction begins.

"Ahhh!"

Zee Zee crouches in front of me. "Stop screaming and push, girl. Push."

Viviana holds me steady when I waver. "Hold your breath in and bear down."

Breathe. Hold breath. Bear down. I do that every two minutes until I'm exhausted and can no longer hold myself in a squatting position. "I can't do it anymore."

"You should rest for a moment and regain some strength," Zee Zee says.

Gemma and Viviana help me up because my legs are shaking, too weak to hold my weight.

Viviana strokes the wet hair away from my forehead. "That's it. Rest, Emilia."

My eyes close on their own because I don't have the strength to hold them open any longer.

"Giada, go into the bathroom and get a fresh wet cloth for Emilia's head."

When Giada returns, Viv strokes the cool cloth over my face and neck. "You're doing a great job."

"Shouldn't the baby have come already?"

"The first one always takes the longest. And if this one is anything like his father, he's going to take his time. I didn't think Luca would ever come out."

Oh God.

"What if I'm too small to have him?"

"Shh… you're letting the exhaustion get in your head. Just rest a few minutes and get some energy back."

"My mouth is so dry."

"Giada —"

"I've got it, Mamma."

Gemma helps me to a sitting position, and I take small sips of water. I'm thirsty but nauseous at the same time.

The next contraction begins, and my body won't allow me to lie on the bed through it. "Oh God. I have to push."

"Come on, ladies. Let's help Emilia get into position."

I resume the squatting position and bear down, hard as I can. Over and over and over. And he still doesn't come out.

This baby is too big for me to push out. Because of that, I'm going to die in childbirth. The baby and I both are because no one can get me out of here and to a hospital where they could cut him out.

I need Luca. I need him to come home and kill every one of those men surrounding our compound.

He should have been back hours ago. Where is he?

38

LUCA ROSSINI

Almost home. Almost back to Emilia. Almost lying next to my wife in bed.

"The heater in this truck is shit." Stephan briskly rubs his hands together. "I hope Gemma is ready to warm up her man."

I know for a fact that he hasn't had her yet. "You fucking wish."

"What the hell is that supposed to mean?"

"Mom will have your ass if you step foot in Gemma's bedroom."

"What she doesn't know won't hurt her."

"You better be careful pulling that kind of shit. Mom's a sharp lady."

"Oh, come on, Luca. You banged your wife before marriage. You even got her pregnant before you put a wedding ring on her finger."

We haven't talked about it, but I suppose Stephan is smart enough to do the math.

"I banged my wife before marriage at *my* house. Not at our parents'. Big difference."

"I've got money. I can buy a house if I want."

"You're getting married. You should do that, Steph. Because let me tell you something. I lived in my own home with my wife for months, and now we're living under the same roof as all you fuckers. And I hate it."

I blame the Gasparis. When the opportunity comes, I'm going to fuck them up good.

"Maybe a house could be my wedding gift to Gemma."

"I think she would really like that."

I survey the perimeter of the compound as we approach the front gate. "Stop the truck, Sal."

Stephan sits taller. "What is it?"

"Something is off." Very off.

"There was fresh snowfall while we were gone so why are there tracks all in the snow?"

He sees what I see.

"That's an excellent question."

"Guys, looks like we may get to try out our new hardware. Start loading."

"Luca—"

"Fuck." I see the garage door, or at least what's left of it, at the same moment Stephan says my name. "The motherfuckers attacked while we were gone."

"How did they know we'd be gone?"

"That's a very good question. One that we will find the answer to after we kill these fuckers."

"What's the plan, boss?"

Think. Think. Think, Luca. "Okay. They're surrounding the compound. We have soldiers who can fire on them from inside. When we approach from the outside, they'll be trapped between us with nowhere to go."

"It's a great plan, bro." Stephan slaps my back. "This is going to work."

"Yeah." It has to.

~

One Rossini man lost. Two more wounded. I have no idea how many Gaspari men we took out, and I don't care. I left the scene of the fight before it could be determined because I have to get to Emilia.

Please let her be safe.

Dashing up the stairs, I take them two at a time. Maybe three. Hell, I might have even sprouted wings and flew.

"Emilia!"

Gemma comes out of our bedroom, meeting me in the hallway. "Thank God you're here."

"What is happening?"

"She went into labor a couple hours after you left."

"Fuck." She told me she wasn't at ease about this trip. She asked me to stay, and I went anyway. I left her here, vulnerable to the Gasparis.

Gemma steps aside. "Go to her. She needs you."

I step into our bedroom, and Emilia is crouched on the floor, her forehead covered in sweat, and her normally delicate features distorted by a grimace. She's surrounded by every woman who lives under this roof, Rossini and otherwise.

"Ahhh!" she screams.

"You have to push harder," Zee Zee tells her.

She's pushing? What the fuck?

"Luca," my mother says. "I've never been so happy to see you."

"Luca," Emilia says, her voice cracking and weak. "Luca."

I go to her and she collapses in my arms.

"I'm here."

"I'm dying, Luca. I feel it happening."

"No, love. You are not dying. You're bringing our baby into the world."

"I am dying. I see it in Zee Zee's eyes. The baby is too big for me to have. I've been trying to push him out for such a long time, but he's not coming. I've tried so hard."

"Why hasn't someone called for an ambulance?"

My mother wipes Emilia's face with a cloth. "We tried, but they cut the phone lines. And they fired on us when we tried to take her to the hospital. We had no choice. It was safer to keep her here."

Sons of bitches. I hope they're all dead.

Zee Zee rises from a crouching position. "Help Emilia onto the bed. She can rest while you and I talk about things."

Lifting Emilia in my arms, I feel her grip my shirt. "Don't leave me, Luca. Please."

"I'm not leaving you. I will never leave you." I lower her to the bed and kiss her drenched forehead. "Close your eyes and rest a moment while I talk to Zee Zee. Okay?"

Her only response is a weak nod.

"I'll be right back."

I follow my grandmother into the hallway, knowing that there's a reason she doesn't want to talk in front of Emilia.

"She's suffering, Zee."

"That's what childbirth is, Luca. Suffering. Then there's joy and the suffering is forgotten."

"Are she and the baby in danger?"

"She's been pushing for a long time. The baby needs to be born as soon as possible."

"I love her. I can't lose her. We need to send for help."

"And we will now that we're able. But until help arrives, she can't stop. I know she's tired, and I'm sure the baby is too, but the safest thing at this point is to get the baby out."

"What can I do?"

"Encourage her. Tell her to push your son out. If she's going to do it for anyone, it's you."

"She's so small. Are you sure it's possible?"

"I've only been part of one birth like this where the mother pushed for hours, and the baby didn't come."

"What happened to her?"

My grandmother shakes her head and says nothing.

"No! That's not going to happen to Emilia."

It can't. We've only just found happiness together. It can't be taken away from us.

"She needs you to stay and help her through it."

Our men don't stay during childbirth. It's not the way. But I don't care about *the way*. I'll do anything for Emilia and our child.

"Tell me what to do and I'll do it."

Returning to Emilia, I kneel next to her at the bedside. Taking her hand in mine, I kiss the top. "I love you so much."

"I love you too."

"You're doing a wonderful job, and I know you're tired, but you can do this, love."

"I'm so weak."

"You are this baby's mother, and you can't quit. I need you to keep going. *He* needs you to keep going."

"I don't want to quit, but all of my strength is gone."

"Do it for me, love. Push him out."

Emilia opens her eyes and looks at me, nodding. "I'll do my best."

"That's my good girl."

"We're going to try something a little different this time," Zee Zee says.

I help Emilia up, and Zee Zee points at the side of the bed. "Luca, you're going to sit there, and Emilia is going to squat between your legs. She'll use your thighs to steady herself while you loop your arms through hers and support her weight with your arms.

"Yes, that's it. When your next contraction comes, give it everything you have and be done with this, girl."

I kiss the back of Emilia's head. "You are so strong, and you can do this. I believe in you."

She nods. "Okay. Okay. A contraction is coming."

Emilia grips my thighs and squeezes as she groans and bears down.

"Don't stop, Emilia. Keep going," my mother says.

She stops and leans back against me. "Ahhh! It's so much pressure down there."

"That's because the baby is moving down. Don't stop."

"Ohh, it's burning. It's burning. It's burning."

"Push through the pain, Emilia, and he'll be here."

My mouth hovers over her ear. "He's coming, baby. Don't stop. Keep going."

She grips my thighs, squeezing again, and the agonizing scream that leaves her mouth rips my heart in two.

"Towels," Zee Zee says.

I hear a gush of fluid and then nothing. No cry.

Emilia's upper body collapses against me, and I hold her up with my arms.

Stretching my neck, I kiss the side of her face. "You did it, baby. You did it."

Emilia breathes deeply. "I did it."

We wait a moment for the first cry, but it doesn't come.

"Why isn't he crying?" Emilia's voice is weak, barely audible.

No one answers her.

"Zee? What's happening?"

"Hold on, Luca. Just a minute."

I see her wiping our baby with a towel, and nothing is happening. He's blue and flaccid in her arms.

"Come on, baby. Breathe. Breathe for Zee Zee."

"You have to do something, Zee. Please."

My grandmother shakes her head and then grips our child by the ankles, turns him or her upside down, and slaps its butt.

And then a piercing cry fills the room. Not Emilia's. Our child's first cry.

My grandmother chuckles. "Oh, he's a fat one. It's no wonder he gave you so much trouble about coming out."

"It's a boy?" Emilia asks.

"Yes. A beautiful Rossini boy."

"Show me. I want to see him."

Zee Zee lifts our son, and Emilia reaches out, touching his cheek.

"A son," she whispers. "We have a son, Luca."

I'm a father. I can hardly believe it. I thought this day would never come.

I reach out and upon contact, my son grips my finger inside his tiny hand. "Alessandro."

Emilia holds out her arms. "I want to hold him."

After his lifeline to his mother is severed, Zee Zee wraps a clean towel around him, giving him to Emilia. She pulls him close and studies his face. "He is beautiful and perfect and everything I dreamed he would be."

I love the way she looks at our son, as though he's her greatest accomplishment.

"Thank you for giving me this precious gift, Emilia."

"I love you."

"I love you, too."

39

EMILIA ROSSINI

Nonna, Micaela, and Isabella greet me at the front door, throwing their arms around me. All of our I've-missed-yous and I-love-yous and I'm-so-happy-to-see-yous overlap at once, and it's hard to make out anything we're actually saying to each other.

Nonna leans over, looking at Alessio in my arms. "He's beautiful, Em. Can I hold him?"

"Of course, you can hold him."

I place my son in my grandmother's arms. "His name is Alessandro, but we're going to call him Alessio."

"You are named Alessandro after a great man, little one," she says, studying his face. "It is my greatest hope that he will be the boy who brings peace between the Bellinis and Rossinis."

Isabella leans over, looking at him. "I want to hold him."

I see that not much has changed with my impatient baby sister. "Don't worry, Issy. You'll get to hold him."

I want my sisters to love their nephew.

I want my grandmother to love her great-grandson.

And I want my mother to love her grandson.

"Sofia's waiting for you in the living room."

I had hoped Mamma would be eager to see me and might greet me at the front door. But no.

Nonna holds out Alessio and I take him from her arms. "She won't let on, but your mother is eager to meet this boy."

I'm relieved to hear that. It gives me hope that today might go well.

Mamma is sitting in her chair and doesn't rise when I come into the living room. She's being cold and formal.

This is me, Mamma. Your eldest daughter. The girl you raised for twenty-one years.

"Thank you for seeing me."

"I've missed you, Emilia."

My heart rejoices. "I've missed you, too."

Her attention shifts to my son in my arms. "I hear that I have a grandson?"

"Yes. This is Alessandro. Alessio for short."

"I'm thrilled you named him after your father."

"It was Luca's idea."

"Yes, I remember the announcement he made about it."

"Do you want to hold him?"

"Yes, I would love to hold my grandson."

I place him in my mother's arms. She studies his face for a moment, smiling, and rocking from side to side. "I knew you were a boy the whole time, Alessio."

I watch my mother with him, and I see it—I see her falling in love with him. But how can she not when he's so precious?

"I see Rossini in him, but there's something about him that reminds me of the Bellinis. Maybe his lips."

"I don't know. I only see Luca when I look at him." Their baby pictures look like twins.

"Either way, you have a handsome son."

"Yes, he is my perfect boy."

My mother rocks from side to side just as she did with my younger siblings. "Hold him close, Emilia, for as long as they'll let you."

She believes the Rossinis will take my son, but she's wrong. "Alessio is Luca's son, but he is also mine. No one is going to take him from me."

"Don't fool yourself. This boy belongs to the Rossinis. You were merely the vessel who carried him and brought him into the world."

"It isn't like that with Luca, Mamma. He and I love each other."

"Well, I see that your opinion about your husband hasn't changed."

"It hasn't, but other things have changed since we last spoke."

"Yes, I'm sure this little one has brought many changes into your life."

"Alessio's not the change I'm referring to. I'm talking about your allies."

My mother shakes her head. "I chose a weak family to align with. That was my mistake."

"And now all of your Gaspari allies are dead."

"Yes. Your husband has managed to annihilate the entire male line of a second family. He's becoming very good at that."

"He's become known as 'the annihilator' by the five families. Did you know that?" I haven't decided how I feel about my husband being called that name.

My mother looks up at me. "Yes, I've heard that name being tossed around."

"The Rossinis have made a name for themselves. Not one of the five families would dare to rise against us now."

"*Us*. You truly do consider yourself one of them, don't you?"

"I do. Nothing has been as I expected it to be. They've been good to me, Mamma. And Luca loves Alessio and me with all of his heart. He would die to protect us."

"Congratulations, daughter. You are on the winning side. You chose wisely this time."

"I don't want there to be a winning or losing side. And I know that deep down you don't want that either."

"No, I never wanted any of this. But I wasn't the one who started this war, was I?"

"In the end, it doesn't matter who's to blame because I've lost too many people. I don't want to not have you and Nonna and Micaela and Isabella in my life. I need my family."

"You're a traitor to us. How do I forgive you and move beyond that?"

"You and your allies nearly killed Alessio and me. How do *I* move beyond that?" Her eyes widen. "I have to make a conscious decision to forgive you and move forward. That's how it must be."

"How did my allies and I nearly kill you and Alessio?"

"I went into labor the night the Gasparis attacked us. They fired at us when we tried to go to the hospital. It was a miracle that I escaped being shot."

"You delivered this baby at home?"

"Yes. Luca's grandmother delivered him in our bedroom."

"Zorah?"

"Yes, with Viviana's and Luca's help."

"Luca was with you when you gave birth?"

"Yes."

"I can't believe he stayed. Men don't do that."

"It was a difficult birth. I pushed for hours, and Alessio wouldn't come out. I believed with all of my heart that I was going to die because they couldn't get help for us."

My mother looks up at me, and I see the deep regret on her face. "I didn't know."

"Zee Zee and Viviana were wonderful, but I always thought I would have you to help me through that."

"I'm so terribly sorry that happened to you and that I wasn't there when you needed me."

I smile at my son when he coos. "Alessio is here and he's perfect. That's all that matters now."

"Luca must be proud to have a son?"

"You can't imagine. He loves this boy so much."

"I'm sure he does."

"Luca came with me today. He's waiting in the car. He wants to talk to you."

My mother shakes her head. "No. I can't talk to that man."

"*That man* is your daughter's husband and the father of your grandson. You can talk to him."

"I don't want to hear anything he has to say."

"Yes, Mamma. You'll want to hear this."

"What could he possibly say that I would want to hear?"

"A lot, actually."

She says nothing, looking down at my son. And I know I'm taking advantage of what she's feeling at the moment, but I don't care. "If you won't do it for me, do it for Alessio."

"That's not fair. You know I'd never say no to this precious boy."

"I absolutely know. And I have no intentions of being fair if it makes you agree to speak to Luca."

She hesitates a moment. "All right. I'll see him."

"Thank you, Mamma. You won't regret this."

Luca opens the car door when he sees me coming out of the house. "She agreed to see me?"

"She isn't happy about it, not even a little bit, but she did agree."

"Okay. All right."

"Are you nervous?"

"Whaaat? You know I don't get nervous, baby."

He's such a man. "Despite what you may believe, you aren't made of steel. You're human and you get nervous. It's okay to admit it."

"Okay. I'm a little bit nervous but not for myself."

"For me?"

"And Alessio. I know how much you want your family to be in your life and his. I don't want to be the one who blows that for you."

I glide my hands up his chest and wrap them around his shoulders. "You aren't going to blow it. I believe in you."

"For you and Alessio, I'll do whatever it takes to make this right."

"I know you will."

Mamma remains seated when Luca and I enter the living room. I go to her, taking Alessio because I don't want her to be distracted. I need all of her attention to be focused on the conversation she and Luca are about to have.

"Hello, Sofia," Luca says, taking my mother's hand and kissing her ring.

She nods. "Luca."

"Thank you for seeing me."

"I can assure you that it's not because I want to."

My mother's eyes widen when Luca kneels on one knee

before her and bows his head. "I have come to express my deepest regret to you for what I've done to you and your family. I understand that you are unable to give me your forgiveness today, and you may never, but I humbly ask you to not hold a grudge against Emilia and our son for my wrongdoings."

Luca pauses a moment, and my mother's mouth gapes.

"I would like to return the Bellini assets to you and your family, which I wrongfully took from you."

Mamma looks at me and then back at my kneeling husband. "I don't know what to say."

"I only want to hear you say that you accept Emilia back into the Bellini family. And with her, your grandson, Alessio."

"And Gemma," I add.

"Yes. I welcome my daughters and grandson with open arms. And in return, I ask that they forgive me for my wrongdoings."

"Of course, Mamma."

Luca lifts his head. "This means the world to Emilia. Thank you."

Luca is afraid to ask for anything on his behalf. Whether he says so or not, he fears my mother's rejection.

"What about Luca and Stephan?"

"I don't offer them my forgiveness today."

I'm not surprised. I didn't expect an absolution from her at this point.

"We understand why you're withholding your forgiveness for the time being, but do Luca and Stephan have your blessing to return here as your sons-in-law?"

My mother inhales deeply, looking at me and then Luca. "I can see that you're doing this because you love Emilia and my grandson. For that reason, you are welcome in our home. Gemma and Stephan too."

"Thank you, Mamma. I can't tell you what that means to me."

My relationship with my mother is still broken. It's going to take time to heal, but this is a step in the right direction. Because Luca made it possible.

EPILOGUE

EMILIA ROSSINI

Four Years Later, New York, 1983

"Hello, love."

Looking over my shoulder, I see Luca standing in the doorway. "You're back earlier than expected."

"I promised Alessio I would be home in time to read a bedtime story to him."

"Well, that explains why he spent all evening going through his books."

"Our boy loves his bedtime stories."

"He does indeed."

Alessio gets his love of books from his dad. And I think he may have also inherited Luca's artistic skills. He certainly didn't get his talent from me.

Luca comes into the nursery and stands beside me, tickling Lorenzo, our second son, beneath his chin. "Hey, boy. Were you good for your mamma today?"

"He's been cranky. I think his ear is bothering him again. He's tugged on it all afternoon."

"Do you think he needs to be seen by Dr. Meyers?"

"Yeah, I'm going to call the office in the morning and make an appointment."

I lift Lorenzo from the changing table, freshly diapered and dressed for bed, placing him on my hip.

My sweet baby boy Lorenzo. I can't believe he's already eighteen months old and Alessio, four. Where has the time gone?

"Everything go well at your dinner tonight?"

"You could say that. I had an offer."

An offer. I've come to hate those two words.

My husband is rich, powerful, and handsome. I'm never surprised when he receives *an offer* from a woman. She makes a pass at him and he tells me, always, so there are no secrets between us. That's the kind of marriage we have. We openly tell each other everything, but I must admit that sometimes I get tired of hearing about women who throw themselves at him.

"You know I don't care about the offer. I only care that you refused it."

"Baby… I didn't refuse this offer."

My head jolts, turning to look at my husband, and my stomach feels as though it's dropped to my feet. "What do you mean you didn't refuse the offer?"

"Let's do this: I'll read to Alessio and put him to bed, you get Ren down, and then we'll talk about the offer when we're not distracted by the boys."

I pull Lorenzo to me, hugging him. "Don't you dare do that to me—tell me that you didn't refuse one of those fucking offers and then expect me to wait and discuss it after the kids are in bed."

Luca wraps his arm around me and pulls me close, chuckling. "Baby, you know me better than that. It's not *that* kind of offer."

Now I just feel like a silly, jealous wife for jumping to

conclusions. But in my defense, *an offer* is what he always calls it when a woman tries to sleep with him.

"What kind of offer was it?"

"I told you, love. Let's put the boys to bed, and then we'll discuss it."

"All right. But I don't like it."

"Believe me, I know."

I'm relieved when Lorenzo goes to sleep without a fight. But Alessio? My boy always begs for just one more chapter, and Luca has a terrible habit of giving into him.

Luca stops reading when he sees me in the doorway. "We have to stop here for tonight, son."

"No. Keep reading. Pleeease."

"It's your bedtime, little man. We'll pick up here tomorrow night."

I come into Alessio's room and pull up his covers. Tucking them beneath his arms, I place a kiss on his forehead. "I love you."

"I love you too, Mamma."

"Sweet dreams, my perfect boy."

With our children tucked into bed, Luca and I retreat to our bedroom. It's the one place in this enormous compound where my husband and I are able to have an entirely private conversation.

"Tell me about this offer you didn't refuse." Before I burst.

"Vitale Lazarro has proposed a betrothal between Alessio and his daughter."

I can't believe Luca would even propose this idea to me. He knows how I feel about arranged marriages. "No."

"Please hear me out before you refuse."

"All right. I will hear you out and then refuse."

"I'm a free man because Vitale's connections within the police department managed to *lose* evidence that would have put me away for at least a decade. I'm here with you tonight because of him. I get to see my boys grow up because of what he did for me."

"And I will be forever grateful to him for that."

"If we refuse this offer and insult Vitale, it's possible that his man on the inside who lost the evidence against me could find it again."

"Is he blackmailing you?"

"No, but I believe it's wise to stay in good graces with the family. As you know, I have run-ins with the law on a regular basis. They could prove to be useful in the future."

"You knew before we had children that I didn't want them to be betrothed."

"I know and that's why our son's betrothal would be different from ours. We and the Lazarros would raise Alessio and the girl together, so they would know each other from the start. They would never be strangers to one another."

Alessio and his betrothed would know each other as Nic and I did? That changes things.

"If they don't want to marry when the time comes, they may dissolve the betrothal themselves. I told Vitale that's the only way you would agree to one."

"He agreed to those conditions?"

"He did, but the real question is do *you* find those terms agreeable?"

"I find the terms agreeable enough to consider the betrothal." Luca smiles and I know he believes he has me. "I said *consider*. That's very different from agree."

"Thank you for considering this."

"You expected me to outright say no?"

"I did."

He's right to assume so. I would have if not for the conditions accompanying the offer.

"Tell me more about the girl."

"Her name is Serafina. They call her Sera. She's a year younger than Alessio, the youngest of the Lazarro children. Their only girl."

All parents of young girls within the five families want their daughter to be betrothed to Alessio. And now, they're starting to inquire about Lorenzo for daughters who've yet to be born.

I hate it. My children aren't pawns. They aren't rungs on a ladder for someone to use in their efforts of climbing to the top of the Mafia hierarchy.

"Because I can see how important this is to you, I agree to meet with the Lazarros and discuss it. But that's all I'm promising at this point."

"That's all I'm asking for, love."

"I'm giving you something you want. I think it's only fair if you give me something I want in return."

"I know what you want." Luca's brow lifts. "Your fertility window is open?"

Sitting on the bed, I place my heels on the bedrail and allow my dress to slide up my thighs when I spread them. "It's wiiide open."

Looking beneath my dress, he chuckles as he reaches for his tie. "Looks like that's not the only thing wide open."

"Nope, it sure isn't."

I sit on the bed, watching, as he kicks out of his shoes and begins unbuttoning his shirt. Piece by piece, he undresses until he is bare, and I am looking at over six feet of masculine nakedness.

Damn. I have a beautiful husband. I love every inch of him, but I especially love every inch when he's inside me.

His bare feet thump against the padded shag carpet as he comes toward me, motioning for me to stand. "Up, love."

I stand and turn around, lifting my hair, so he can unzip my dress. He's so close that I can feel his breath falling on my back's bare skin, sending chills down my spine.

He pushes my dress down my hips, and it falls to the floor, followed by my bra and panties. When I'm as bare as he is, his powerful arm hooks around me, pulling my body tight against his. His mouth lowers to my ear, my neck, my shoulder, kissing me hard.

Turning me around, he grips the back of my thighs and lifts. I instantly wrap my arms around his shoulders, and together, we tumble backward on the bed. I love the feel of his weight on top of me, pushing me into the mattress.

My fingertips dig into his muscular back as he slides every hard inch inside me. When he's in all the way to the hilt, he stops and groans. "Fuck, you're wet."

His sculpted body rocks into mine as his muscles flex and tighten, his knees pushing my thighs apart. With this man deep inside me, I feel the connection not only between our bodies but also between our souls as though we are one entity.

His strong arms hook behind my thighs, bringing my legs up, spreading me wide apart. His thrusts are so deep that I can feel his tip hitting my womb, causing me to ache, but it feels so good that I don't want him to stop.

And then he fucks me hard.

My fingertips dig deep into the flesh of his back, and my thighs squeeze him tightly. We'll both be sore tomorrow, I'm certain of that.

This is how love is supposed to be—an all-consuming desire where you can't get enough of your beloved no matter how many times you're together. And that's how I feel. I don't think I'll ever get enough of this man.

"I'm close, baby."

His thrusts slow and deepen, like he's trying to bury himself as far inside me as possible when he explodes. He moves at a steady pace between my thighs. Hovering over me, his eyes focus on mine, and I stretch upward to kiss him.

"Give me a girl this time," I whisper against his lips.

He nods and whispers back, "A princess. Our little princess."

With his face buried against my neck, he writhes on top of me, his sweaty chest rubbing against mine. Groaning, his cock twitches inside me, filling me with every drop of him. Hopefully, giving me the baby girl I want.

Gradually, his muscles relax, and his breath becomes regular again. He kisses the length of my throat, worshiping me. His queen.

I don't see an ideal love when I look at Luca. Far from it, actually, and nothing like the kind of perfect love I once dreamed of having.

I am looking at a man who would fight until his last breath to protect me. A man who would sacrifice his life in place of mine because that's how deeply he loves me. I don't doubt that for a second.

Our love story didn't begin as a romantic one. Neither has it been easy. The truth is that it's been brutally painful. But it's our love story, and I adore it. Nothing is dearer to my heart.

Hard as I tried, I couldn't escape loving this beautiful monster.

The End.

ABOUT THE AUTHOR

Georgia Cates is the New York Times, USA Today, and Wall Street Journal Best-Selling Author. She resides in rural Mississippi with her wonderful husband, Jeff, and their two beautiful daughters. She spent fourteen years as a labor and delivery nurse before she decided to pursue her dream of becoming an author and hasn't looked back yet.

Sign-up for Georgia's newsletter at
www.georgiacates.com.
Get the latest news, first look at teasers,
and giveaways just for subscribers.

Stay connected with Georgia at:
Twitter, Facebook, Tumblr, Instagram,
Goodreads and Pinterest.

SIN SERIES STANDALONE NOVELS

Endurance

Unintended

Redemption

THE BEAUTY SERIES

Beauty from Pain

Beauty from Surrender

Beauty from Love

The Beauty Series Bundle

GOING UNDER SERIES

Going Under

Shallow

Going Under Complete Duo

THE VAMPIRE AGAPE SERIES

Blood of Anteros

Blood Jewel

Blood Doll

The Complete Vampire Agape Series

Printed in Great Britain
by Amazon